W9-COJ-578

MAY - - 2023

THRESHING OF STRAW

PEABODY INSTITUTE LIBRARY
PEABODY, MA

THRESHING
OF
STRAW

Kim Catron

BELLWETHER

BELLWETHER

SINCE 2009

Copyright © 2021 by Kim Catron

All rights reserved. This book, or parts thereof, may not be reproduced in any form without permission.

LCCN: 2021922155

Paperback ISBN: 978-1-63337-578-9
E-book ISBN: 978-1-63337-579-6

1 3 5 7 9 10 8 6 4 2

To Peyton and Beckett.
Always, always, always follow your dreams.

Chapter 1

HARRISON, GEORGIA
MACEY MAY JOHNSON
1962

"NOW LOOK UP, Macey May, so I can wipe that off your face." Mama spit into her handkerchief and skirted it over my chin, her wet saliva making me squirm. "Why you can't seem to keep chocolate off of you is beyond me. Once piece and it looks like you took a bath in it."

"I can't help it," I said, shrugging my shoulders.

"Ladies don't shrug, and watch your sassing in case you forget who you're talking to. Now, give me the rest of it." She held out her hand, her fingers motioning for my contraband. "Come on. I'm not having you get off this bus at your grandmother's covered in chocolate. It's hard enough sending you all alone. You don't need to arrive needing a bath."

"But Mama, I bought it with my own money." It was true. I had saved ten cents working for our next-door neighbor Miss Eunice, sweeping her porch clear of leaves for the whole month of October. She had a crazy old maple tree that wept yellow, orange, and red like it was trying to repaint the ground, as if God made a mistake when he decided on green. In the afternoons, Miss Eunice liked to sit on the porch and watch the goings-on of the neighborhood and said she was afraid she might trip on all those hues. She just might have too. I had seen her shuffling over to her folding chair she

1

had perched next to the right side of the front door, "a less obstructed view," she said, and between her feet in those camel-colored orthopedic slippers and her cane, stumbling didn't require too much of the imagination.

"Macey May...now."

I rolled my eyes, reached into my pocket, and surrendered the Sky Bar. So much for saving my favorite section—fudge—until later.

Mama stowed it in her purse and crouched down next to me. "Grandma or Otis will pick you up at the station. If they aren't there, find a bench and wait. Don't go wandering around getting in trouble."

I rolled my eyes again. I was nine but you'd think I was some sort of juvenile delinquent the way Mama was always reminding me to not get into trouble. Her fingers fumbled over my coat buttons, and she adjusted the scarf around my neck. "Quit, Mama, it's too tight. You're strangling me."

She stood up, smoothing down the waist of her coat with her hands like she always did when she was nervous. She thought I didn't notice, but I did. Daddy used to tell me I could be a private investigator like Perry Mason someday, I was so good at focusing on everything going on around me. Though it seems, not when it really matters, like it did a few months ago when he went outside and never came back.

"You know I wouldn't be sending you there if it wasn't absolutely necessary." She turned her head, looking down the road for the bus. "It's just...well, with your daddy being gone so long and all."

"He's coming back, Mama. You make it sound as if he's dead or something." I loosened the scarf and let the sides fall down by my arms.

"Macey May Johnson!" Her hands were swift, and my throat was double wound before I could say anything more.

We had been having a cold spell in Harrison. Forty-eight degrees. The coldest recorded November in history.

"Keep your scarf on," she said, and looked at her watch. "The bus should be here in five minutes. Can't you just cooperate for that much longer?"

I looked down at my boots. They were too small (a hand-me-down from one of Mama's friends) and my toes pinched at the end. I stomped my feet. "My toes are getting numb," I said. "Can't we wait inside the station?"

"Stop complaining. Your feet are just fine."

If my feet were fine, I wouldn't have complained about them, but I knew better than to contradict Mama when she was getting herself riled up. I slid my hand into hers. She squeezed it.

"Now, it will only be a week, and then I'll be there for Thanksgiving. Adele has too much going on at the bakery for me to leave her right before the holiday."

"Will Daddy be back by then?"

"Macey May." She bent over and kissed my forehead, her voice softer, her breath smelling of peppermint leaves. I looked into her eyes, the whites almost glowing against the rich darkness of her skin, and I felt a twinge of envy. Mama was midnight, and I was early dawn. High yellow. Enough to know the color was there, but not enough to make me feel beautiful like Mama. Mostly, I felt plain.

She smiled and pushed some pieces of my hair back under my cap. They were always springing up no matter how much product she used to keep them down. "Daddy's not sure how long this job is going to be. It's you and me now. At least for a while."

It's just me, I wanted to say, but I didn't.

Mama had a sister, my Aunt Ruby, who lived in New York City and worked at Macy's department store. In my whole life I'd only seen her three times. She never seemed to leave the city, but this year she'd be at my grandma's for Thanksgiving. She's got to head back first thing on Saturday morning, but at least we'll all be together, minus Daddy, that is.

I used to think the department store was named after me, but Mama says it wasn't, that the store was there long before I was born, and I have an "e" in my name anyway. Mama said I was named after my daddy's grandmother who raised him and passed away on his eighteenth birthday. I always thought that would be awful—someone dying on your birthday. Every year as you cut the cake and then opened your presents, you'd be thinking about death and feeling guilty that you were alive. Daddy seemed to do okay with it, though. I'd look for signs on his birthday that he might be sad, but he never showed anything other than his big smile full of white teeth as we placed the cake in front of him. He'd wink at me before he'd make his wish and then clap like a little kid when all the candles blew out. "Macey May," he'd say, picking the candles out of the cake and giving me one to lick, "it's going to be a good year."

And they were good, until this last one.

I had been folding up the wrapping paper; Mama always saved it to use the next birthday. I didn't hear the doorbell ring or even a knock at the door, but then there was Daddy getting to his feet as if someone had whispered in his ear that it was time to go.

He tugged on one of my braids and pointed to the cake between us. "Best one you've ever made, Macey May."

I beamed.

Red Velvet was his favorite, and Betty Crocker and I had spent the better part of the morning creating one from scratch. Mama didn't tolerate boasting, but I knew it was good, so I was glad he had said it. He left the front door open, the late August air seeping in through the screen and cooling down the house. The sun was just settling in for the night, and the blinking lightning bugs out the front window reminded me of the white Christmas lights we put up on the outside of the house every year. I remember thinking that I'd have to ask for an empty jelly jar so I could catch some of them. They'd be the last of the season. Daddy poked his head around the corner and lifted his chin toward the kitchen and the sound of Mama's favorite radio show coming from under the door. "Tell your Mama I'll be back in a little bit."

"But Daddy," I pointed to his piece of cake half-eaten, the fork saluting out of the frosting like a flagpole, "it will dry out, and you didn't even finish it."

"Then I'll just have to cut me a brand-new slice when I get back. Maybe two."

I smiled. "Two? Mama will kill you. You know the rules about sweets."

Daddy laughed out loud. He blew me a kiss; I caught it before it could get by. "Rules are made to be broken sometimes, Macey May." He grabbed his hat from the coat tree and glanced at me one last time. "Be sure to let your Mama know."

That was over two months ago, and we haven't seen him since. Mama tells me he has a job way out in California, but I don't believe her, never have.

It seems the world has a lot of rules my Daddy likes to break.

"Macey May, look at me now. The bus is here."

Mama took a step back and put her hand to her chin, nodding slowly. "It's as good as I can do. I suppose your grandmother will find something wrong anyway. I don't even know why I try."

The bus sighed and opened its door. "Mama?" My stomach was knotting up. I had never done the trip from Harrison to Crawford by myself. Usually me, Mama, and Daddy would borrow a car and drive down a few times a year. The beginning of summer was the best. Grandma hosted a strawberry festival in her front yard and everyone from the neighboring farms came. I never made it through a full one, always falling asleep on the front porch double rocker while the fiddles were still playing, my stomach filled with shortcake and lemonade. "Mama?" I said again. Shortcake and lemonade made for the best dreams.

"I heard you the first time, Macey May." Her head was bent down, as her hands rummaged through her purse. "Here. This is Grandma's phone number just in case. Don't lose it. And besides, Grandma is looking forward to spending time with you. Last week she told me she was going to show you how to make her chocolate pecan pie. That's special, you know. You're the only grandchild. It's up to you to make sure that recipe doesn't die out. I was about your age when she taught me." She looked at me with her beautiful violet eyes, the ones I coveted ever since Miss Eunice taught me the definition of the word "covet." "Actually, now that I think about it, I was a year older."

I nodded and folded up the piece of paper and stuck it in my pocket.

"Also," she handed me a brown paper bag, ruffled and crumpled from being in her purse, "a bologna sandwich. Sorry it's smooshed. There's an apple, too. Make sure you eat it."

"Where's my thermos?"

"No drinks. You don't need to be askin' the bus driver to pull over so you can do a toilet on the way there. It's only a two-and-a-half-hour trip. You won't die of thirst."

"Ma'am?" The bus driver looked at his watch. "We've got to head out if I'm to stay on time. Don't you worry. She'll sit right behind me. I'll keep an eye on her."

Mama smiled and thanked him. She had a great smile, the kind you see on the screen at the pictures. "That Rose Johnson," people would say and whistle, shaking their heads, "now there's a true beauty." It was usually followed by another shaking of heads and the debating what she ever saw in my daddy. Lately there's been some other talk, but I paid no attention to that. At least I tried.

"Mind that paper now," she said and bent over to kiss me one last time on the cheek. Mama rarely hugged. That was Daddy's role. "I'll call you when I can."

I swallowed the lump in my throat and walked up the stairs into the bus.

"Sit right there, little lady." The bus driver tipped his hat to me and motioned to the seat behind him with a nod of his chin. "The one on the other side ain't no good for no one. Seat's a mess and the window's painted over. I've been asking them to fix it for months."

I looked across and saw cracked red vinyl, a crack so wide across the middle that the sides were rolling up and splitting away from the foam underneath. Just thinking about sitting there on a hot summer's day made the back of my legs itch.

"One behind me is better anyway. Window's nice and big, that way you can look out as we go. Make the drive seem not so long. Some pretty country we'll be seeing as we make our way...cows...and hills...yes'm, some mighty pretty country."

The door strained shut. If Daddy were here he'd tell the driver to oil the hinges. Daddy always knew how to fix things. The medicine cabinet upstairs in the bathroom, the kitchen table leg that made dinner a wobbly affair. I lengthened my neck like a giraffe to get one last look at Mama. She had crossed over to the curb and was waving goodbye to me. I motioned back.

"I'm Louis, by the way," the bus driver said, looking out his side view mirror as he turned the bus onto the street. "You need anything, you let me know."

"Mama doesn't let me call grown-ups by their Christian names," I said.

"Your mama is one proper lady then, isn't she? In that case, call me Mr. Cotton. I wouldn't want you going against your mama's rules."

The diesel fumes snuck in through the vent, and I swatted them away nonchalantly, trying to clear the air like I had seen Mama do when we had walked past the elephants at the zoo once. I had plugged my nose then and said "ew," but Mama told me that wasn't the proper way to act in public. A lady didn't ever touch her nose unless there was a tissue in her hand, and then only in dire circumstances.

"That smell will clear out soon enough. It happens after we've been idling. I've gotten to where I don't even notice it anymore." He laughed like he had just had a joke with himself.

I nodded and looked out the window. We were going through town and passing the house that we rented right next to Miss Eunice. She was a retired schoolteacher. Yesterday when I went over to say goodbye and wish her a good holiday, she had pulled out a wrapped present for me. "In case I don't see you at Christmas this year," she said.

"Oh, we'll be back, Miss Eunice. Only going to be away for a week or two."

"Never you mind. Take it now anyway, and open it up so I can see you enjoy it." Her eyes looked real sad for some reason. I wondered if she had anyone to spend Thanksgiving with. Usually she'd spend it with us. Mama said Miss Eunice couldn't come to Crawford, that she wouldn't be up to such a long bus ride. Even so, I didn't feel right leaving her alone.

The wrapping paper was stiff underneath my fingers as I tugged it open. I knew it was a book by the size and weight and hoped beyond hope it would be the one I wanted. I saw the large curved "A" first followed by two "Gs." "You remembered!" I wrapped my arms around her. "Thank you, thank you, thank you, Miss Eunice."

Anne of Green Gables.

She had been telling me stories about Anne all year. Kindred spirits, that's what we were—Anne and me. The fact that Miss Eunice thought I was ready to read it made me swell with pride.

"I expect a full report when you get back."

"Yes, ma'am."

I was hoping Miss Eunice might be on her porch for one last wave, but it wasn't her time yet. I imagined she was sitting at her kitchen table eating her early lunch of wheat toast with orange marmalade and sipping her tea. I waved just in case she happened to be glancing out her window in my direction.

"What are your mama's rules about sweets?" Mr. Cotton looked at me through the big rearview mirror above his head. His pepper gray hair, shorn close to his scalp, outlined the bottom of his cap. It looked velvet to me, like those pieces of felt in children's books when they want you to feel the fur of a bunny. "Do you think she'd let you have a lollipop? I've got a bag up here I keep for all the kids." He gave me a big smile, the space between his front teeth big enough for two toothpicks to nestle. His skin was dark, darker than even my Grandpa Otis's whose was a nighttime sky when the moon had run away to hide. There were a few black freckles surrounding his eyes. I bet he played Drop the Handkerchief or Pickle in the Middle with his grandkids on Sunday afternoons and shot chinaberries at the crows from sling shots when he was a boy. He had that look to him. It was a good look, and I decided I liked him.

I thought for a moment about the lollipop. Surely there was no harm, and it would be impolite to refuse. Mama said it was always important to be polite, especially to my elders. "That would be nice, thank you." I sat up straight and pretended that Mama was there giving me an imaginary nod.

"What a little lady you are," said Mr. Cotton. He handed me the entire bag and told me to pick whichever I wanted. Purple was my favorite, and I was happy to find one toward the bottom. I took the wrapper off and dispensed of it in my coat pocket. "Have you ever been to Taylor County before?"

"Oh, yes," I said. "Plenty. But never by bus. I'm going to my grandma's farm while my Mama finishes up work. She works at a bakery, and Adele, her boss, is short-staffed. They've got lots of pies to make, as you can imagine, on account of Thanksgiving coming up. She'll be here next week. My Aunt Ruby is coming home, too. She works in New York City."

Mr. Cotton whistled. "New York City? My, my. Isn't that exciting."

"She works at Macy's in the shoe department." I closed my mouth. Maybe I was telling too much. Mr. Cotton must have sensed it because he smiled at me once more in the rearview mirror and began humming some song I hadn't ever heard before. It was real pretty. I thought about telling him I liked it, but I wasn't sure Mama would want me to. Although he had been awfully nice to me the whole trip, I still didn't know him. Mama had rules about what you could and couldn't say to strangers, especially outside of Harrison. It was one of the things she and Daddy agreed on.

The bus made three more stops along the way, and by the time we entered Crawford it was almost half full. I had eaten my bologna sandwich minus the crust but left the apple in case Grandma was late in gathering me and I got hungry. Other than a little boy who practiced counting to ten for most of the trip, I was the only child. And even I knew not to annoy the other passengers. His mama must not have taught him that lesson. Lucky for us, he and his daddy got on at the last stop before Crawford, so there were only twenty minutes or so of math class. It seemed he had his one to six skills down but struggled something awful with seven and eight, always messing them up and then starting all over again from one. I'm sure Miss Eunice would have cringed if she had been here. I couldn't understand why it was the order that messed him up. Daddy told me once that seven ate nine, and I've never forgotten it. I wondered why the boy's daddy didn't know that.

Mr. Cotton pulled the bus into the parking lot of the station. "Now, you wait right here, miss, until I let these other people off, then I'll take you on in."

I nodded and looked out the window. Crawford was a blink of a town. With only seven square miles, most people missed it the first time through. The post office and the Five and Dime were across the street. The Five and Dime had counter service, although I'd never been allowed to eat at it. Chuck's Luncheonette was on the side of the bus station. I could make out the green and white awning a ways down, but the smell of their French fries floated through the air right into the bus. My stomach grumbled. The last time we had come to visit we had stopped there for cheeseburgers and chocolate malteds. It had only been Mama and me that trip; Daddy hadn't been able to come on account of another construction job that he needed to finish. His jobs always seemed to take him away more and more often of late. "How about that cheeseburger you're always asking for?" Mama had said as Chuck's came into view.

It was true. I asked every time we visited Crawford, and Daddy would always say no while Mama would look straight ahead, her posture proper and hands folded in her lap. There I'd be with my nose pressed against the side window as we drove past, my mouth salivating for mustard, relish, and grease.

I hoped Otis would be there to pick me up. I was sure I could convince him to take me to Chuck's. He was always going and doing things behind Grandma's back like giving the stray dog that hung around their place table scraps and singing to the cows while he milked them. Grandma said it wasn't never a good idea to believe that animals were human; it made it that much harder when you had to put them down when their time came. That didn't seem to stop Otis, though.

Cora Lee Jenkins was my Grandma. I never met my Pap. He died long ago before I was even thought about. I used to think he died in the war fighting against Hitler, but Grandma said no; he never lived long enough to do anything as heroic. He died only six years after they were married, a few years after they had bought the farm. Mama had been five and Aunt Ruby only two when one morning Grandma awakened to Pap cold and stiff in the bed next to her. They never did find out why. Heart attack or something. Grandma says he was grinning ear to ear though, so she was pretty sure he was happy wherever he'd gone. He's buried behind their farmhouse down at the tree line where the crops stop with his headstone facing the creek. Grandma said he loved to fish, and this way he could watch the water all he wanted. I'm not sure if she believed in heaven. I heard her talking to Jesus all the time, but it never seemed like she was waiting for an answer, more like airing her grievances. I thought it would be scary, waking up next to a dead person. And even though it terrified me, I couldn't ever stop thinking about it. What would it be like to roll over and be staring at death right next to you? I saw a dead possum once on my way home from school. I turned it over with a broken branch and then ran all the way to Miss Eunice's house. The image of its wide, open eyes, and swollen tongue was etched forever in my brain. Sometimes at night, I still see those eyes.

"Gracious, child," Grandma would say whenever I asked her to tell Pap's story again, "why do you want to hear about that? No good can come from talking about the dead. It's like walking on their grave. Let him have his peace."

I thought maybe hearing about Pap's grin would erase the possum's eyes.

Sometimes she'd get real quiet when I asked, and then Otis would tap me on the shoulder and lead me out to the barn, leaving Grandma sitting at the kitchen table not doing anything but looking. Otis and Grandma had never married, even though Mama said Otis had asked her to marry him plenty of times. I had even witnessed the aftermath once a year ago. We had all been sitting around the formal dining table for Sunday dinner, finishing our collard greens and ham, when Otis threw down his napkin and stood up to his feet, knocking the table so hard that my milk spilled over the edge of my glass. He wasn't a big man, barely a hair taller than Grandma, but you knew he was there when he wanted you to. "Cora Lee, you…you…you'd make a man—" His face was beet red, and he clenched his fists in the air, hitting toward something I couldn't see, before he walked out into the kitchen, the door swinging through behind him. Mama raised an eyebrow and Daddy coughed. "He asked you again? And I assume you said 'no'?" Mama asked Grandma.

Grandma sighed. "This morning. He hasn't talked to me all day. Old fool. He'll miss the shoo fly pie I made for dessert." She put her napkin down and started clearing the table of the mismatched china, remainders of my grandma's and great-grandma's legacy. Mama told me they'd be mine one day. Sunday dinners were served on china and always in the formal. Other days we ate in the kitchen or on the porch if the weather was fitting, our plates balanced on our knees. "Serves him right," Grandma said.

I don't really think she was paying much attention. I wasn't done, and the greens were good, lemony and peppery at the same time with bits of crispy fried bacon on top. I looked at Mama for help, my fork suspended in midair, but she shook her head, so I grabbed one last bite before Grandma swooped my plate out from under me.

"Grandma, why won't you marry him?" I asked.

"Macey May. I already was married. Otis and I get along well enough the way it is. He's just stubborn. Don't you worry, honey. He'll come around." She leaned over and kissed the top of my head. I stuck my finger onto my plate she was holding for one last taste of the lemony juice. I figured this was the one time Mama wouldn't mind. I was right.

From what Mama told me later that night when she tucked me into bed, Otis had been asking my grandma to marry him for the past fifteen years. Grandma's answer was always no, and Otis always got angry and walked away. "It's their way," Mama said.

I loved Otis. He was the only grandpa I had ever known, and he was a great storyteller. At night when I was visiting and couldn't sleep or was scared of the thunderstorms that would rock the farmhouse, he'd come sit at the end of the bed and tell me stories about a little girl who swam with alligators and a talking chicken who thought it was a cat. That one made me laugh so hard that Mama would yell up at us to go to sleep or she'd come up with a wooden spoon. Otis would make a big "O" with his mouth when he heard her words as if he were truly scared, and we'd giggle more. Lightning would flash outside and the rain would knock against the windows, but I'd be laughing away while that stupid chicken tried tirelessly to climb a tree.

I trusted Otis. He was my friend.

He was the only one I continued to tell about the White Lady sightings, and he didn't laugh, not even a little. He simply looked me in the eyes and nodded, serious like. It was as if he was contemplating what I was saying and thinking on it, hard, as if I was his equal. Not many people would trust that you saw a ghost. But he did. Otis didn't even need me to pinky swear to prove that I wasn't fibbing. That was the way he was—accepting.

I told Mama one night about seeing the White Lady from my bedroom window when we were staying at Grandma's, but she refused to hear anything about it. She told me I had "an overactive imagination." She then suggested that maybe I was reading too many books. I kept it from her after that.

But not from Otis. I always told Otis.

Mr. Cotton poked his head back in the bus. "So, little lady, why don't you come with me and we'll see about finding your grandma."

"It might be Otis picking me up instead," I said. I could almost taste the cheese on one of Chuck's burgers.

"Either way, let's go poke around and see who we can find."

Mr. Cotton offered me his hand to get down. I accepted.

"It's so small," I said as I stepped into the waiting area. There were a few worn benches, back-to-back, tired and holding each other up in the center of the floor across from the ticket counter. A Coca-Cola machine hummed against the far wall next to a bench that looked even older than the others.

"Crawford may be the center of Taylor County, but there's not much call for coming here." Mr. Cotton smiled at me. "It sure ain't no Union Station, that I do know."

The clock on the wall read 1:25. Mr. Cotton had made good time. We were five minutes early. My throat was dry as a desert, and when I saw the water fountains against the wall, I didn't even stop to think. It was Mr. Cotton who grabbed me by the shoulder. "Whoa there, miss. You'll be wanting this one." His finger pointed to the fountain on the right, the one labeled *For Colored*. He kneeled down next to me, his voice softening to almost a whisper. "You might find things a little different down here in Crawford, especially in town. Out on the farms is another thing, but here, there's, well…" he paused and breathed loud out through his mouth, his lips bumping together. "Well, in town, there's ways, that's all." He looked like there was more he wanted to say, but instead he stood up and stretched, his hands pressed into his back.

I cleared my throat like I had heard Mama do those times before she made an important announcement. "Well, thank you very much, Mr. Cotton. I don't want to waste any more of your valuable time. Mama told me to sit and wait, so that's what I intend to do."

15

Mr. Cotton chuckled. "Those are some big words. How old are you anyway?"

I giggled back. "Almost ten."

"Soon to be twenty, I'd imagine. I don't feel right leaving you here alone, but I do need to go out back and complete some papers before I have to head out to Macon. Now that's a big station." He tapped his hands against his thighs. "I've only got about fifteen minutes to do them too. Are you sure you'll be fine?"

"Sure as shootin'!" I said, smiling.

He tipped his hat at me and bowed. "It was lovely meeting you, miss. You wait right here until your grandma comes. And…" his eyes shifted a little, "and if you need the bathroom, ours, yours is outside and around back. Remember, okay?"

He patted me on the head, and I nodded.

Harrison didn't have a Whites Only drinking fountain or a Coloreds Only bathroom. It wasn't really even a town—just ten blocks at the edge of Spencer that had taken on a name and a space of its own. No one from Spencer seemed to mind that we weren't a part of them. Strangers rarely ever passed through. If they did, I doubt they ever realized they still weren't in Spencer proper. Mostly it was just those of us who lived there. We had one school, one church, and one grocery with an ESSO gas pump and garage next to it. There wasn't even a motel, but Widow Madison had two rooms she let out for people passing through needing a place to stay for a night. Her name was in the Green Book for Negro Motorists you could get free when filling up your car. She served a breakfast for her guests consisting of sausage biscuits and gravy with grits on the side. I heard they were so good that sometimes people would stop over again on their way back home just to have her cook for them once more.

For the rest of us in Harrison there wasn't much need to leave except to work, and there wasn't any need to separate where we drank our water from or where we ate. Daddy was the only white man in town, and he fit in with the rest of us just fine.

I tapped my fingers against the bench and looked up at the ceiling of the bus station. An old ceiling fan dripped with cobwebs, dirty strings waiting to float down on someone's head. I pictured one falling on my grandma and her doing her own version of the Lindy Hop. Oh, Otis would find that funny! Thinking about Otis laughing made me think of his stories. Just thinking about that chicken made me laugh and laughing made me have to go pee. I remembered what Mr. Cotton had said. My bathroom was outside, but Mama had said to stay in the station until Grandma came. It was 1:40. I swung my legs and tried to do times tables in my head, anything to take my mind off of the building pressure. Mama always said if you're stuck somewhere doing something you didn't want to do, keep your body and mind active, and the time will go by before you know it. 1:41. I shook my head. Times tables didn't work for peeing.

No one was behind the ticket counter, so I picked up my suitcase and walked out the door around back to the bathroom. It was next to a line of garbage cans and between the leftover exhaust from the buses and the smell of rotting trash. I held my breath to keep from inhaling it all. I turned the knob with my free hand and leaned my shoulder into the door. It was stuck.

"Let me help you there, sugar. Those doors sure are heavy, aren't they?"

I felt the door give way before I saw the hand pushing it above my head. It looked like Daddy's hand, and for a minute I thought it was him come to surprise me.

"Isn't your mama here to help you?"

I looked back. His smile was wide and bright. Mama always said you could tell a person by their smile. He had a nice one, with clean white teeth, smooth and straight. I doubted he could even fit one toothpick between them. She also said you could tell a man by his shoes. I took a quick peek down. Freshly polished, shiny black.

"My grandma or Otis is coming to get me," I said. "They'll be here in a minute. I couldn't wait anymore, though."

He laughed. "I'm sorry then. Keeping you from doing your business. You go right ahead in. Here," he reached down and put his hand on the handle of my suitcase, his soft skin touching my fingers as he did. Daddy's hands were rough with calluses and smelled like gasoline and burnt wood. "Why don't I watch this for you so you don't have to take it in there?"

I looked inside the open door to find gray walls and a gray floor that looked damp. The white sink seemed to be running a thin steady stream. Pee trickled into my underwear. "Thank you. I'll be right out." I stepped inside and rushed into the closest stall, sitting down as fast as I could. The balloon inside of me deflated, and I let out a sigh and closed my eyes with relief. My underwear was only a little wet, and I wiped them with some toilet paper when I was done. I'd change at Grandma's and stick them in the hamper. They'd be dry before she even washed them. My stomach grumbled again, and I thought of French fries. Maybe Otis would let me get extra ketchup. I bent over to pull my sock up that was slouching down at my ankle, and it was then I heard the soft click as the outside bathroom door locked. I watched as the tips of the black shoes, freshly shined, appeared across from mine on the other side of the stall, and my suitcase was placed on the floor.

I pulled my feet up onto the toilet seat and tucked my head into my knees.

For some reason I'll never understand, he knocked.

A girl who swam with alligators. A chicken who thought it was a cat. 2x2 is 4. 3x3 is 9. 5x5 is 25.

Chapter 2

CRAWFORD, GEORGIA
CORA LEE JENKINS
1962

CORA LEE LOOKED at the clock above the sink and wiped the flour from her hands onto the green kitchen cloth she had tucked into the front of her pants at the waist. It was a few minutes past one o'clock. If Otis planned to be at the station in time to pick up Macey May, he was going to need to leave. She walked to the back screen door and shifted it open with her hip. The November cold was crisp, and she felt it in her chest when she breathed in, but the house had felt stale to her that morning. Filled with mourning air for some reason. Mourning air was her mother's superstition and her mother's before that. Cora Lee remembered thinking her mother was crazy when she'd go on about the restless spirits. She couldn't ever imagine herself doing anything but rolling her eyes about it. "You can tell," her mother would say, "when the spirits are restless. The air stills. Mourns. That's how you know. The only way to fix it is to give them the wind to breathe. They'll attach to it and be on their way." Cora Lee was twenty-six when she finally believed in it. Three months after Hi died. She'd believed in mourning air now for the past twenty-five years.

She had been airing out the house since the early hours of the morning, but the ghosts didn't seem to be budging. That was never a good sign.

"Otis! Hey, Otis!" She tilted her head a little to the left. Her right ear was losing some of its hearing. Most of the time it rang with a high-pitched squeal as if someone were easing a bow across the tight strings of a violin, other times it sounded like waves in the ocean. It didn't bother her and, if truth be told, it helped out at night with Otis's snoring. All she had to do was roll over in the bed, and she slept as tight as a bug in a rug, or she slept like a top. She was never sure what either saying meant, but it didn't matter. She knew she slept better now that the sawing from the pillow next to her was shut out, and that's all that mattered. Whether that made her a bug or a top made no difference to her.

"Otis!" She yelled louder this time, her voice skipping over the wind like the flat rocks she used to throw into the pond when she was growing up.

From the direction of the barn she heard her name. "Hold on, Cora!"

The screen bounced shut behind her.

The kitchen was yellow, Meyer lemon, bright enough to make you smile even if you didn't want to, even without you knowing you were doing it. It made Cora Lee smile. Every time she entered it a grin would spread across her face, and "Thank You Jesus" would whisper across her lips. She was lucky—always had been, mostly. Lucky to have married Mr. Lehigh Jenkins when she was nineteen (Hi to everyone who knew him). Lucky to have raised two baby girls with him, for a while at least. Lucky to have the yellow kitchen that stood proud under a roof that stood prouder over her. All life was lucky if you thought about it, even the sad parts.

She was making cornbread to go with her chili for later that night. It was Macey May's favorite, and with the nip in the air, they could all use something to warm them up. She had two secrets for her recipes. The first was only using white cornmeal in the mix for the bread but sprinkling yellow cornmeal in the bottom of the skillet with a little lard to make sure it didn't stick. A cast iron skillet, old and seasoned, was also a must, so maybe she had three. Cocoa powder in the chili was the biggest secret, the one she'd carry with her to the grave. The words had never crossed her lips, and a pen had never leaked its ink anywhere on a recipe card indicating it. It didn't bother her that people would never know, would never be able to exactly replicate her chili. Maybe it was good to leave people talking, wanting, missing her even.

"Cora Lee!" Otis burst through the door, his breath coming quick and loud.

"What's wrong?"

"It's Mabel."

Cora Lee shook her head. "I told you not to name those cows."

"Look, she's laying down and won't get up, not even for a bit of apple. Her stomach doesn't look right to me either, and her breathing's labored. I think I better call Denim and have him come take a look."

"Pasture bloat again, you think?"

"Probably. But I'd be happier hearing it from him."

She turned the oven off and covered the raw cornbread mixture with a clean dish towel. It would keep until she came back. "Fine, call him, but I'm going to have to go into town to pick up Macey May. You'll be here without the truck."

"That's fine. I'm not planning on leaving. He'll probably bring the trocar again and give her some relief."

"It's the third time this year. There has to be something more permanent."

"I know. I'll ask about our options."

"Well, let me run and change out of these clothes. You think she knows enough to stay in the station? I'm going to be late. There's no way around it."

Otis nodded. "She's a smart girl. She'll stay. I'm sure there's someone there'll keep an eye on her. Little thing, all by herself."

"I still don't know why Rose couldn't just tell Adele she needed to bring her down. It doesn't seem right sending her alone on a bus." Cora Lee folded the green kitchen cloth from her waist and placed it on the counter.

"Rose said there were too many orders with the holiday coming up. That other girl they hired didn't work out, and she didn't feel she could leave Adele all alone. Besides, maybe she needs a week to herself. With Curtis off working in California, I think she feels the need to get going, get in charge of things, make sure everything is in order for when he comes back."

Cora Lee left the kitchen and walked into the bedroom off of the downstairs hallway. Her voice was muffled in the distance, but Otis heard her. "She's never had any control in her life to start with. Don't understand why she thinks she's going to get some now. First it was Willie and then Curtis. Why that girl makes the choices she does, I'll never know."

She looked at her reflection in the mirror above her bureau. Her skin had sallowed, the darkness becoming more a ghostly hue of the deep gloss it used to be. *Yes*, she decided, pulling her cheeks back with her hands and lifting up her eyebrows, *I do believe I'm fading*. She'd see fifty-two come the spring. Five years longer than her mother got to live and six years longer than her grandmother. Aging was something she never thought she'd do, but once forty-five passed, and the doctor gave her a clean bill of health at fifty and fifty-one, she started thinking about what she might do with the years ahead that she never planned on getting. She thought about it, made a list, and then crumpled it up and threw it away. If she knew anything, it was that plans had a way of changing on you.

Otis was getting off the phone with Denim when she went in to grab the keys out of the bowl next to the door.

"You'll be okay going to get her?" He hesitated. "You'll have to take County Road. There's no time to skirt around on Route Ten."

She could hear the worry in his voice, trying to disguise itself below the surface of his words. It was always there when she had to make a trip into town alone. "And why wouldn't I be?" Cora Lee pulled her shoulders back and closed the kitchen door on her way out with more force than was necessary. The ghosts seemed to have decided they were going to stay for a while.

His was a pointless question, the answer inevitable. She wouldn't be okay going into town, but she'd do it because it needed to be done. He also knew that when she came home there would be no cornbread or chili that night. Otis would have to grill some cheese sandwiches for him and Macey May, and Cora Lee would sit in the rocking chair on the porch long into the night, long after they had gone to bed, the soft creak of wood against wood the only sound that she was out there. In the morning they'd possibly have to forgo her homemade pancakes shaped into hearts and have oatmeal instead.

Sometimes memories were that powerful.

Cora Lee drove the pickup truck down the long driveway to the road, the dirt billowing beneath the tires and in through the open windows. Too much mourning feeling everywhere. If the ghosts were in the truck also, she wanted them to have a way out. She raised a hand to wave the dust out of her eyes when the wheel hit a divot and bumped her up from the seat. "Heaven's mercy!" she said. "Damn if Otis doesn't get out here and plane out these holes before I kill myself."

She turned the radio on, found only static, then turned it off again, resigned. She knew Otis was busy, and she knew Otis would make sure the driveway was fixed before the winter set in. He always did. It was the trip that was tying her up, getting to her in that place that she didn't like to be.

County Road.

How she hated that stretch into town. She preferred Route Ten. It was longer by at least twenty minutes, but it brought her in from the other direction, down Main Street with the library and courthouse on her left. Unlike County Road, she could get to the bus station and never have to see *IT*.

Macey May was waiting and didn't know and wouldn't understand why her grandmother didn't like driving County Road. Cora Lee didn't want her to either. Only Otis knew the truth, and Denim, his brother. She owed Denim more than she could ever repay for keeping hidden what he knew all these years. Even Rose and Ruby didn't have any idea. She'd protected them from it and intended to go right on doing so. It didn't even matter what it cost her—Rose's disappointment in her, Ruby's distance. She'd take it all, carrying it on her back like a basket of penance. It didn't matter to her as long as her girls never had to live with the image that haunted her most times her eyes closed. She never wanted them to know what hate could do when it wanted to.

She took a deep breath and forced her foot down on the accelerator. The turnoff for Route Ten blurred by in her side mirror. "No going back now, Cora Lee," she said in case the ghosts were listening.

Taller and with a trunk too big now for arms to ever get around, *IT* would still be there, she knew, an overseer of sorts, pushed back from County Road up on the little knoll behind the dilapidated stone wall left over from a war fought to fix inequality. As if fixing it would ever be that easy. The tree held a power in Cora's eyes that had taken on a magical, menacing quality over the past twenty-five years. Cora was sure that its roots would rip out of the ground one day, and she'd wake up to find that it had walked the miles and planted itself smack dab in front of her doorway, branches squeezing the farmhouse until the windows blew out. One last attempt to destroy her entirely.

She had tried for years to hold on to the other memory of that place and that tree. The one of Hi courting her there, carving their initials into the bark with the old switchblade he kept in his back pocket, the Spanish moss secluding them away. He had brought her over there one night right before dusk to show her the farmland and tell her his dreams. It had been half an hour's drive to get there from their parents' homes in Avery, but Hi had insisted. He had even borrowed the Reverend Gardner's car for the purpose. There was a harvest moon then, the sky an autumn oil painting of rust, amber, and ochre splashed against a gray-blue canvas, and stars twinkled like candles. They had spread out a quilt and eaten some molasses hermits she had brought with her. He promised he'd marry her, buy her a fine house, a farm right there in Crawford where the land was cheap and the soil good. They could both work it and call it their own, a safe haven in the crazy world. She believed him. She needed to. And he did.

The memory didn't hold, though. It couldn't. And now all she wanted was to hollow that tree, to gut it like it had hollowed her out, and burn it to its core. Instead, it stood there overlooking County Road, mocking the injustice it had unwittingly perpetrated in her life, an accomplice to her own years of mourning.

Chuck's Luncheonette blurred by, the awning a green and white taffy pull in Cora Lee's peripheral vision. Macey May would be hoping that Otis was picking her up, she knew this. The two of them conspired all the time like they were best friends behind the schoolhouse, the cross my heart and hope to die kind. If they weren't thinking about some way to scare her—a snakeskin on her pillow, a dead mouse in freezer, anything to make Cora Lee cry out (which she never did)—he was showing her how to run the tractor or allowing her to name the new calves. The forty-four-year age difference didn't seem to matter. Most of the time she assumed that Macey May was the more mature of the two.

Otis had told her the night before that he planned to take Macey May to Chuck's after picking her up, a surprise. He said he was going to say no when she asked but then pull in anyway. Maybe Cora Lee would take her there. She smiled at the thought. She and Macey weren't that close yet. Rose was headstrong, and visits to the farm happened only two or three times a year. When they did come up, Macey May became Otis's shadow unless Cora Lee was baking. Then the girl was underfoot so much that more than once Cora Lee had to do the two-step around her to keep from falling. Invitations to Harrison were given with reluctance, and she had no desire to be where she wasn't wanted, so Cora Lee had never been. It was regrettable, and she knew she needed to change her thinking on that if she was going to see Macey May more often. Yes, lunch at Chuck's would help them bond.

Macey May was three months old the first time Cora Lee laid eyes on her. And oh, how she took her breath away with her light brown skin, deep dark eyes, and sheeps' black wool covering her head. Her first grandchild. She thought her heart would burst. Lifting her up and catching her in the rays of the sun that darted through the parlor window, she said, "She looks just like Hi."

Rose had taken her back then. "Does she? I wouldn't know."

It was true. Other than telling them about him dying in his sleep, Cora Lee said little about Hi. It was her fear that kept her mouth closed.

Afraid that if she talked too much, the girls might ask too many questions, might start bringing him up in conversation around town, might go looking for answers other than the ones she had given them. She knew Rose wasn't the type to let go once she latched onto something, or someone. Better to not have her reach out at all.

The first time Rose stood on the farmhouse porch hand in hand with Curtis, Cora Lee saw the look of defiance in her eyes, the piousness in her stance, and had wanted to take her by the shoulders and shake her. Not for bringing home a man whose skin was as white as the flour she used to make her cornbread, but for thinking that the world would accept it. That it was safe.

Cora Lee had seen Rose's car coming down the driveway from the upstairs window, the dry earth clouding from the tires almost making it up to the second floor in mini tornadoes. It had been a hot summer. The sun was up then early, rousing the roosters who only wanted a few more minutes sleep. Sweat made your skin prickle before noon, and the dry dust tripped your feet up when you walked. It was barely ten in the morning when Curtis got out of the car and walked around the passenger door to let Rose out. Rose's hair was covered in a pink scarf, and she wore big sunglasses as if she were a movie star in hiding. Cora Lee would have laughed at the ridiculousness of it all had Rose at that moment not placed her hand upon her belly in a way all women do when they have created a life within them.

Cora Lee shook her head at the memory and slowed the truck down to pull into the bus station. *At least she's not waiting outside in the cold*, she thought. *At least Macey May has sense.* She shut the car off and left the keys in the ignition.

"Macey May? Macey May, honey. Wake up." Cora Lee nudged her with her hand. "Why, you've gone and fallen asleep on the bench. Are you that cold? You're all wound up like a ball of string. I didn't even realize it was you when I first came in. I thought someone had left their coat all pushed up like. I could barely even see you in that corner, tucked in behind the soda machine. You weren't hiding from me now, were you?"

Macey May looked up at her grandmother and shook her head.

"What's wrong with you? Cat got your tongue?"

Macey May shook her head again.

Cora Lee sat down next to her and placed the palm of her hand against her forehead. "No fever. Your stomach bothering you? Were you scared because I was late?"

With that, Macey May burst into tears.

"Oh, child. Come now. It's okay. Probably just from the trip. Those buses are so bumpy to ride in, why, I'm surprised the drivers aren't sick every day. We'll go on home, and I'll get you a bicarbonate of soda. It will fix you right up, I promise."

Cora Lee reached into her purse and handed Macey May a tissue. "There now. Wipe those tears away. I'm here, you'll be fine. Otis is home with Mabel. She's not feeling well either."

Macey May's lip quivered as the tears continued to fall, her voice caught in her throat. "Grandma, there...there...was..."

Before she could finish, a man was standing next to Cora Lee. "Everything all right here? Anything I can do to help?"

Cora Lee looked up. "Hey there, Junior! I didn't even hear you come in. She took the bus all the way from Harrison, and it did a number on her stomach, I'm afraid. This is Macey May, Rose's little one."

He looked at Macey May and smiled, a perfect smile, with teeth that couldn't even hold one toothpick between them. "Sure she is. I remember seeing her picture the last time I was at your place." He kneeled down. Macey May could smell his breath on her face. It smelled of black licorice and cigarettes. "What you need is a Coke. I hear it helps with upset stomachs." He stuck his hand in his pocket and picked out a few coins. "Here you go."

Macey May shrunk into Cora Lee.

"Child, stop that," Cora Lee said. "Junior's being kind to you. I know you don't feel well, but that doesn't mean you can be rude. I know your mama taught you how to act proper."

"Ah, nothing to worry about. I'm sure Rose told her never to talk to strangers." Junior dropped the coins into the machine. There was the sound of the money falling into the inner coin box and then a click. He opened the side door and took out a glass bottle. With one swift motion, Junior hit the top of the bottle against the opener using his other hand to stop the cap from falling on the floor. He held the cold drink out to Macey May. "Here. Feel better, sugar."

Cora Lee stood up and stepped aside, leaving Macey May unprotected, and motioned for her to take the bottle. "Go on." She crossed her arms in front of her.

Macey May reached out. Their skin touched as the glass passed between them. Junior tweaked her ear and tapped the tip of her nose with his finger. "See, that wasn't all that hard now, was it? Well, I better be going, Miss Cora Lee. I saw your truck in the parking lot and thought it might be Otis. I was hoping to talk to him."

She picked the suitcase off of the floor and put her hand on Macey May's shoulder. "He's back home, but I'll tell him you were looking for him."

Junior raised his hat in a goodbye. "Sure thing. Tell him to stop by the store later this week if he's in town. Daddy wanted to talk to him about those acres in the far field. And tell Rose hey for me when you speak with her. Ruby, too." He looked at Macey May and winked. "Your mama and me have been friends forever."

Macey May stood up and retreated behind Cora Lee's shoulder.

"You can say 'hey' yourself. They'll be here for Thanksgiving. Both coming in the day before and staying until Saturday. Why don't you stop by for a piece of chocolate pecan after you're done with dinner? I seem to recall it's your favorite. I'm teaching Macey May the recipe this year."

Junior smiled and bent his head down. "Thanks just the same, but I'm not sure Rose would be up for seeing me."

"Come now." She looked sideways at Macey May and stepped aside, leaving her exposed again. "It's been almost ten years since your quarrel."

"What do they say about a woman's wrath? Hell has no fury or something like that?" Junior's laugh filled the hollow waiting room.

Cora Lee touched his arm. "Water under the bridge, Junior. Besides, you never scorned her. You both had a disagreement is all. Stop by. I know she'd love to see you."

Junior smiled at Macey May. "Your grandma makes the best chocolate pecan pies in the whole county, you know. She could sell 'em if she wanted to. Thank you, Cora Lee, for the invitation. Maybe I will stop on over."

Cora Lee helped Macey May into the truck and waved goodbye to Junior. "Nice man, most of the time, that Junior. I hear he can be nasty, though, when he's been playing poker and drinking. His real name's Thomas just like his daddy, so folks have called him Junior ever since he was born. That poor family…been through some tough times." She stopped the car at the intersection to the main street and looked both ways. "Your mama ever tell you about them?"

Macey May shook her head.

"I reckon that's for the best. But my goodness, did Junior have a crush on your mama growing up. Never seen a boy so taken."

Junior had a shine for Rose; it wasn't a secret. He had ever since the two of them were little, and Cora Lee would watch him during the mornings while his daddy went to work. Mrs. Walsh was a fragile sort, ever since she lost her second baby when Junior was only four. Never seemed quite right after that. People said they'd see her sometimes walking the roads at night, singing lullabies and missing her sweet little girl. For a while she spent some time in the state sanatorium until Mr. Walsh brought her home and hired a live-in nurse who was supposed to watch her twenty-four hours a day. She couldn't be much of a mother to Junior, so when Mr. Walsh asked Cora Lee to sit for him for four dollars a week, she thought it made sense. Ruby was still a toddler, and this gave Rose someone to play with. Hi had died less than a year before; she was thankful for the distraction. The farm was in her name and established enough by then that she felt she could continue on with it. There were plenty of workers, hired hands making their way across the country with the crops. Otis was made the full-time manager, so taking care of another young'un along with hers didn't seem like something she couldn't handle. And she knew Mr. Walsh could use the help.

Every morning Mr. Walsh drove Junior out to the farm and then picked him up late afternoon after he closed his grocery. By the time Rose and he were six and kindergarten was about to start, you would have thought their little hearts would break when they realized they wouldn't be going together. She never thought she'd seen anything so sad as the way Junior hugged on to Rose, neither one of them understanding why they were being torn apart because of the color of their skin. She'd still watch him over school vacations and a holiday if Mr. Walsh needed her to, and they'd be back to peas in a pod, walking in step around the farm, Rose showing him the baby chicks and even how to milk a cow. Cora Lee knew even then that Junior loved her.

"Yes," Cora Lee said, "I'm not sure he ever stopped caring for her." She patted Macey May's leg. "You're too young to understand this, but love can be hard. When your mama found your daddy, I'm pretty sure it broke Junior's heart in two."

"Did Mama love Junior?"

Cora Lee thought a moment before she answered. By then she knew enough about her daughter to know that much of what she did and how she acted was aimed, for some reason, at her. A punishment for a crime that she was still in the dark about; a reprimand of sorts to show her that her views were wrong and out of date, as if Cora Lee were somehow single-handedly responsible for the state of race relations. When she had refused to register to vote no matter how many times someone from the NAACP knocked at her door, Rose didn't talk to her for a month. If Rose had been uncivilized enough to spit on her, Cora Lee was sure she would have. When reports came in of a young black man being senselessly killed on the streets of Atlanta, Rose would call her up and spew out a diatribe that ultimately ended in her blaming Cora Lee—as if Cora Lee's inaction against injustice was the same as her finger pulling the trigger.

Cora Lee sighed. "No, Macey May. I don't think your mama ever loved Junior in that way. She loved his attention, but I don't think she ever thought of him as anything more than a brother."

Macey May leaned her head against the coolness of the car window, her hand still wrapped around the untouched Coca-Cola bottle that was leaving droplets of sweat on the skirt of her dress. They passed Junior walking down Main, and Cora Lee beeped. Junior raised his hand in a parting wave, and Macey May watched as his freshly polished black shoes continued on their way.

Chapter 3

HARRISON, GEORGIA
ROSE JOHNSON
1962

"I'LL BE FINE, Miss Eunice. Honest. Just nerves is all. My stomach's been acting up with Curtis gone. The peppermint leaves help a bit." Rose wiped the perspiration off the top of her lip and sat down again at the kitchen table. "And I don't like lying," she said. She placed the teacup down in its saucer. The china clinked together, reminding her of the wind chimes on her mother's front porch. It was how you knew a storm was coming, the cling-clanging of the wind chimes. Sometimes, if the wind was right, you couldn't hear anything but their music, a personal symphony, and before you knew it they'd quiet down and the storm would be over. Her hand shook and the teacup rattled again. No music was going to ease the power of this storm.

"Secrets aren't lies," Miss Eunice said, putting another gingersnap on Rose's plate. She closed up the bag, reopened it, and added another two. "Here, a few extra for settling your stomach. Never easy on a mother to have to leave her child. You're lucky you only have a smidge of indigestion."

Rose was in Miss Eunice's kitchen, had arrived straight after seeing Macey May off at the station. A bus passed by the window not long after she got there, and Rose found herself ducking out of the way in case Macey May had obtained see-through vision somehow and knew she was sitting at the Formica table partaking in tea with their neighbor. "If they aren't lies, then what are they?"

"Nothing as big as you are making them out to be. People need to keep some things to themselves, especially when they don't know what those things might bring or do to someone else. Take Macey May. She's only nine. I'll give you sharp as a tack and just as smart, but she doesn't need to worry about this. You figure it out, and then you tell her. No sense in throwing grown-up problems onto her little shoulders."

"But I lied to my mama too." Rose's chin fell to her chest.

"Did you? How?" Miss Eunice dipped her gingersnap into her tea, the end becoming moist and soft.

"I said I needed to stay home to work."

"Aren't you?"

"Miss Eunice, you know…"

"Aren't you?" Her voice was adamant.

"Yes, but only for two more days. Adele's closing up shop and going to Irving's family for the holiday. Mama thinks I'm working morning, noon, and night until Thanksgiving Eve."

"And what harm is there in her thinking that?" Miss Eunice lifted the teapot and refilled Rose's cup. "It seems to me you are doing exactly what you need to. Curtis is gone, and it looks like you and I are the only two who expect something isn't right. If you told your mother or your sister that you haven't heard from him in almost two months, or that no checks have ever come, why, they'd probably tell you to forget about him and think about moving on…probably say things they'd later regret when he does come home. This way you are saving everyone from hurting."

Rose reached out and clasped Miss Eunice's hand. Her skin was smooth and her nails newly polished. It was Miss Eunice's one extravagance.

Every week she had a manicure over at Bertha's Beauty shop at the corner of Bishop and Walker across the street from Adele's where she'd also get herself a fig bar. Primrose Luster was her color of choice; Rose had never known her to wear anything else.

"What if I'm wrong, though? What if he's really left us for good? The last time it was only a few days, the time before that a week at most. Macey didn't question it. I'd say Daddy had a job and needed to be away, but now it's been too long, Miss Eunice. And you know, he never told me—any of the times. Never once did he explain where he was or why he'd left. And I wouldn't yell or scream or challenge him because I didn't want Macey May thinking anything was wrong. I'd make him dinner and tell him I was glad he was home when he finally walked through the door." Rose's fist hit the table. "What is wrong with me?"

"Nothing, child. You love him. Sometimes our hearts let us do things our heads never would. Your head probably wanted to kick him out the door, but your heart felt differently."

"Is love always like this?"

"I wouldn't know, honey. Seems that's one thing God didn't seem fit to give me. Now, I know love. My children," Miss Eunice stopped and smiled, "my students, I mean, forty-two years of them. They showed me love, allowed me to be a mother when I didn't have any of my own. But the love you are talking about…no one ever seemed to cross my path that way."

"There's always time."

Miss Eunice let out a laugh. "I'm afraid not for me. Too set in my ways now. I wouldn't know what to do if a man started showing me some interest. Who's around here? Floyd at the Auto Shack? Old Peeper at the grocery?"

"Mr. Byrd seems to like your company?"

Miss Eunice blushed and sat up properly in her chair. "Thanks, but no. I've got my books and you and Macey May to take care of. I don't need stars in my eyes. That's for you young ones."

"But was I wrong for not telling her that I don't think he's coming back this time? How long do I keep pretending? What do I tell her about the house?" Rose looked out the window of Miss Eunice's kitchen. What if this was it? What if she had to raise Macey May all by herself? Of course she had her mother and Otis, but they were in Crawford—a world away from the last ten years of her life, a world too closed up in the past. Just going into town there and seeing those signs everywhere—blacks here, whites only here—made her so mad she could spit. And her mother, sitting on her farm, just taking it, not trying to change anything.

Rose hadn't wanted to go back to full-time at Adele's Bakery, but then Curtis's paycheck started getting sporadic, and they needed the money, especially with the holidays coming up. Macey May had been looking through the Sears catalog, it had come so early (mid August). She was enraptured by all the games and toys, circling everything with a big black marker that she wanted Santa to bring her. Rose knew they'd be hard pressed to even buy her a doll from Woolworth's on Curtis's undependable salary alone, never mind presents from Sears. Her moving to full-time work was the only option. She had always heard that men didn't like their women working, took away some of their manhood. So it surprised her when Curtis rubbed his chin and nodded. He went on for five minutes explaining how Macey May deserved that little red and white bike she'd been wanting. Rose knew he was right. There wasn't a week that went by without Macey May coming into the house out of breath from running home after school, bursting to tell them about the kids riding their bikes down the hill with playing cards in the tires, clicking and clacking through the spokes while the colored pompoms streamed from the end of the handlebars. Rose hesitated a second, and he filled the space with a quiet suggestion—they could use the money.

The next day she told Adele she'd take the job.

Rose stood up and walked over to the sink to put away her teacup. "This time is different though, Miss Eunice. I feel it." Rose crossed her arms. "The money's gone."

"You mean he cleaned out your savings?" Miss Eunice shook her head.

"Not savings. There's nothing in it to clean out except twenty-three dollars. I mean the other money."

"Rose. You better come back and sit down and tell me what you're talking about."

Rose thought about the last time she had seen the money. It was a week before he disappeared, the day before she told Curtis she had accepted Adele's full-time position as baker. And it was a lot more than twenty-three dollars that she found tucked far back in his sock drawer, balled together with elastic. She wasn't snooping. She was looking for his lighter. The gas burner on the stove had been acting up again, clicking in vain. It needed to be lit manually. Curtis promised he'd fix it that weekend, but she had used the last match that morning for breakfast, lighting the flame for his fried egg with a soft yolk. By afternoon the weather had turned nasty, rain and wind pelting against the windowpanes; she wasn't walking to the corner grocery for matches. The lighter had been a present to him for his birthday the year before. Shiny silver and smooth as a rock taken out of the creek that ran behind her mother's farmhouse, with a red rose engraved on the front. He kept it in his sock drawer "where it would stay nice and pretty" like her. He'd take it out to use at home, but he never took it to work with him. "I don't want it scratched," he'd tell her.

The money ball was big and wound tight, so tight that after she unfurled it she worried if she'd be able to get it small enough again. Five hundred and thirty-seven dollars. Five hundred and thirty-seven dollars. She could see it still in her head. The two hundreds, the one fifty, the six twenties, some tens but no fives, and the ones. So many dollar bills, green, wrinkled, dozens and dozens of them. Dollars. Instant. Easy. Accessible.

Rose's stomach knotted remembering that night. It turned her insides out remembering the pleading in Curtis's voice as he gave his reasons for her taking on the full-time work, trying to make it seem like this would make her a modern woman of the world. All she felt was put upon. What man couldn't provide for his wife and child?

"It's like he planned it, Miss Eunice. Planned me taking the job so he could leave…wanting to be sure that I could take care of us without him. He'd know my mama would watch Macey May if I needed her to. When I think it about it now, he seemed relieved to hear about the job, like God had cleared a path for him, made a way."

Rose looked at the wallpaper next to the table. "You know, I never noticed it, but this is the same paper we have in the kitchen except yours is pink and ours is brown. Funny, isn't it, the things we don't notice that are right in front of us the whole time."

Miss Eunice's eyes narrowed. "Rose. What money?"

"Five hundred and thirty-seven dollars rolled up in his sock drawer. I don't know where he got it or how long he's had it, but it's gone now, just like him."

Pushing back her chair, Miss Eunice stood up. "Are you sure?"

Rose nodded. "I'm sure. I counted it twice. I thought maybe it was a surprise, thought he was saving for that house he's been talking about over at the edge of town."

"A house?"

"Ever since he started working for that developer, all he does is talk about buying us a home. There's that eighteen acres on the outskirts of Harrison, the southern part where it borders Newton. Thirty starter homes, Curtis calls them—cute little single-family homes in rows of ten, back-to-back. He took me over there not long ago and started spinning dreams in the air. Even said we'd have another baby, how he always wanted a son to call CJ for Curtis Junior. I told him I didn't know of any bank that would give a white man who had a family with a Negro a mortgage, but he told me not to worry about it, that things were changing, and to leave it to him. He said he was looking into a different way of getting the money. He promised me it wasn't illegal, but maybe I just wanted to believe the lie."

Miss Eunice clucked a few times and nodded her head. "Yes, honey. Sounds to me like this went a different way than even Curtis imagined. Have you talked to Willie?"

At the mention of his name Rose's eyes grew dark. She sat up straighter in the chair. "Why would you even say that, Miss Eunice? I'm not speaking to Mr. William Price for no one. I've kept my silence with him since the day he left me, and I'm not about to break it now."

"Rose."

"I said no, Miss Eunice. That's the end of it. Curtis may be gone, and I may be a fool when it comes to him, but in everything else, I will not beg." She sat up straighter to emphasize her point.

"Asking isn't begging. And besides, as I recall, it was Willie doing the begging, not you."

Rose folded her napkin and placed it on the table next to her saucer. "Willie left me, Miss Eunice. I don't owe him anything."

Miss Eunice placed her hand on Rose's shoulder. "But he came back."

"Seven years too late."

Miss Eunice sighed. "Rose, it was war. Rules are different when it comes to that. There's no timeline."

"Since when is dodging the draft at Howard University *war*? He was supposed to stay there for a year. Then we were going to get married so we could be together while he finished medical school and did his residency. One year. Just to wait for Korea to end. He said it was his parents' idea, and I believed him. He made me believe." Rose paused. Her throat constricted and her voice became tight. "I couldn't visit him with working all the time, trying to keep that stupid roof above my head at the boardinghouse. And the one time I thought I could—had changed my shift and everything—he told me not to come, that his parents and sister were going up that weekend. Miss Eunice, we had been together for eight months. I had a promise ring on my finger. We were supposed to be married that fall, and they didn't even know I existed. I was supposed to be Mrs. William Lewis, a doctor's wife!"

The radiator on the kitchen wall breathed to life, its lungs tired and achy. Rose put her head down on her forearm against the blue Formica table and let the sobs come.

It was true, all of it. When Rose thought about what she had given up for Willie, so much. Everything nearly. Her mother had called her a fool when she left the farm, told her not to chase any man ever, but Rose wouldn't listen. Willie wasn't any man. Tall and proud with skin a high yellow, no one told him no and even if they had, he wouldn't have listened. At least not then. They had met at one of her mother's strawberry festivals in Crawford. He was a neighbor's cousin visiting for the month. Rose saw him the minute she walked out the front door holding the punch bowl. He was lounging under the shade of the chinaberry tree in the yard on one of the old quilts that were scattered about, his white shirt sleeves rolled above his elbows, his tan pants inching up above his white socks and black shoes. He was lighter than most of the people out on the farms—not enough to pass for white but enough to not make whites skittish around him. She knew he'd be able to go far on that alone. When she found out he had just graduated college and was planning to continue on to medical school, she knew he'd touch the stars.

She heard Willie laugh then, could remember it still as if it were a soundtrack playing in her ear from a movie she'd never forget. The deep bass to it that made her belly vibrate, the warmth she felt crawl up her

as his secretary was something Rose would never understand. The size of her mouth was only to be beaten by the largeness of her backside. No, there would be no food for fodder on the end of Odella's phone when she started making her calls if Rose could help it. Although, Rose was smart enough to know that Odella would not want for things to say—real or fictitious. When Willie came out he wouldn't catch her reading one of those magazines or filing her nails, her leg crossed over and bouncing, like she'd seen so many women do in waiting areas, as if they didn't know how to present themselves in public. No, when he appeared she wanted to be sure he knew without hesitation that she was not there for *him*.

Fifteen minutes later laughter came from the hallway leading to Willie's office down the hall, and Rose's heart began to pound in her ears. "Oh, Dr. Price." The words jangled like keys. "How can I ever thank you? I mean, I truly believed I was having a heart attack."

Rose brought her feet in closer and sat up straighter.

"Now, Mrs. Parker, if you ever think it is a heart attack again, please don't walk over to see me. Better to call for an ambulance, and head right on over to the hospital in Spencer to be safe."

A giggle erupted from Mrs. Parker, who appeared, Rose noticed, to have taken the time to put on her best mustard yellow dress with matching hat before rushing over to be saved by Willie. She hated women who acted coy, who pretended to be incapable of their own lives. She especially hated women who acted this way around Willie. For some reason they always had. "Who would have thought…just itty-bitty indigestion. I feel so very foolish."

Willie's low voice was louder, closer. "Now, don't worry. There's never a reason to feel foolish. Odella here is going to call the pharmacy and get that prescription for antacid filled right now so you won't have to wait for it when you get there. Twice a day for five days should do it, and stay away from the boiled crawfish for a while."

He was standing at the desk now, his back to her. She watched as Odella raised one eyebrow and motioned with her chin for him to turn around.

Rose smoothed down the front of her coat and stood up. "Dr. Price."

She saw it in his eyes before he could cover it up, and she hated herself for doing anything to put it there.

Hope.

"Rose?"

Odella coughed and handed the prescription to the woman at the desk, who seemed more intent on the meeting she was witnessing before her than anything that could cure her indigestion.

"Willie...excuse me, Dr. Price, is there somewhere we could talk?"

"Your next appointment will be here in ten minutes." Odella smiled at Rose. "I told her you were booked all day, but she didn't want to listen. Walked right in here."

"Certainly. In my office. Please, this way."

Odella stood up, exasperation on her face, her large bosom heaving, reminding Rose that everything about her was large. "But—"

"Odella, please call whoever it is and see if they can reschedule. If they arrive, tell them I'm sorry but I will have to see them tomorrow." He stopped and looked at Rose behind him. "And please call the other patients and reschedule them too. I don't seem to recall anything of great urgency on the docket for today."

Rose was happy to see that the industrial blue hadn't seeped into his personal office. The walls were a light beige tweed patterned paper, like stray pieces of hay and sawdust on a barn floor. A large mahogany desk took up most of the space with two dark leather chairs facing it. It was too big and not her style. She looked at the diplomas on the wall. Bachelor in science from Tuskegee Institute. MD from Howard University. There were a few more citing accolades and recognitions, but Rose lowered her eyes and sat down. He *had* gone far. Without her.

Willie was nervous, she could tell. He had a habit of wiping his palms along his thighs if he found himself in a particularly uncomfortable situation. When he finally came back to Harrison after his first year at Howard, he made it clear he was only home for a visit and he intended to be gone for another three years. More if his parents had anything to do with it. She had thought he'd rub a hole right through the cloth of his pants as the words tumbled from his mouth. When he asked for his promise ring back, she knew his pants didn't stand a chance.

He took off his white lab coat and hung it on the back of the door, which he closed with one hand on the knob and one on the wood, quiet like, as a child might do who didn't want to be heard or a mother backing out of a sleeping baby's room. The black stethoscope encircled his neck, the silver sphere hanging midway down his chest. If she had been there at another time for any other reason, she might have actually congratulated him. After all these years, she might be able to do that. He had done so much, achieved greatness. It was hard not to be proud of that. Now he was moving ahead, changing the lives of those in Harrison, traveling out to the farms and bringing medicine and medical advice to those who'd never had it before. It didn't matter if they couldn't pay. Rose was sure it wasn't the path his parents had wanted him to take.

She'd even heard that he had created a scholarship at the high school for any girl who wanted to study nursing and had the grades to do it. Imagine that, she thought, a girl going to school and becoming a nurse, a professional! A black girl! Rose smiled in spite of herself at the thought. Maybe it would be her Macey May. Wouldn't that be irony?

"Rose. It's good to see you." He motioned for her to take a seat. He went behind his desk and then turned around and took the chair next to her. Their knees were close. She angled her legs, afraid they might touch. Rose could smell his cologne, see how his tie hung loosely around his neck. In all the years, he hadn't changed at all.

She reached out and touched the mahogany. The wood was cold and smooth. "Nice desk. A little grand for this space, though."

He laughed slightly. "A present from my parents when I graduated Howard. I guess they hoped I'd stay in Washington, gain a larger office, better clientele."

She nodded. "Instead, you came back to little ol' Harrison."

Willie coughed and looked out the window above her head. "I came back to you."

Rose stood up and stepped back. "Willie—"

He took her hand. "I'm sorry. Please sit down. I don't mean to make you go away."

She brushed her hand on her coat trying to get the feeling of his skin off of her. "Curtis is gone."

Willie leaned back in his chair and bit his lip. "I know. A few months now, right?"

"Almost two." She pressed her back against the wall, resting her head. It felt like the wind had been knocked out of her, hearing the words out there in the air. *Almost two.* "Miss Eunice thought you'd be able to help. Might know something I don't. Might have heard something from someone?"

Down the hall Odella's voice rang loudly on the phone. "No, I'm sorry. Dr. Price has had to reschedule. He can see you tomorrow at nine. I know, I know. But I'm just telling you what he told me." Her voice lowered, and Rose shook her head.

"Sorry about that," Willie said. "That was for my benefit. Odella likes a tight ship—doesn't like when things need to change up."

Rose shrugged. "The loud may have been for you, but the muffled was for me. You know she's telling whoever she's talking to that I'm here. It will be all around town before I've even left."

"Yeah, I guess you're right. Let the whole town know you won't speak to me, and then actually don't do it for four years, and there's bound to be talk when it finally happens."

"Three. It's been three years since you've settled back down here. And I never told anybody anything. It's none of their business. Let them think whatever they want anyway. It's not like I haven't known what it's like to take some of their sass or shunning. Not with the way I have chosen to live my life."

Willie smiled and stood up. "Oh, I'm pretty sure it hasn't bothered you one bit if you're still the same Rose I knew." He walked next to her and leaned on the wall beside her, their shoulders almost level, their breath in sync. He ventured out with his hand and held her fingers. "I'll help you, Rose, as much as I can."

On instinct, she squeezed his hand and then let go, putting her hand in her pocket and turning to face him. "Willie, you have to know—"

Willie looked down at his shoes and sighed. "No strings, I promise. But once we find him and we are on even playing ground, can we at least talk?"

"Talk? I'm married. There's nothing to talk about."

Willie walked to his desk and sat down behind it. He raised an eyebrow and leaned back. "Married? Did something happen in the Supreme Court of which I am unaware?"

Rose clenched her jaw. She had promised herself she wasn't going to let him get to her. "You know what, Dr. William Price, Miss Eunice was wrong. I should have never come here. I don't need your help, and I certainly don't need you."

"Rose. Sit and stay."

"And why should I do that?"

"Let me tell you what I know."

Later that night, Rose helped Miss Eunice with the dishes and ushered her into the living room to sit down. *The Lloyd Bridges Show* aired at eight o'clock and Miss Eunice didn't like to miss it. During the summer, Macey May would watch it with her and then come home for bed. Rose turned on the television.

"Pull that curtain across, would you, dear? No one needs to see me getting excited over that Lloyd Bridges." Miss Eunice sank into her chair by the front window.

Rose laughed. "Miss Eunice!"

"It's his hair and, boy, that deep voice of his. Sometimes his sons are even on the show with him." She picked up the *TV Guide* and began to leaf through it. "You need to let him help you, Rose."

"Who? Lloyd Bridges?"

"Of course not. Willie. What did he say?"

Rose went back into the kitchen to put the tea on. "Nothing I care to talk about yet."

She took two mugs down and sliced two pieces of pecan pie. No, she wasn't ready to talk about what Willie had said. He had been over in Dobson meeting an old college friend when he thought he saw Curtis come out of a bar across the street from his hotel. She didn't want to consider what it meant, didn't really even want to think about it. Didn't want to think about why she bristled at the way Willie had said "friend" and why her heart clenched at the word. She hated the fact that, try as she may, she had never gotten over Willie.

Dobson was thirty miles east of Harrison. They didn't know anyone in Dobson. Rose had never even been there.

Chapter 4

HARRISON, GEORGIA
CURTIS JOHNSON
1962

I HAD NEVER SEEN a prettier girl than Rose Jenkins in my life. Her black hair, smoothed down around her face with a flip at the end, skin that looked like burnt coffee and eyes a shade of lavender straight out of some field over in France. *Fairy eyes*, I thought the first time I looked into them. Eyes like that could get a guy in trouble. Eyes like that could make a guy think any dream is possible. Even when it wasn't.

I had been home from my tour in Korea for three weeks. Long enough to know that no one was going to give me a handout. Maybe a "thank you" and a cup of coffee for my service, but not a job. It was August of 1953. I had joined the U.S. Army on August 18, 1950, the same day I buried my grandmother. My friend Johnny enlisted too. We were eighteen years old with high school diplomas and believed President Truman when he told us that we were trying to prevent a third world war. The atrocities of Hitler were still pretty well etched in my mind. Now that I was old enough, I couldn't sit back and let murder happen. Besides, I had nowhere else to go, seeing that the bank was taking my grandmother's house. But Johnny was looking for adventure...and women. "The girls, Curtis," he'd say. "They love a man in uniform." Six-four with gangly legs and ears that stuck out like corn cobs, Johnny needed all the help he could get, so I wasn't going to begrudge him any attempt he wanted to make. It didn't seem to help, though. Neither did the folded flag given to his mother nine months later. Even in death he couldn't seem to make any girls, other than his mama, weep over him.

His mama was a widow with no one in the world except Johnny. She took me right in when I got back—put me up in Johnny's room even. I think she hoped that I could fill the empty space she felt. I knew I couldn't do that for her. Knew even then that the hole the war had left me would only get bigger until it swallowed me whole. It was strange sleeping in his bed when I knew he never would again. The walls were as he had left them. Our high school pennant in gold and blue. Pictures of our baseball team the year we won the state championship. (He did have a great pitching arm.) Photos tacked randomly next to the window for better light. Johnny's dream was to become an artist. He hoped the Army would let him be a combat photographer. He imagined his images from the Korean War splattered over *Life* magazine in full color. Instead of a camera, they gave him a gun. He didn't seem to quite have the same talent for that.

The Army Corps of Engineers had jobs building the connector between Savannah and Atlanta for the railway line that would cut right through the towns of Spencer and Harrison. It seemed a mountain stood in their way that they needed gone before they could start laying track. I figured I had the same chance as every other guy needing work, so I gathered what little money I had saved plus a ten that Johnny's mama gave me, hopped a bus, and went to try my luck in Spencer. I was put in charge of surveying and demolition setup—thanks to Uncle Sam for teaching me a skill that I could use in the civilian world. Blowing up bodies wasn't much different than blowing up mountains. The job came with decent pay and a bedroom to sleep in with a shared bathroom. Meals were made for us and deducted from our weekly paychecks. They were square, and three of them—nothing to write home about, but they filled your belly.

Basically, I carried a yellow pencil behind my ear and a rolled-up blueprint under my arm most of the time. I was barely twenty-one; it was enough.

Five Negroes worked under me. From eight until five every day, I pointed here and there and watched as the men laid the wires, making sure everything was connected like it should be. We got along all right. War makes you not care about the color of someone's skin if the gun they are holding is saving your life. I never considered myself a racist before I went to war, but I wasn't holding signs trying to get them their rights either. Separate but equal? Jim Crow? What did I know? I knew they were fighting now for kids to go to school together, but I also knew it wasn't that simple. Saying things and doing things, I've found, are not usually the same.

I hadn't seen color, any color, in a long time.

They were men, plain and simple. I think they found me an okay boss.

The sound the explosions made unnerved me: rock splitting under dynamite, shards flying through the air singing some warped patriotic song. It was the bullets all over again, never stopping in my mind. It was men screaming and lost limbs, and blood. Always blood. It was Johnny.

Most times I'd have to will myself to breathe as we huddled far enough away from the detonation to be out of the line of the explosion and remind myself that I wasn't in combat anymore. That it was only rocks and not the discharge of ammunition that I was hearing.

We all handled it differently over in Korea with the noise of the mortars exploding overhead, machine guns volleying fire back and forth inches away. The sounds of war. Johnny would draw when it got bad. Crawl to some space inside of himself where the battle didn't seem to reach him. He carried around a little sketch pad bound in leather, a graduation present from his mother. It was tiny, small enough to fit inside his helmet, held in by an elastic band. He'd take it out, grab the nib of his pencil from his pocket, and start drawing the trees, or the sky, or the waves of the ocean. Leaving out the death that was all around. Leaving nature undisturbed and innocent. Sometimes he'd draw us. He had a habit of leaving our eyes out. They'd be there, the outline, but nothing inside of them. Emptiness. I asked him once why he did that, but he never really had a good answer. "Eyes tell too much," he'd say. I think now I'm only beginning to understand what he meant by that.

Most of my guys on demolition were over there too, but we don't talk about it. There's no need to, the explosions at the site don't let us forget—mini reminders twenty times a day. After each blast I'd catch the eyes of the other guys, but that's as far as the reminiscing went.

Until Charlie. He joined the team five months in. Most of the mountain had been blown by then. He was the only other white man on my team, a little slow, simple. The type that makes you wonder what the service board was thinking when they allowed him to enlist. A disposable body? A human shield? Simply another to make us look stronger? There were less than a dozen detonations left to do that morning, so Charlie only needed to wire a few. Once this stage was over, we were moving to rebuilding if we wanted, laying down the beams for the rails. I was looking forward to it, actually. I thought it might be nice after all that time to finally create something rather than destroy it.

"Mr. Curtis?"

"Yeah, Charlie? What is it?" I could see droplets of sweat forming on his temples and his left eye twitched.

"I don't know if I can hear this?"

"Hear what? The explosion?"

He took off his helmet and ran his fingers through his hair. "I've got no problem lacing the rocks to blow, but, well, I don't do so good anymore with loud noises." He looked down at his boots. "I should have told them when they gave me the job, but they didn't ask, and I need the money."

I took a cigarette out and offered him one. His hand shook as he took it. Shook more while he tried to keep it steady as I lit a match. I noticed track marks on his arms. "You start that before or after you went over?" I asked, motioning toward the lines. A lot of guys took their coping mechanisms home with them. I threw the burning match down on the ground and snubbed it with the steel toe of my boot. So many men, boys really, realized if they mixed heroin with amphetamines and injected it, they'd stay high longer. Anything to forget where they were and what their own government was asking of them. There were guys who did it every day and those who only did it after the memories wouldn't let them sleep. I tried it once. Found myself sitting in the middle of a field a quarter of a mile away from my unit counting blades of purple grass. One time was all I needed.

He looked down at his feet, then off to his left. "Smoked some before I went, thought that would get me through." He shook his head. "It didn't. Trying to get off, but it's hard. I've got a wife and a kid." Our eyes met. "They're depending on me."

I blinked and swallowed hard.

Charlie only lasted three days. It could have been any one of us.

I had heard that there was a great bakery in Harrison, where a few of my guys lived. It was only a stone's throw away from the mountain, and supposedly they made the best strawberry-rhubarb tart in the county. My grandma made the best, so I couldn't pass up the comparison.

"Yeah, Mr. Curtis," Elwin said to me one day after the last stick was placed, and we were walking to the safety zone. "You've got to get over to Adele's Bakery."

Lucas pipped in with a low whistle. "Mmmm....hmmm. Now that place has some sweets, if you know what I mean."

Elwin laughed and winked at me, nodding his head in that knowing way he always did. I hopped a ride on the rear of the pickup later that night that brought them back home, and that's when I saw Rose walking past on the sidewalk. More of a sashay, actually, her maroon chiffon skirt swirling around her legs. I slapped the side of the truck twice with my hand and jumped off the back when it slowed down. Lucas's whistle floated out the passenger window.

Her hands were delicate and covered with white gloves that matched the flower in her hair. It's funny to think about it now, but, boy, was I jealous of that flower for touching her. It was my luck when she walked right into Adele's, walked around the back of the counter and wrapped her pretty little waist with an apron. I think she knew I had been following her because she asked me what I wanted before she even turned around to face me. I reached up to my hat and bowed a little bit, and she smiled back. I ordered a half a dozen strawberry-rhubarb tarts. It was then I knew I'd be staying in Harrison.

Chapter 5

HARRISON, GEORGIA
MACEY MAY JOHNSON
1962

MY ARM HURT. I swallowed hard, my throat burning from the bile that made its way up, looking for a way out.

"Honey, why you so quiet, child?" My grandma reached over and touched my shoulder. "You can tell me."

We were almost back to the farm. The ride had been a silent one. I guess she had held out as long as she could before trying to find out what was going on with me.

She was wrong. I couldn't tell her. Couldn't tell anyone. Never. I shrugged my shoulders instead. "Don't know," I said.

"Here, baby." She handed me a red and white peppermint wrapped in plastic. "See if that helps."

The plastic wrap crinkled as I undid it, and I popped the candy into my mouth. The sweetness made me gag, but I kept my mouth closed and prayed the ride would be over soon. I didn't want Grandma to keep worrying over me, asking me what was wrong, fretting over my answers that wouldn't be good enough. The tears worked their way up again from somewhere down deep in my toes, overtaking every vein in my body, like that Old Faithful geyser I learned about in school, bursting up from the earth whenever the pressure got to be too much. I didn't know a feeling could be so powerful. I leaned my head against the window and watched the road curve behind us in the side view mirror. The mint burned into the side of my cheek. When I moved it, my tongue caught in a crevice, the salty taste of blood filling my mouth.

I felt heavy. Heavy with secrets, too many secrets for my nine-year-old heart to hold in. The car wheels started to jump and bump, a sure sign we were on the drive to the farm. I sat up and took a deep breath. "Is Otis home?"

Grandma smiled at me. "Sure is. Probably still working with Mabel. Denim was coming over to see what he could do. I'm sure he'll come into the house once he knows we're back, though."

I bit my lower lip. "Could I lie down in your bed for a little bit?"

"My bed? I've got your room all made for you upstairs. Wouldn't you rather be where it's familiar? Mr. Jumpers is waiting for you. Snuggled right up there on the top of the bed between the pillows."

I smiled when she said that. Mr. Jumpers was a stuffed bunny that stayed at Grandma's house awaiting my visits. He was small and gray with a pair of blue overalls and a red bandana wrapped around his neck. His ears were long and made of velvet and reached down to the top of his feet. Whenever Grandma wrote to me, Otis was sure to include a line or two regarding Mr. Jumpers's latest adventures. Once Mr. Jumpers went all the way to Washington, D.C. to meet with President Kennedy only to be thrown on his bushy tail when he was discovered to be eating the radishes out of the White House garden. At night I'd rub his ears against my cheek until I fell asleep, the softness like a pussy willow against my skin.

I thought about the room on the second floor, so far away from the kitchen and familiar noises. "Just for a little bit. I'll sleep up there tonight. Promise. Please?"

Grandma winked at me. "It's probably as good an idea as any. That way I can hear you if you need anything. Now, come on. Let's grab your suitcase and go get you rested."

The farmhouse was large and white with green shutters sandwiching the windows. The porch was as long as the entire front of the house and wrapped halfway around on the left to meet up with the kitchen. The screened-in sleeping part was off to the right. The bright yellow door on the front, Meyer lemon, left over from the kitchen walls, welcomed anyone who wanted to enter. Grandma's door was always open. She even kept an extra bedroom in clean sheets because she never knew who might need to come for a stay. Two red wooden rockers, seasoned from the years, sat like an old married couple who had fallen into a comfortable nearness under the sky blue of the porch ceiling. I asked Grandma once why she had painted it blue, and she said it had been Pap's idea, first thing he had done to the house, even before fixing the few broken panes of glass or the screen door on the side that hung off its hinge. "No one owns the sky," he said.

I let her guide me by my shoulder into the house. I hadn't been there since the summer, but nothing had changed. Nothing ever changed there. That's why I liked it so much. I never understood why Mama had such a sore spot when it came to the farm. I'd hear her and Daddy in their bedroom the night before we came for a visit, words like "racist" and "bigots"—big words that I didn't quite know what they meant, but from the way Mama was saying them I knew they weren't good. Daddy's voice was always softer, trying to calm her down. I didn't know why she couldn't see what I saw, what I felt when I was here. If I had a choice, I'd leave Harrison and live on the farm. Mama and Daddy could work it. I know Otis would love my daddy's help, and Mama could cook with Grandma in the kitchen or open up a bakery of her own downtown. Miss Eunice would have to come. I wouldn't feel right leaving her all alone back home. I was confident Grandma would understand. I could hear her now, "Why, of course, Macey May. Wouldn't have it any other way. You go on ahead and tell Miss Eunice I'll have a room set up for her all proper-like with books and everything."

It wouldn't be no trouble.

"Grandma." I closed my eyes and let the yellow brightness of the kitchen sun me. Mr. Jumpers held tight against my chest while I spoke. She had taken my suitcase to her room, told me to go get a cracker from the tin on the counter on account of my stomach, and had returned promptly with him. "Mama doesn't think Daddy's coming home." I kept them closed, not wanting to read her face, to see if she agreed. I knew she'd try to disguise her voice, but few people could hide their eyes.

"Oh, Macey May. What makes you say that? He's away on a job all the way over in California. She said he'd be done by the end of the month and then be on his way home. Wouldn't be surprised if he shows up here this week before your mama's even done working. He'll probably bring you something nice from the ocean. Maybe a shell so you can hear the waves."

I turned and hugged her, thankful in my heart for her attempt at the lie. I knew what Mama had told her, that he was off over on the West Coast doing some contracting, but I could sense that Grandma wasn't fully believing it. I could still see Mama talking on the phone to Grandma, a cheery lilt in her voice that I didn't see on her face. Her eyebrows were knitted together and her knuckles were white from clenching the side of the table so tightly. "He'll be gone a month, Mama. Left the other day and won't be back until Thanksgiving. It's a good job with good pay, he says. More than he could make here in almost a year. He'll come to the farm and meet us there when he's finished. He thinks he'll have enough to put a down payment for our own house even." I must have looked at her strangely because she held her finger up to her lips, the unspoken indicator that told me to pay no mind, and scooted me out of the kitchen with a swift push from her free hand. The door almost hit me on the behind as I left. I asked her that night why she had said that, lying that Daddy had left only the day before when he had been gone by then for a month. "You wouldn't understand, Macey May. Grandma can be difficult at times. It's easier this way."

She was right. I didn't understand. Didn't understand her. Didn't understand Daddy. But I had heard him talk about wanting to buy us a house, so maybe she wasn't completely fibbing. Maybe she was only spinning parts of a tale and mixing it with truths.

"He's been gone before, you know." It was barely a whisper, part of me hoping Grandma wouldn't hear.

Those times Mama would make up some grand story about Daddy being needed at a job site over the state line. When I asked her when he'd be back, she'd look at the calendar and point somewhere in the middle. "About there," she'd say and then she'd tell me to go read a book or see if Miss Eunice needed anything. I knew she wasn't being truthful. I could tell by the way she'd pull back the living room curtain and look down the road every night before we ate dinner, Daddy's place set and waiting for him. Whenever he was gone, she wouldn't let me go get the mail none either. I'd watch her from the porch flipping through the envelopes the minute her hand snatched them from the box as if one held a notice telling her she'd won the King Arthur baking contest and a new refrigerator was on its way. Mostly it was bills, the pile of them getting higher and higher as they stayed unpaid on the counter.

Grandma put her hands on my shoulders, her eyes giving me a once-over. "What do you mean he's been gone before? When? For how long?"

I looked down at my socks. Now that I had said it, I wondered if it would have been better to keep it to myself. I shrugged.

"Macey May, don't you lift your shoulders at me pretending like you don't know an answer to my question. When has he gone before?"

I inhaled. If she talked to Mama I knew there would be no way for me to escape a few smacks across my backside and a lengthy tirade of all of my past indiscretions. Mama was good at remembering everything I'd ever done that I wasn't supposed to. The list, in her mind, was long. "Please. You can't tell Mama I told you. I guess she didn't want you to know… didn't want you worrying or nothing." I added the bit at the end hoping she'd be able to see the predicament I had gotten myself into and feel some sort of sympathy for me.

"Macey May?"

"All right. I'll tell you. I don't know if he ever left when I was real little. He may have, but I don't remember. Last year he left twice. Once was only for a couple of days, but the other time was almost three weeks. I remember because he came back home right before we were leaving for the annual Bake Off fundraiser at the school. He and Mama spoke some words in the kitchen, but I couldn't make out any of them. At first I was afraid we might not go since he'd been gone so long and just come home, but then they came out and Daddy kissed me on my forehead and pulled one of my braids and said he wouldn't miss it for the world.

"Mama got mad at him later for spending five dollars on one of Miss Eunice's banana puddings when we got them for free anytime she was invited over for dinner. Besides the fact that she had spent nearly every penny from the rainy-day jars around the house trying to keep enough food on the table while he was away, and here he was doling out bills like he was made of them. He grabbed Mama with one arm, his prized banana pudding in other, and spun her around the gymnasium floor and laughed. Once he got Mama to smile, he reached into his pocket and pulled out a quarter for me and told me to go buy as many sweets from the candy table as I could fit in my pockets."

"Sounds to me like he was off on a job. A good paying one, too."

I shook my head. "I don't think so."

"Why do you say that?"

She wasn't going to accept a shrug again, but I wasn't sure how much to tell her about what I saw that night. Mama was downstairs and I had already said goodnight to both of them. I got up to use the toilet and saw the light on in their bedroom. The door was open an inch or two, and when I peeked in, I saw Daddy rolling up money with an elastic band. It was bigger than a softball. He looked at his watch and then opened up his sock drawer and reached as far back as he could go, then he petted his socks down like he was trying to get them to look like they'd been before.

I chose my words carefully. "I saw him put some money in his sock drawer, but Mama is the one in charge of the money. Every week Daddy gives her money from his paycheck and tells her to make sure she takes care of everything that needs to be done with it. If this had been work money, what was it doing hiding away like that? How was Mama supposed to get it?"

Grandma looked thoughtful for a moment. "You're too young to understand how grown-ups work. I'm sure your Daddy always keeps some money out for himself. How else does he buy you things or take you out for a special soda? Men like to have what they call pocket change for occasions like that. Now, why don't you go take a rest? I'll wake you in a bit."

She kissed my cheek and pressed her hand against my forehead, lingering there a moment before I turned to go. This time it felt more like a prayer than checking for a fever. I didn't tell her that Daddy didn't buy me stuff; most things he gave me were someone's discards that he fixed up with paint and a hammer. I didn't mind, though. I knew we didn't have a lot. When we went to get a soda from the grocery, he always grabbed a dime from the old pickle relish jar on the kitchen window.

I didn't tell her that he never said where he'd been those times he was gone. He didn't even acknowledge that he'd been away. He acted like he had never left, like he didn't realize the calendar had turned or that seasons had changed. I didn't tell her that Mama pretended everything was fine or how clumsy she'd get when Daddy was home. These past two months with him gone, she'd been right as rain—no walking into doors in the middle of the night or tripping on the laundry hamper left in the hallway.

Even her old bruises had healed. But I wasn't meant to see them.

When I walked away I heard Grandma talking to herself about morning air, which was funny since it was the middle of the day. I guess she was right; I didn't know grown-ups.

I loved Grandma's room. Her bed was so high that she had a small stool down at the end that I would use to hitch myself up when I was smaller. Now I didn't need it, but I stepped on it anyway, pretending for a moment that I was a princess climbing up into my high tower, so high up that no one could get me. I shimmied under the covers, the quilts heavy against my skin, the sheets beneath surprisingly warm. My body shivered but not from the cold. If Grandma wouldn't believe me about Daddy being gone, how would she ever believe me about anything else?

4x4 is 16. 3x2 is 6. 7x5 is 35. 2x4 is 8. 9x3 is 27. 6x4 is 24. 5x5 is 25. 10x3 is 30. 8x4 is 32.

The sun disappeared behind the clouds darkening the room.

He had touched my knee, his fingers making little circles on the edging of the dress fabric. His hands cold on my skin. "Don't," I said. More of a squeak. My face felt hot, and my heartbeat found its way into my ears.

He must have known I wouldn't be able to hear him from the loudness of it because he leaned in and whispered.

I rolled over in the bed, squeezed my eyes shut and covered my ears with my hands, his words refusing to leave me alone. *Macey May... Rose's girl...* His breath condensed against my cheek... *You're pretty... like your mama.* I sat up in bed and knew I was going to be sick. And then his face in the depot, smiling at Grandma that way he did and asking about Otis and the land. Giving me a Coke. His fingers touching mine, making it out like he was someone to be thanked. Someone who could be trusted.

I made it into the bathroom, my feet clattering loud enough on the wooden floors to send Grandma from the kitchen to see what was wrong. "Macey May?"

The tears came, and between being sick and crying I seemed to be splattering everywhere, the toilet trying its hardest to catch all of my outburst. Grandma grabbed a towel off of the rack and held it over my head as I knelt there, the sides draped down over me, covering my face and the bowl. "Dear Jesus!" Grandma's voice rang off the bathroom walls.

I started coughing and couldn't stop. Now I was crying and choking and sputtering. I had never thought about what it would feel like to die, but at that moment I imagined I might be headed that way. Snot leaked out of my nose and down my chin, the salt crossing over my lips. His tongue had slithered into my ear like a poisonous snake. *You taste like her, too.* My body heaved.

Grandma started saying things I'd never heard her talk before. Telling the Devil to leave me be, that I was washed in the blood. Blood? My knees started to shake against the cold wooden floor, and my crying had become a wailing. I heard water on behind me and then Grandma's hands were under my arms, lifting me up into the standing clawfoot tub. The shock of the coldness stopped my tears midstream, but then my legs gave way and white spots clouded my eyes. I heard Grandma's voice distant-like and then Otis's even farther away, and then there were firm hands catching me as I fell.

"Macey May…Macey May?" The words were muffled, sounding in my ears like someone was talking through water or some distant fog. "Come on there now, open your eyes." I felt a soft touch on my cheek and someone petting my head. "There you go."

I looked around the room. I was on the floor of the bathroom leaning with my back against the tub. I was in my grandma's big yellow robe, and she held a cool cloth to my forehead. Otis sat on the toilet seat holding a cup of water out to me. "Take a sip," he said. "Just a small one, though."

My throat was dry and achy, like someone had made me swallow a pin. The cold water felt good. I put both hands around the cup and gulped.

"Whoa now," Grandma said, pulling it away from me. "What goes down may come up again. I can guarantee it will if you drink it that fast. Small sips." She gave the cup back to me, and I did as I was told.

"What happened?" I asked. Out of the corner of my eye, I saw my wet clothes piled in the bottom of the tub.

"You got sick and then passed out. I haven't seen an episode like that since your mama was about your age, and she ate an entire bar of baking chocolate. What did you eat on the bus?"

I thought back. "Bologna."

Otis scratched his chin. "Think maybe that done it?"

"And a purple lollipop." I stuck my tongue out, trying to see if any of the hue remained.

Grandma thought for a second. "I doubt Rose would have put any mayonnaise on it knowing it wouldn't be in a refrigerator. Even so, she probably only had it for an hour or so before she ate it."

They talked as if I wasn't there, which was fine with me. I was going to tell them that Mama had put butter on my bologna like she always did, but I gathered it wouldn't have made a difference. I sat on the floor sipping the water, letting it cool the scratchy burn that had lit my throat on fire. "My throat still hurts," I said when the cup was empty.

"I'm sure it does. Bile will do that. Nasty stuff. It will get better in a bit, though. Otis, can you go into the kitchen and get a piece of the horehound? You know where they are." She looked back at me and winked. Her horehound candies were hers and hers alone. No one, not me or Otis or Mama, no one was allowed to take one. They were by invitation only. The Five and Dime didn't carry them all the time, so when they did, Grandma would grab up as many bags as she could. Then she'd hide them in her special places around the house where no one could find them and open only one bag at a time to fill the glass candy jar she kept on the kitchen counter. Her glass candy jar.

At night she'd sometimes put a kettle on and melt one in a teacup with hot water. She'd take it out on the front porch and rock and sip. Sometimes she'd sing softly to herself. One day I planned to ask her what she was singing about so quietly out there. *Ruminating,* Otis told me once when I asked what she was doing. He said it like he assumed I knew what the word meant. I nodded my head as if I did even though I didn't.

If it was a cool night when she was out there, she liked to open my window up a touch for circulation she'd say, and then I could listen to her singing. A pretty melody that made me think of creeks and butterflies and feathers of sunshine that tickled your face. It was sad at the same time, but I couldn't explain why. Something in my bones told me.

She smoothed down my braids with her hands. "Whatever it was, I'm sure it's done now. How about we get you back in bed?"

I nodded and tried to stand. My legs were weak under me, so I hung onto Grandma's arm. Otis came back down the hallway and scooped me up. "Let me carry you. Don't need you falling down again." He put me on the bed and patted the top of my head one more time and gave me a big smile. Sometimes I felt like I was one of his cows with all the petting he did, but I knew he loved them cows, and I knew he loved me.

"Otis?" I whispered before he walked away.

"What, honey?"

"Have you seen her?"

"Seen who?"

"The White Lady?" I whispered again.

Grandma turned around from my suitcase, a nightgown in her hands. "Who?"

Otis put his hands on his hips and looked at me. "Thought you were too old to believe in the White Lady anymore. That's what you wrote in your last letter."

I hugged Mr. Jumpers. Before the bus station today, I had decided that ghosts and scary things weren't real, but now I wasn't so sure.

"Otis, what tales have you been telling her?" Grandma stood shaking her head at him in that scolding way she did when she wanted you to know she was disappointed in your choices.

"Don't be mad at him. He hasn't told me nothing. I've seen her, Grandma, honest."

Grandma gave a look to Otis that I'd seen Mama give to Daddy when the conversation was over and meant to be talked about later without my presence. "*Anything*, Macey May—not *nothing*."

Otis petted my head again. "Oh, I don't think you need to worry none about the White Lady. I've been watching, and she hasn't come 'round. Not once. Reckon she's made her way to wherever she wanted to be. You rest now. Denim's leaving for a spell, but he's coming back over later. Wants to see you and give you a big hug." Otis leaned over and kissed my cheek. "Now you get some rest." He looked at Grandma one last time and left the room.

Grandma gave me a horehound to suck on for a minute while she put the nightgown on over my head. It was a strange flavor. Now that I finally got to have one, I wasn't sure if I liked it or not. It tasted like mint and root beer, a combination my nine-year-old palate didn't find that refreshing. But I knew they were special to Grandma and her giving me one had never happened in all my life, so I kept it in. She made me spit it out into her hand once I lay down. "I'll wrap it in some foil for you in case you need it later," she said. "Only put it in your mouth if you're sitting up and then no more than a minute or so."

"Thank you."

"You're welcome. Now try to rest some." She left the door open an inch or two. "Sweet dreams, baby girl."

Grandma hadn't called me baby girl since I was seven. For some reason that year it had started embarrassing me, and when we had come out for a visit and she hugged on me and called me that, I crossed my arms and told her "I am not a baby anymore." I remember Mama giving me a nod, but Daddy shook his head and said, "Sorry, Cora Lee." Then he shrugged his shoulders and went out back to find Otis.

I know I felt sorry after I said it. It seemed to break her heart to not be able to call me that. The whole week it would start to come out—*baby*— and then she'd catch herself and call me by my name instead. Today it felt good to let her call me that again. I decided I would tell her that I didn't mind anymore, that it was fine with me if she wanted to call me baby girl until I was eighty and then even after that if she'd like.

I took the piece of tinfoil off of the nightstand and held it up to my nose. I could smell the horehound through it. I wanted Daddy to come home so we could be a family again. I wasn't ever scared if Daddy was around. Even when we were visiting the farm and I'd see the White Lady at night out my window, knowing Daddy was down the hall made me feel safe.

The first time I saw her I had been looking out the window unable to sleep and listening for screech owls. She was beyond the tree line along the ledge of the creek, pacing back and forth, staring at the ground like she was searching for something lost. The next morning I found scratch marks in the dirt. Another time she disappeared down the embankment only to come up a moment later, her white dress wet and stuck to her body from the creek's water. She hadn't scared me either time for some reason, just made me sad for her. That was the last time I had seen her, but something told me she was still around, waiting.

I looked up at the ceiling and the walls of the bedroom. Pictures of Mama and Aunt Ruby when they were children were scattered about. The house was quiet except for the wind chimes on the front porch. But even they were reverent, sounding like the music Miss Eunice listened to on her radio on Sunday mornings when she claimed she was attending service as a Bedside Baptist, though I had never heard of that denomination before. A tractor started up in the distance, probably Otis getting one last mow in before the grass died, and he could put it away until after the winter.

My eyelids drooped. Grandma had told me to sleep. I wanted to tell her I was afraid to close my eyes, afraid of what I would remember. I pulled my knees up into my chest and hugged Mr. Jumpers. If only Daddy were here. Mama told me that you could tell a man by his shoes. She was wrong.

Maybe she was wrong about other things, too.

Chapter 6

CRAWFORD, GEORGIA
CORA LEE JENKINS
1962

"NOW OTIS, I'm telling you. Something ain't right." Cora Lee sat at the dining room table, her hands folded in front of her.

"Shhh," Otis said, signaling to the bedroom door down the hallway. "We don't need to be waking her up. It seems to me she's been through enough already."

Otis had reached the bathroom at the moment Macey May collapsed in the tub. His arms were the only thing preventing her head from hitting the porcelain side. When he saw the truck was back and went in to see how the trip had gone, he never expected to hear a church service going on in the bathroom, especially since Cora Lee wasn't one for asking Jesus into anything anymore.

"I told you. I knew it. Mourning air. I felt it the minute I woke up today, even felt it in the truck on the way to town. I don't know why, but the ghosts are restless, and now something's wrong with that poor child."

Otis sat down next to her and took her hand in his. "This has got you all in a twitter, hasn't it? I don't think I've seen you like this before."

Cora Lee lowered her head and leaned in. "Something's not right, Otis. When I was changing her clothes, I saw bruises on her arms. Like someone had latched onto her right there." She grabbed Otis's upper arm with her hand. "And squeezed real hard."

"You know kids. They are always playing and getting hurt. She probably got grabbed a little too roughly playing tag on the school yard. Don't they still play Red Rover?"

"I think I should call Rose. I don't feel right keeping this from her."

Otis stood up and pushed in his chair. He had to get out to Denim and make a decision about Mabel. "Rose doesn't need the worry, and you know that. She has enough to handle with Curtis being gone so long on this job. No, we'll take on this one. Macey May's sick from the bus ride and unsure about being alone here with us. It's got her stomach turning on itself is all." He walked toward the kitchen and paused. "Her mama's gone and, now, don't hate me for saying this, but heaven knows if her daddy plans to come back. It's a wonder all she did was faint. I imagine there's a lot of emotion going through that little girl's body. Let her shut down a bit and get some rest. I'm sure by the time supper is ready she'll be her old self asking us to take her into Bennie's for a double hot fudge sundae."

Cora Lee hesitated. Those bruises couldn't be from any game of child's tag. No, those were made from hands much larger than a nine-year-old's. Large hands. A man's hands. Curtis had been gone too long for them to be leftover. Maybe the ball of money wasn't from a job. Maybe he was mixed up with men he shouldn't be. Cora Lee hadn't even known Curtis Johnson existed until he appeared at her door hand in hand with Rose; Rose far enough along in a pregnancy by then to know there was no going back. It wouldn't surprise her now if Rose was keeping other secrets from her, too.

She knew Otis wasn't in the mood for discussing. His head was thinking about Mabel, and she didn't know how much more there was to say anyway. Until Macey May woke up and she could ask her, everything was speculation, nothing more. "You're right, Otis. I'm sure she'll be fine once she gets some rest and distance from the day and that long trip." She walked back into the kitchen with him. "So what does Denim think about the cow?"

"Mabel," Otis over-pronounced the name for effect, "needs the trocar again, and then we'll have to think about something more permanent. There's a surgery could fix it, but Denim's not sure it's worth it to spend on her. She'll be past her birthing time in another year."

"And that's why I told you not to name the animals. How are you ever going to put her down?"

He kissed her on the cheek and rubbed his chin. "We'll see when the time comes. Now, I want to talk to you about the drive into town, but I've got to get outside. You good enough?"

With everything that had happened with Macey May, Cora Lee hadn't had much time to contemplate the trip. She opened up the fridge. "Don't you worry. We'll talk about it later." She saw the look of uncertainty in Otis's eyes. "I'm doing just fine. Shoo." Grabbing the cornbread mixture, she placed it on the table. "Seems to me I've got some chili to fix up for supper."

The night sky came in early. Out the back window Cora Lee could make out a small group of Brown Thrashers foraging under the bird feeders, their yellow eyes and speckled breasts barely visible under the waning moon. Otis and Denim were still outside with Mabel, or perhaps they were done with Mabel and talking about things. The business dealings were bothering Otis, she knew this. Not the day-to-day taking care of the farm—no, Otis lived and breathed the soil and everything that came from it. It was something else.

Ever since the sit-in over at the Woolworth's counter in Greensboro a few years back and the Freedom Riders activities in Birmingham, Klan activity had stepped up. Crawford itself felt like it was perched on a tinderbox. Lately little explosions—statements supposedly—started happening around town.

She heard that Bennie's Ice Cream Parlor had its power cut off one night and lost almost twenty gallons of ice cream. It seemed he had gone with a new milk distributor from the next county that offered him a better deal. A black distributor who was starting out with his own business just like Bennie. Supposedly Tiny Jimmy's chicken coops had mysteriously opened during the early morning. People suggested foxes had fingers to pick locks with now. Rumor was that Tiny Jimmy had asked for two more cents on every dozen eggs from Mr. Walsh. It didn't pass by Cora Lee that Mr. Walsh was white, and Tiny Jimmy was as dark as the proverbial raisin in the sun. She had heard it all and wanted nothing to do with it.

Cora Lee knew Otis heard these stories, everyone had. But she had never had problems with any of their buyers. Mr. Walsh had always bargained fair. She wouldn't go so far as to call him a friend, but she didn't expect Mr. Walsh would pour chlorine on her sweet potatoes or poison the cows if they didn't reach an agreement of predetermined prices he liked. They were neighbors, separated by acres, but their lands abutted one another.

The soulful call of the Chuck-will's-widow made Cora Lee walk outside. She loved their song—its endless, rolling melody that seemed to dance off the wind in an intricate pas de deux. Melancholy and beautiful at the same time, she wondered what story it told, what the widows were crying for. It seemed even birds had their own mourning.

The air had chilled; they'd have to turn the heaters on in the barn later before they went to bed. The news had said it might hit twelve degrees after midnight. Across the way, the barn light was on. It was close to seven. Supper was almost ready, and she wanted to talk to Otis before Macey May woke up.

"Hey, Cora Lee. How's it going?" Denim looked up from the bale of hay he was sitting on. He reached down to a thermos at his feet and lifted it to her. "Coffee?"

She shook her head and made a face. "Chicory ain't coffee."

He smiled and shrugged his shoulders. "Suit yourself."

"You know, if you had a woman, she'd say the same thing."

"Lucky I don't then." He winked at her and took another sip.

"Where's Otis?"

"Stepped around back to do his business. He'll be right along."

Cora Lee sat down on the hay bale next to Denim. "You know, Eugena's daughter is in town visiting. Newly divorced, they say. Maybe you could take her out while she's here. I'm certain she'd like something to do other than those crosswords that Eugena does every night."

Denim put his arm around her shoulder and pulled her close. "Ah, Cora Lee. Why you always trying to fix me up? You want me out of your hair?"

"Nonsense. You can stay in my hair as long as you want. I have eyes, though, and I see how women look at you, and you won't give them the time of day."

Denim motioned to his watch. "Seems to me they should be smart enough to tell time. Don't think I want a woman who couldn't."

It was a conversation that could go rounds, and she still wouldn't get a straight answer out of him. The closest thing he ever shared with her was that he had loved a woman once and didn't think he could love another. Who the woman was stayed a mystery to Cora Lee, and if Otis knew, he was keeping that secret. The bond of brothers. Cora Lee pushed his arm away. "I saw Junior at the bus station earlier. Said to tell Otis to call him.

It looks like he wants to talk about those two acres along the water again."

Denim took a cigarette out of his pocket and lit it. "How many times does he have to hear you're not selling? I know Otis has told him it's not for sale, that it will never be for sale. How long he's been trying to buy it from you anyway?"

She thought about it for a minute. It had been so many years she had lost track. Mr. Walsh's asking had started not long after Mrs. Walsh was put in the sanitorium. "I remember when that easement went up on the auction block. Hi was so excited, couldn't believe his luck. Thought was that the town was going to put a road in there, but then they decided against it. Hi bought it to round out our acreage to a full ten. Mr. Walsh hadn't been able to attend." She shrugged. "Not sure why he thought it should have been put on hold until he was there to bid on it, but Lord knows he did. Said the same to most anyone who would listen. Didn't put his complaints to rest until Mrs. Walsh had another bad spell and his attention had to be elsewhere."

Owning ten acres had been Hi's crowning moment. And hers, too. She had never been so proud. Hi had gone to school, had a degree in agriculture from Morehouse College. He wasn't going to just be a farmer. His plan was to revolutionize the farming industry. She knew he'd do it.

"Over twenty-five." Cora Lee looked around the barn. "Mr. Walsh knocked on our door. How my heart pounded when I opened it to see a white man on my porch. It was the first time I had ever met him. I don't know what I would have done if Hi hadn't been around. He came up behind me and invited Mr. Walsh to make himself at home on one of the rockers, as if he were some old friend who had come to pay a visit, and told me to fetch some iced tea with lemon and a few of my hermit bars. My hands were shaking so much I almost couldn't carry the tray outside.

"I couldn't even serve it, just left it all next to Hi and went back inside, praying to whoever was listening that there wouldn't be a storm brewing under the roof of my house. Hi came in a little while later with a funny grin playing on his lips. 'Cora Lee,' he said. 'Do you like this farm?' I told him I loved it. That I planned on dying here and being buried beside him down by the river in the back so the two of us could watch the water running by. 'Good,' he said, 'because Mr. Walsh offered to buy it from me, the whole thing, not just the easement. But I told him I didn't think I'd be selling—any of it.'

It turns out Mr. Walsh had upped the price that Hi had paid by an extra hundred dollars. I think that's one of the reasons he asked me to babysit Junior. He was hoping I'd realize how difficult running the farm would be on my own after Hi passed, and I'd sell it to him. But with Hi's life insurance policy, I didn't need to worry about that. Even if it hadn't, I wouldn't have been able to break my promise to Hi. I still don't under-stand why he wants it so bad. It's two acres, but it's just a long strip of bowling alley along the creek that eventually meets up with the road. Can't plant on it. He'd own behind our house if he had bought it, and we'd lose access to the water."

"Wants what so bad?" Otis stepped into the barn.

"Those acres behind the house down by the river's edge. Junior was asking about them today in town." Cora Lee looked into Otis's eyes.

He wiped his brow with his handkerchief. "Man, oh man. Those Walshes are like clockwork. One month off, one month on. I don't know how else to say no to them."

Denim put his cigarette out on the bottom of his boot and stood up. "Sometimes a man simply doesn't want to be told no for no other reason than that. What's the offer up to now?"

"I stopped keeping track. Not even sure I know anymore. Haven't actually returned one of their calls in at least four months." Otis reached out and gave Cora Lee a hand. "I'm not worried, though. I'm sure they'll keep asking."

Years ago after one of Otis's proposals, Cora Lee had gone to the county clerk to see about having his name added to the land deed, including the farm. It was going to be her way of telling him that she wasn't going anywhere, ring or no ring. But when she saw Hi's signature there, Mr. Lehigh Jenkins, signed above hers, his "H" high and sloping in the dark ink, she couldn't bring herself to do it. It was their land, and as much as she had come to love Otis, it didn't seem right.

But time and experience had taught her that a man, even a black one, was apt to get better deals on selling crops and livestock than what any color woman would get in negotiations, so she gave Otis the official title of Farm Manager. Contracts were never signed until she had read over them, but Otis was the one who talked everything out now. Junior only dealt with Otis. As a courtesy, he or his father, Mr. Walsh, would always ask Cora Lee to have Otis call them, and they'd let her know it was pertaining to the land, but they left it at that.

It was one of those things that made Rose flush with anger, always had. "Mama, how can you sit back and let the men talk about your land. It's your property, Mama. Daddy left it all to you." It didn't make any sense for Cora Lee to try to explain. Rose wouldn't have listened. What could she have said anyway? The truth? No, as far as she was concerned, the truth was buried and would stay there. She had taken her stand once; she didn't need to do it anymore. Her one job was protecting her girls, and if that meant playing people's games and keeping her head down, refusing to take part in society's fight, that was what she'd do. She wasn't a fool, but if Rose wanted to think she was ignorant, that was fine too.

Cora Lee stood up. "Still don't know why he'd want it. He's more than welcome to come on down and fish when it pleases him. He knows we let people use it. Denim, you're staying for dinner, right? Chili and cornbread's about ready, so let's go in. You can both finish whatever needs to be done after."

"I wouldn't want to intrude with Macey May not feeling well. Maybe it's best it just be the three of you tonight," Denim said, putting his gloves back on. He picked up the hay barrel and moved it over to the corner.

"Actually, I was hoping you'd stay so you could look at her. Otis told you about the bruises around her arms?"

Denim nodded. "I'm not a doctor, Cora Lee."

"No, but a vet and a coroner is the closest thing I've got on my property at the moment, so you'll have to do. You'd be able to tell if they are fresh or not, and that would be a starting point at least. Besides, what else are you going to eat all alone in that house of yours?" She shook her head. "Now, if you had a woman to take care of you…"

Denim shook his head and laughed.

She let the sentence peter off as they walked out of the barn and into the house. That was one thing Cora Lee could never understand, Denim remaining single all these years. There were too few black men as it was, and there was Denim, educated and attractive without a woman. It seemed wrong.

Otis took out two beers from the fridge and handed one to Denim. "You know if you'd just go on one date, she'd leave you alone for a while?"

"And then what? Would I have to get married to keep her quiet forever?"

Otis chuckled. "Probably. But you know…"

Denim put his hand up to stop what was coming next. "I'll stop you right there, brother. I'll take it from Cora Lee but not from you. You're supposed to be on my side."

"Fair enough." Otis raised his hands in mock surrender.

Cora Lee put the butter on the table and the large soup tureen filled with the chili in the center. A plate of steaming cornbread rounded it out. "You men go ahead and get started. I'm going to rouse Macey May. Even if she doesn't want to eat, it will be good to get her up or she won't stay sleeping until morning. She'll be as restless as a pig before butchering time by midnight."

She walked quietly into the bedroom, the moonlight illuminating Macey May's face on the pillow. She looked peaceful, and Cora Lee debated over waking her at all. She turned on the soft yellow light on the dresser in the corner, adding just enough light so she could see. Macey May's suitcase was propped open on the chair by the closet. Filled with socks and underwear, a few pairs of pants, tops and two dresses, there was only one other short sleeve except for the nightgown she was sleeping in. Cora Lee bit her lip. Rose would have a fit if she let Macey May come to the dinner table in her nightgown; it wasn't something she'd normally allow in her house either, but there was no other way for Denim to see the bruises. The last thing she wanted to do was to make Macey May feel uncomfortable, and having her lift up her sleeves to show them would certainly do that. No, tonight she'd let her come with nightgown, slippers, and all.

"Macey May…wake up, little girl." Cora Lee tugged at her toes under the covers. "Let's get you up and put a little food into that stomach of yours."

Macey May rolled over and sat up. "Hey, Grandma. What time is it?"

"Oh, almost past seven. Otis and Denim were late in the barn working on Mabel, and I thought you could use with the extra rest, so we're finally getting 'round to eating. How you feel, honey?"

She dangled her legs off of the bed. "Okay, I guess. A bit empty, maybe."

Cora Lee passed her her slippers. "You stay right in your nightgown. There aren't any strangers here, and I want you back into bed not long after you eat anyway. No sense in changing clothes when it's only me, Otis and Uncle Denim at the table with you. I've made chili, but I think eggs and toast would work better for you tonight. You can have some of the chili for lunch tomorrow once we're sure you're on the mend."

Macey May nodded. "Could I bring Mr. Jumpers with me?"

Something clenched in the pit of Cora Lee's stomach. There was something wrong; she could feel it. Macey May had never been a child who carried dolls, blankets, or anything else around with her. Not even as a toddler had she needed anything to comfort her. "Mr. Jumpers?"

Macey May nodded again. "Please?" She held him tight to her chest, the bruises peeking out from under her sleeves.

"Come on. But tell Mr. Jumpers he's not having any chili either."

Otis and Denim were talking about Mabel when they walked into the kitchen. "There she is!" Otis said, getting out of his seat to envelop her in a hug. "And Mr. Jumpers, too!" He raised an eyebrow and looked at Cora Lee. She shook her head.

"Hey there, sleepy head. Come over here and sit on your Uncle Denim's lap and tell me what you've been up to. What's Miss Eunice making you read nowadays?"

Macey May crawled up and wrapped her arms around his neck, Mr. Jumpers hanging down Denim's back by a paw. "She gave me *Anne of Green Gables* to read and told me she expected a full report when I got back."

Denim whistled. "*Anne*, huh? Miss Eunice must think you're pretty smart if she gave you that book and you're only nine."

"I'm almost ten, Uncle Denim." Macey May giggled and leaned her head against his chest.

Denim lowered his eyes and glanced at her arm. "Macey May, you want to play 'Trot, Trot to Boston'?" He felt her head shake no against him. "All right, maybe another time."

She stayed on his lap and ate her eggs and a few bites of toast, and then Cora Lee brought her back to her bed. "You stay in here tonight with me. Otis will sleep upstairs. I'd feel better. If everything's fine tomorrow, we'll move you up to your room." She tucked Macey May in and shut the light off.

Denim left an hour later. Cora Lee and Otis sat in the small parlor room at the front of the house. He had been clear. Fresh bruises. Not more than a day or two old.

"I don't understand it," Otis said, his brow furrowing.

"Neither do I."

"And Rose didn't mention them to you?"

"I think I would have remembered that."

Silence crept between them. The clock on the wall chimed its half-hour note and paused. It was eight-thirty. Momentarily the phone might ring. Rose would be home from work and calling to check on Macey May. There were things they needed to decide on, what they would say, and what they wouldn't. Yes, Macey May had bruises around both of her arms, made by grown-up hands or at least a teenager's. It was not some childhood mishap on the playground.

Glancing over at Otis, she could see his mind spinning, spinning in the same direction hers was. Going to places neither wanted to be.

Otis cleared his throat and said what they'd both been thinking. "Are there bruises anywhere else?"

Chapter 7

HARRISON, GEORGIA
ROSE JOHNSON
1962

ROSE LOOKED AT HERSELF in the bathroom mirror and combed her hair back on the right side, fastening it with a butterfly-shaped silver pin. It had two emeralds and two amethysts on either wing—a first anniversary present from Curtis. Her hands shook as she secured it, and she swore at herself for being nervous.

When she left Willie's office yesterday afternoon, he promised that he'd do a little more digging and see what other information he could find out. He had a friend in Dobson who owed him a favor. If Curtis was still there, he'd track him down. If he had already left, he'd find out where he was going. Rose closed her eyes and leaned into the vanity. Would it be wrong if she didn't care if Curtis was in Dobson or where he might be going? As the months had passed, she had begun to realize that she might not be bothered if he came back at all. Life would no doubt be easier if he didn't. In some aspects, at least. Like her mama used to say, "The grass *looks* greener on the other side, baby. It doesn't mean that it is." Life with Curtis had straddled both sides of the fence.

Willie suggested Pete's for dinner at seven. It wasn't a fancy place; there weren't any fancy places in Harrison. If you wanted something more than collards and chicken, or chops and potatoes, you were out of luck. Pete's was quiet, though, during the week. Not too many people would be there—a few at the bar, the regulars, and maybe a couple or two. Pete didn't bother with a complete menu until Friday when he could count on the place being filled. There were limited options during the week; he usually brought you whatever he felt like cooking for you. It was always good, so no one complained.

"Miss Eunice, I don't know about this." Rose walked back and forth in the living room, her coat in her arms.

"Stop your worrying and get going. As it is, unless you run, you're going to be late."

"But it's Willie. You know people are going to talk. Curtis gone not even two months, and here I am going out with Dr. William Price."

Miss Eunice clucked from her chair by the television. "Let them say whatever they please. For a woman who took up with a white man, I don't think now is the time to worry over what people might think."

Rose stopped and sat down on the couch. Miss Eunice was right. She'd never cared what anyone said before, so why should she worry now? Her heart fluttered under her dress reminding her why. If she were to be honest, although she hadn't been honest about her life in a long time with anyone, she wanted to go out with Willie. She hated that she did. Willie wasn't a part of her life anymore, but in all the years, her heart hadn't reached that conclusion.

"Willie is your only way to find out about Curtis. It's dinner. No one can fault you for eating, now can they? It doesn't matter where you meet him. If he showed up on my porch, they'd talk. It's probably better that you're eating at Pete's, less private."

Kissing Miss Eunice on the cheek, Rose put on her coat and went to meet Willie.

The radio was playing "Baby, Won't You Please Come Home" when Rose walked in. The lights were low and the short stumps of candles flickered in the clear glasses on the table. It was a few minutes past seven. She scanned the room for Willie and found him at the bar. Even from behind he had poise. The way he held himself, his shoulders strong and confident. He laughed at something Pete said as he passed him a scotch with one ice cube—his drink of choice, Rose knew—and his voice filled the room, the deepness of it reverberating in her belly like it always had. And then like the first day they had met on her mother's porch, he was beside her guiding her to a table and signaling to Pete to bring her a gin and tonic with a lime twist.

I have tried in vain
Never more to call your name

Willie sang the words low enough for her to hear. "Let me take your coat."

Rose softened her shoulder and slid her arm through the sleeve. Her pulled out her chair and hung her coat on the vacant seat next to them.

"You look beautiful, Rose."

She felt her face blush. "Willie, please. That's not why I'm here."

He smiled. "I know. But it's the truth. Just as pretty as the day I saw you holding that punch bowl at your mother's strawberry festival."

It was this way for them. Their thoughts in sync, their memories resurfacing at the same time. She could remember every word they said under that tree, spread out on the blanket years ago.

The blues guitar poked its slow rhythm around them. Rose's drink came, and she took a sip. She had imagined that they would be together until they got old. It was Willie who had backed out of that belief.

"Did you hear anything?" The sooner she found out whatever information he had about Curtis, the sooner she'd feel free to relax.

Willie looked around the room.

"What?"

"Nothing. Rooms have ears is all. Making sure no one's listening when they shouldn't be."

"Willie, what did you hear?" She reset the knife and spoon next to her plate and placed the napkin in her lap.

"My friend checked around. It seems like Curtis had been playing some high-stake poker games. Did you know he played?"

Rose nodded her head. "A little here and there, but what man doesn't?"

"From what my friend says, he's kind of a regular. Been at least two or three times."

She wasn't about to confess to Willie what she knew about the extent of Curtis's gambling problem or about anything else. It maddened her that she cared what Willie thought about her, her choices, her life, and what he'd think if she told him everything, knowing that she still stayed. Rose remembered the gambling binges—sometimes a day, never more than two. Then he'd appear as if a haint out of thin air, flashing dollar bills and buying Macey May treats, kissing on Rose's neck, telling her it wouldn't happen again. Until the next perfect hand came into town.

Sometimes, when his absences were longer, she understood now it was the memories of the war haunting him, digging at him, stealing from him again, keeping him away. Their hold was tighter than any card deck would ever be. Sometimes he'd come home as if nothing had happened, oblivious to his being away or his erratic behavior.

Other times, when the memory was too deep, he'd be a different man and go to bed and sleep twenty-four hours straight. If Macey May was home, he'd walk right on by ignoring her "Hi, Daddy," and Rose would have to make up another excuse. *Daddy was sick. Daddy had worked overtime and could barely stand from exhaustion. Daddy was tired.* When he finally did get out of bed, a part of him was gone, a puzzle piece lost somewhere, and Rose didn't even know where to begin to look for it. Soon so many pieces were missing she wasn't sure what the picture would look like with the ones she had left over if she were to try to put them together. So she didn't.

The thought scared her.

They certainly wouldn't make up the Curtis she had met with all those years back in Adele's Bakery over the strawberry-rhubarb tarts. She didn't know how to talk about it, though—to him, or anyone else.

She wasn't sure which one she hated more: his choice to gamble when he should have stayed with her and been a family, or the times when his thoughts gripped him in their clutches and refused to let go and turned him into someone she didn't know. Someone who scared her.

Pete came by with their orders. Two specials of fried catfish with hominy grits and mustard greens. Rose nodded a thank you.

Willie cleared his throat. "Rose, were you in trouble? I mean, did you need money? I thought Curtis had a steady job now?"

Rose's mind was working overtime, trying to digest all that Willie was saying, keeping her lies intact, telling him just enough. "No, I mean, not that I know of. Our bills were paid on time. He always had money to give me for groceries. He never told me that we needed to cut back." And then she thought of something she could tell. "But he did encourage me to start working full-time again in the bakery. Said we could use the extra money to make sure Macey May had a nice Christmas. Said he didn't know how much longer the job would be there when the winter hit."

Willie lit up a cigarette and offered it to Rose. She took it. "That makes sense. Construction does usually stop for a bit come those February cold spells." He leaned in and met her glance. "Rose, are you sure there's nothing else? Besides being your friend, I'm also a doctor. Doctor-patient confidentiality?" He smiled. "I won't tell, but the more information I have to go on, the more I'll be able to help you."

She inhaled deeply on the cigarette, the smoke filling her lungs and then exhaled into a ring of Os. It felt good to smoke again. She had given it up years ago when she was pregnant with Macey May. It calmed her now. She thought about what she should say, truth or lies. Did it even matter? "I found some money in his drawer a while ago. A few hundred. I know that doesn't amount to a lot for you, but…" She stopped her sentence midway, not sure how to continue it. She didn't want Willie to think that she was comparing him with Curtis or, worse, that she knew Curtis didn't come anywhere near to him when it came to success. "But I don't know where he got it. Didn't think he was playing in any big games. It's gone now. He must have taken it with him."

She waved off another drink as Pete came with a refill for Willie and asked for a seltzer with a twist of lemon. She needed her faculties about her, and one drink was enough. Rose relaxed. At least there was direction now. It seemed like Curtis had finally forgotten about them, her and Macey May, lost in a memory so dark and fathomless that he couldn't come back even though he wanted to. If Macey May wasn't part of the equation, Rose couldn't be sure that she wouldn't have been forgotten about much sooner than now. Macey May seemed to be the tie that binds, a tether to reality for him.

At times it was so hard for Rose to hold onto him. To bring him back from wherever he was. In the beginning she'd hold him in her arms and sing to him a song about angels that her mama used to sing to her. Eventually his muscles would slacken, his breathing slow, and he would fall asleep. That hadn't worked in a while.

Sometimes his talk got so crazy that she couldn't tell if he even knew where he was, that he was there in Harrison with her. Instead his mind seemed to play tricks on him, leaving him somewhere in Korea screaming about Johnny and how sorry he was. During those times, she never could tell what he might do. But, even understanding that and knowing that sometimes things were out of his control, when his mind got where it went she couldn't completely absolve him. Surely, somewhere deep down inside, the piece of himself that he was fighting to hang onto, he would know how hard it would be without him. The rent. Food. That realization scared her most of all. If he could allow her and Macey May to lose everything, he was too far away to come back.

A week after he hadn't returned, she had discreetly gone to the bank to make sure he hadn't taken out what little savings they had. He hadn't touched it, and there was more than she remembered. It wasn't enough, though. It covered the rent for the next month and a few weeks of groceries, an electric bill. Her salary could only cover things for so long. And here she was now, eviction notice in hand and two days to get out of their house. She'd never felt so shamed.

"He likes to play cards, but he doesn't have a gambling problem, if that's what you are insinuating." Rose felt she needed to say it. She didn't want Willie thinking that she was with a man like that. Even though he was, yet he wasn't. She certainly didn't know how to tell Willie about the other way Curtis was. No one would understand. She wasn't even sure she had words to explain it. *He gets lost in Korea*. People would think *she* was crazy.

When she left Crawford and followed Willie to Harrison, it was to become a doctor's wife—to show people, her mother especially, that she wasn't going to sit around and say "yes ma'am" and "no ma'am" to anyone. Her mama may not have been willing to stand up and break any barriers, but she sure as hell would. She would have a life just as good if not better than the white folks did. Respectable, rich, with a fine house and furnishings. And wait until she drove home with Willie at the wheel of a shiny new Ford. Oh, how she imagined the heads would turn. Instead, she drove home with Curtis. Heads turned, especially Junior's, but not for the reason she was hoping.

Nothing had turned out like she thought it would, more than nothing.

"He's a good man, Willie." Even the words caught in her throat, fighting against perpetuating a lie. Not a lie, so much, her conscience told her; a memory. Curtis *had* been a good man at first—before the nightmares took hold, the crazy talk fought for space in his mouth, and his actions became so irrational that he scared her so much at times that she thought about calling the police. How could she explain to Willie what kind of man Curtis had become when she could no longer find words for it herself?

She could sense the advent of the breaks, though, and see the change in his eyes, like a dog could sense a storm coming over the wind. She'd send Macey May over to Miss Eunice then. Always, always, always she got her to safety. Her little girl never witnessed anything.

Rose picked a sugar packet from the plastic basket and started tapping the edges on the table, turning it round and round. "You know, Curtis always said that he had never seen a prettier girl than me in his life. The way I wore my hair, my eyes." Her fingers absently touched the ends of her hair.

Willie lit another cigarette, and Rose wondered if she should ask for one or perhaps another gin and tonic.

"He called them fairy eyes."

Willie blew the smoke out of the side of his mouth and stifled a laugh. "Did he now?"

Rose nodded. "We were on our first date. I'll never forget. He said the first time he looked into them he knew they were eyes he wanted to get lost in."

"Oh, so he's one of those guys?"

Rose raised an eyebrow. "Those guys?"

"Talkers. Romantics." Willie laughed. "Fairy eyes, that's a good one."

"Stop it. It was nice. No one ever told me that before." In a way she still loved him, and if she wanted to hold onto some of the good times, she would. No one was going to make judgments against him.

"I used to tell you that you had beautiful eyes."

"Yes, but then you didn't."

Willie coughed. "Does Curtis have any family he'd go to if he needed help or money?"

"No. He's from over in Cobb. His grandma died right after he graduated. He'd only been home from Korea a few weeks before he came over to Spencer looking for a job. He's got no one. Except me and Macey May. His best friend Johnny died in the war. But Curtis never talked about him much."

"Did he ever talk about the war? What he saw over there?"

Rose hesitated, then shook her head. "We visited Johnny's mother once years ago. She was real nice. We sat in her parlor drinking weak lemonade and eating Nilla wafers. I guess they were Johnny's favorite. It didn't even seem to matter to her any that I—"

Willie stuck the end of his cigarette in the ashtray and finished her sentence. "—was black?"

"What's that supposed to mean?"

Willie shrugged and leaned forward in his seat. "Nothing. That was right kind of her, though. Did she have you serve, too?"

Rose pushed her chair back and stood up. His nerve. She glanced around and saw eyes were on her. They pretended to be entranced by who might be walking through the front door or what was going on outside the window, but Rose knew she was making a spectacle of herself. She reached for her purse. "Excuse me," she said loudly enough for anyone who might be trying to listen, "I need to use the washroom."

She closed the bathroom door behind her, locked it, and leaned against the wall. Her head was spinning from getting up so quickly, and her nausea from the night before lingered. Her reflection in the mirror showed tired eyes and flushed cheeks. Everything was unraveling around her.

Why did she even ask Willie to help her find Curtis? And now she had brought Miss Eunice into her lies. Poor, poor Miss Eunice with a heart of gold, so sure that Curtis had fallen victim to something or someone. "Foul play," she said. "Such a good man, that Curtis. And oh, what a wonderful father." Miss Eunice, Rose assumed, refused to believe things talked about in the canned vegetable aisle of the grocery, or while she was waiting for her weekly fig square at Adele's. Adele had plenty to say about Curtis. Always had. There were words whispered during the receiving line after the Sunday evening worship service in Curtis's absence or his presence. "I don't listen to gossip," Miss Eunice would tell her, "and neither should you." *If only it was that easy*, Rose thought.

It didn't usually matter to her what people said, but now Rose hated herself for allowing Miss Eunice to believe, for allowing Macey May to believe. For allowing herself to believe for so long. She couldn't even remember what she was trying to believe anymore. Asking for help wasn't in her vocabulary. But what was wrong with Curtis was beyond her, and now it was too late. Maybe if she had spoken up sooner, tried to get him some assistance in one of those VA hospitals. Who knows, maybe even Willie could have helped.

She turned on the faucet and let the cold water rinse over her wrists. Rose hadn't told anyone, but a month ago Curtis had come home. She hadn't told anyone because she knew he wasn't staying. He had left his mark, though. She took a deep breath and winced. The bruising on her ribs had all but faded, only a slight lavender remained. "Lavender," Rose said out loud to her face in the mirror. When it had happened, she thought she might need to go see Willie, the pain had been so bad. Every inhalation was like a knife cutting through to her spine. She had brought

Miss Eunice into that lie, claiming that she had fallen off the chair while cleaning the tops of the cabinets in the kitchen. A fall that jammed her ribs into the corner of the counter.

The truth didn't make sense.

"Don't move, *Jeog*," Curtis had said from behind the back door. It took her a minute to register what it meant. *Enemy*. Korean. Rose dropped the bag of groceries and screamed. Instantly he had her in a headlock and was dragging her through the kitchen into the living room, her heels scraping across the floor, her toes pointed toward the ceiling. "Where are the rest of you?" he whispered in her ear. "Tell me!"

"Curtis?! What are you doing? Where have you been?"

"I know who you are," he said. "Watching me, thinking I wouldn't be able to see through you. I know what you did. Johnny was my friend."

And then the crux of his arm tightened around her neck until there was only black.

She woke up later, a mass on the floor, her head pounding, blood dried on her cheek, the inside of her mouth red and salty. The clock on the wall said Macey May was due home from school in less than an hour. She pulled herself up and went into the kitchen. The expected mess was not there, instead Curtis had left a note on the kitchen table for her. "Working late. Don't wait up. Love you."

The broken milk bottle was in the trash, the apples placed neatly in the fruit stand next to the sink, the bread nestled snug and safe in the breadbox. Rose wet a paper towel, blotted her broken lip, and slowly made her way across the yard to Miss Eunice. She had planned to tell her, was finally going to allow someone to carry her load. Only when she saw Miss Eunice open the door, the look of horror that jumped from her eyes, Rose knew she couldn't burden her. Besides, Rose wasn't sure what she would say or how to say it. She burned the note he left, not wanting to run the risk of Macey May seeing it in the trash, and continued to spin the lies she had become so good at over the years.

Miss Eunice had iced her ribs and wrapped them tightly with an ace bandage. She then made Rose promise that she and Macey May would come over to dinner every night for a week because she didn't want her cooking. Pouring bowls of cereal and cutting sandwiches was fine, but she drew the line at filling pots of water and peeling potatoes.

"You say you're clumsy, Mama," Macey May had said later that night while she was tucking her into bed, "but I've never seen you so much as trip when we are walking around town. It seems to only happen when you're by yourself." Sometimes Rose worried that Macey May was too observant. "And you know, this is the first time it's happened since Daddy's been gone."

Rose reapplied her lipstick in the mirror and spritzed her hair with some water on her hands. This night needed to be over. It was getting too hard now to remember her stories, to remember her feelings, the lies, the untruths, the—whatever she had taken to calling it. Miss Eunice thought Curtis had been kidnapped like in one of her late-night television shows; Willie thought he had made himself scarce after a gambling entanglement; Macey May and her mama and Otis all thought he had taken a big job out in California and his paycheck had been held up. She wasn't even sure if she knew the truth anymore.

He was gone. Simply that.

Willie wiped off his mouth and crisscrossed his fork and knife across the plate when she returned. A cold gin and tonic waited for her at the table, and she lifted it to her lips and took a sip. "He's got a problem, Rose. I don't know what it is, but I think you'll find gambling is only the half of it if you keep digging. What did you even know about him? You took up with him so quick—"

Anger rushed up her neck, finding a way to her voice. "How dare you! I've been with that man for almost ten years." The words hissed out, low and strong. "First you tell me I'm acting like a servant for the white folk, and now you have the temerity to suggest I didn't know him? You of all people have no right to say that. Men do this, Willie. They leave." She shook her head. "You did this."

She waited a moment for her words to sink in. "And you don't know Curtis. You played it safe and comfy in that school while Curtis was out there fighting, seeing things no man should have to see. And only Heaven knows what he did, what he had to do. I came here tonight for Miss Eunice, but she was wrong. You think you're such a big man. Dr. High and Mighty! Well, you know what, Willie? I did okay without you. Macey May and me. Your leaving didn't break me. I survived on my own then, and, if it comes to it, I'll survive on my own now."

He reached across for her hand. "Rose, come on, I didn't mean it like that. It's just my friend knows these people. These are high-stakes games, Rose, played by people who plan to win, who want to win, and if they don't, it can get ugly. Big money gets passed around. They play for other stuff, too—homes, cars, land. He knows of people who have lost everything. Generational homesteads, businesses. There's no mercy in them, Rose, and no court of law is going to step in and help anyone who's been wronged. These are illegal games. They cut off fingers, Rose. Or worse."

Rose looked away. She hadn't thought of the possibility that Curtis's gambling could become her problem.

"I'm sorry. I don't want to frighten you. Maybe I shouldn't have said anything. My friend could be wrong, after all."

Rose tried to compose herself and took another sip. "So, Dobson. A few weeks ago? Any idea where was he before that? These games travel, right?"

Willie raised his shoulders. "My friend didn't know."

Rose thought for a minute. "Willie, what aren't you telling me?"

"What do you mean? I've told you all I know."

"William Price, in case you forget, I know you." She lowered her voice. "I know you very well. You're hiding something from me. You've never been good at it, and times haven't changed. How did your friend know it was Curtis anyway? Games like that I imagine are low-key, on a need-to-know basis. I'm sure names of players aren't thrown around for everyone to hear."

"I told you. He plays in the games. Said he knew Curtis from around. Had played some smaller-stake games with him over the years."

"And?"

"He said something was wrong this time, though. Usually Curtis laughed and joked while he played. That's what made him such a good player, he said. He was casual, like if he won or lost didn't matter. This time was different. Curtis was jittery. Kept looking over his shoulder, like he was waiting or looking for someone. His hands weren't coming up, either. Finally he excused himself halfway through the game. Left thirty dollars on the table and never came back."

"Well, at least he knew enough to get out."

"Rose, he left owing one hundred and forty."

Even she knew you didn't leave a game owing anything. "What are they going to do?"

"My friend said there was talk of going after him, finding him, making him pay. All I know it's a good thing that Macey May is up with your mother and that you are going there in a few days. I don't know if they can trace him back here, but I know I'll feel more comfortable when there are miles between you."

She searched his eyes. There was more, she could feel it. "What else?"

Willie shook his head. "Nothing, honest. That's it."

Rose's arms felt heavy and her head was swimming. How much gin did Pete put in his drinks? If she didn't want to make a fool of herself, she needed to leave. In a few more minutes, the alcohol would have more control over her than she wanted.

"I don't believe you."

Willie opened his mouth and closed it.

She picked up her coat and purse and stood to leave, reserved and polite. "When you're ready to tell me the rest, you know where to find me. I'm a big girl now, Willie. I don't break so easily anymore."

He stood up. "I'll try to find out more for you. Should be able to meet up with my friend again later this week. I've got some business over there I need to check in on."

Rose wondered what size dress his "business" wore and if she had plans on being a doctor's wife too. She shook her head. "No, you've done more than enough." She took his hand in hers. "I'm grateful. Really. But you don't have to worry about me."

He brought her hand up to his lips and kissed it. "I'll always worry about you."

"You haven't told anyone about this, have you?"

Willie hadn't let go of her hand. The warmth from it spread up her arm. "Your secret's safe with me."

Secret? Funny, she thought. Secret? Lie? Maybe there really wasn't a difference.

Chapter 8

CRAWFORD, GEORGIA
CURTIS JOHNSON
1962

THE BUS STRAINED to take the hill, the engine wheezing while the shocks chirped. If I had my tool kit with me, I'd tell the driver to pull on over and let me take a look at it. Shouldn't take more than cleaning out a spark plug or two. We were a few miles outside of Crawford, and I still had no idea what I was going to say to Cora Lee or Macey May when I got there. Maybe I wasn't going there at all even.

Outside we passed a pecan grove. The green heads of the trees swayed in the November air that had turned to an Indian summer ever since the sun had come up. Three or four men stood below them with five-gallon buckets and rolling pickers while a few more sat in the branches shaking them, loosening the nuts, a shower of shells falling from the sky, the last of the late season harvest. These last pecans would be sold by the edge of the road during the holiday weekend, probably wouldn't even leave the buckets they were collected in. Visitors would, no doubt, pull over and buy a pound or two, excited to be getting some authentic Georgia pecans.

I didn't envy the pickers. Pecan harvesting was hard work. I had done it the seasons throughout high school, me and Johnny. It didn't pay well, but when you had next to nothing, anything was something. Every weekend from September through November, we'd show up at the farms around five in the morning hoping to be the guys chosen for the job that day. We didn't complain and were hard workers, so once we proved ourselves, they'd wave us right in. It got to be that the guys in the line knew to let us pass without any grumbling. I'm sure it helped that our skin was white.

Otis would be busy finishing up the sweet potato crop along with the last of the turnip greens. It was that time. There were a few pecan trees nestled near the farmhouse, but those were for Cora Lee's own use—pies, tarts, pecan sandies. She'd roast them in brown sugar and cinnamon and put them around the house in little crystal bowls at the holidays. Their five acres of cotton had already been picked months ago.

Usually we'd come down in September, and I'd help with it even though he had plenty of other hands. Cora Lee's famous strawberry festival was the culmination of the cotton picking, and anyone who had helped, from volunteers to paid workers, were asked to stay around and enjoy the celebration. Cora Lee was like that, making everyone feel welcome and like they belonged. She had always made me feel like I belonged even though I knew she thought I'd bring Rose nothing but trouble because of the color of my skin. In some ways she was right.

On the drive to Crawford the bus had wandered into a vast expanse of bare cotton fields. They looked like someone had a feather pillow fight in them, the white remnants sticking to the thorny brown stubs of bushes. Most people around here still picked cotton by hand; my fingers ached at the thought. Itched to pull a trigger that wasn't there. It was bushes that the Koreans would hide in waiting for us. Bushes filled with thorns—of both kinds. I never thought it was fair. Why did they have to hide? No one had a chance.

The bus backfired, and I jumped in my seat. Sweat broke out under my armpits, and I rested my head back and closed my eyes. The back of the bus was stuffy, the window next to me broken shut. It was the safest place to be. No one had bothered to wander down my way, most choosing to sit up closer to the front where the air was better and they could look out the large driver's window. I looked at my watch. We'd be there in a minute or two, and I still hadn't made up my mind.

The driver came over the speaker. "Crawford Station. We'll be stopping here for fifteen minutes and then heading on to Eggersville. There's a soda machine inside and bathrooms. You'll find the Five and Dime has some ready-made sandwiches that they keep behind the counter for the bus service patrons. If you're hungry, I suggest you try there. If this is the end of your trip, I hope you enjoyed yourself, and thank you for choosing Greyhound."

We pulled into the station, and I waited for people to gather their things and make their way off of the bus. I wasn't sure if it was the best decision, hopping a bus all the way to Crawford, but I didn't know what else to do. Wasn't even aware that I had made the decision to do it. Truth be told, I realized partway into the trip that I was on the bus, not sure how I even got on it. I guess my subconscious was sending me to Rose, hoping in some way she and Macey May would be able to ground me like they had in the past. Although I didn't know if she would ever forgive me for disappearing for this long, excuse or not.

Reasons were never my strong suit, and I wasn't sure what I could give her now that would make her do anything but hate me more than she already did. I didn't blame her. It wasn't her fault. It's just there were times when it all got too much, and my head hurt trying to hold onto something, anything. Some days it felt too hard to remember my name. I'd squint my eyes, trying to see the letters form in my mind, knowing that they were out there skirting the edges of my mind, but all that came to me was my dog tag. Serial number: 5567834294. Blood type AB negative. Religion P. And then I'd see Johnny next to me. Drawing one minute.

Dead the next, his blood forming a suction under his helmet that made a *smmkk* sound when I took it off, like I had broken the seal between life and death.

I never told Rose this, but there were days that vanished on me. Most of the time I lied and said I was gambling, taking in a game the next town over. I knew she'd be mad, but at least her anger over that was something I could deal with. I never could figure out how to tell her that I disappeared on myself—sometimes into a black space of nothingness; sometimes back into the tree-lined hills of Korea, the sky lighted by firefight, bombs bursting in the air as limbs exploded. Even though I know that the war is over for me, I'm beginning to realize that it might never be over for me. How does something like that, the memories, ever end? War. Not sure man was made to do that.

I found that I preferred the black void.

"Excuse me. You getting off?"

The bus driver's voice bounced off the tin roof of the bus. A little bullet searching me out.

"How far to Eggersville?" I asked.

"'Bout an hour or so. This is the last stop I make until we get there."

He had walked down the aisle and was standing four seats down from me, one hand on the back of each headrest. I couldn't tell if he was blocking me from leaving or there to take me off. His suit was nice. Dark blue pants with clean yellow lines down the sides that matched a yellow tie against a lighter blue shirt. Even his belt buckle shone—its own kind of sunshine. I envied him, a bit.

He took off his hat. Sweat formed on his temples, and he wiped his forehead of with a handkerchief. "Sure is a warm one today. This Georgia weather. A few days ago we were worried about frost killing off the potatoes. Today, you could cut them up and fry them without any grease outside under the sun." He took a step closer, one row on my left and sat down. "It's not my business, but you okay? I only ask because it's mighty hot back here. No one usually chooses to sit in these seats unless the bus is full, and they're the last ones on."

I nodded. "Prefer my privacy."

He nodded back. "Well, I'm not allowed to leave the bus with people on it, and I've got to grab some licorice strings." He smiled. "Promised my little girl some red ones. Would you mind getting off so I can lock up? You can sit inside the station if you'd like. There's a ceiling fan in there might be doing something to push around this heat."

"S'pose so."

Macey May liked the licorice string that wound into a pinwheel. She'd carry it around in her hand, one end stuck in her mouth, and unravel it as she went. If I was going to see her I could bring her some or maybe a bag of Mary Janes from the penny candy aisle. She liked those, too.

I stepped off the bus. Outside the heat pressed its weight against me. I took a few steps and then I felt it. My chest tightening, my heartbeat growing in my ears. I knew what would come next. The sign from the Five and Dime narrowed in on itself, and I blinked my eyes to steady it. A few women from the bus sat outside on the benches eating sandwiches and drinking Moxie, the distinct orange and black logos giving the glass bottles away. Their low laughter carried over to me, and I took a deep breath. Perhaps I could keep what was coming at bay if I just focused on the here and now. I looked across at the awning for Chuck's Luncheonette and hoped that Macey May had been treated to a cheeseburger. My palms were sweating and I wiped them on my pants.

Then I saw him. The Korean I had killed. He was walking down the street, right there in the middle, following the center line. Foot after foot. Toe to heel, some sort of grotesque tightrope walker. He smiled at me with that stupid, toothless grin and held up a picture. I squinted. *The* picture. My fingers wrestled aimlessly in my back pocket for my wallet. It didn't make sense. I had the picture; how could he be holding it? The closer he came, the larger the picture, until he needed two hands to carry it, until he was enveloped, and the only thing left that I could see of him were his feet. His marching feet.

I squeezed my eyes shut and counted to three, afraid if I looked up again he'd be there in front of me, asking for my penance or something else I wasn't able to give.

A bottle of Moxie dropped against the pavement, the glass shattering. The women squealed, their own voices startled at the sound, but for me, I only heard the snipers in the distance, lots of them. If I didn't find a place to hide and soon, they'd be all over me. I had to get somewhere fast. I didn't know where Johnny was, but we had a plan, a rendezvous point where we knew to meet if we ever got separated. It wasn't a specific place, more of a "find it" place. The closest rock next to a clump of three trees. If we searched for the same thing, we knew we'd locate each other.

I looked left and right. People were everywhere, any of them could have a gun. That was the problem with this war. You couldn't tell your enemy. Women, children. Young, old. It wasn't just soldiers in uniforms, targets that you knew were there for your taking. The kids were the worst.

How did you shoot a six-year-old?

A platoon had lost eight men when a four-year-old girl had walked toward them holding flowers in her hand asking, *Sada? Sada? Buy flowers, Joe?* As soon as they lowered their guns, shots rang out from all around them, the girl knowing enough to lie down as soon as she heard the first round.

Macey May.

What if they found her?

She was only a little girl.

She'd reach for the flowers, and it would all happen too fast.

She wouldn't know to lie down.

Chapter 9

CRAWFORD, GEORGIA
MACEY MAY JOHNSON
1962

I PULLED THE TIRE SWING back, stuck one foot on the rubber base, and hitched myself up. Nine was my record, but over the past three days my numbers had increased, and today my goal was twelve. Twelve rocks back and forth without needing a push. I had the whole day; there wasn't much else to do.

Grandma had finally seen fit to let me be and stopped her incessant hovering. It seemed no matter where I looked, there she was asking me if I was okay or needing anything. Even Otis seemed overly concerned with my liquid intake, asking every time he came around if I needed something to drink—sweet tea or lemonade. Grandma had succumbed to the notion that the housework did, after all, need to get done, and Otis said I could help him later with the cows, but for right now he needed to spend some time getting the books ready and accounts paid up.

I knew I could do it. It was all about the start. And besides, I had grown a full inch and a half since the summer. If you jumped and brought the other foot up quick, you'd have nothing breaking up your down wind. You needed to hold the tire out as far from the tree as you could and as high as you could with still being able to hold the rope and get your foot in in time. If you didn't, you looked right silly, a leg dragging, the swing twisting. It usually ended with your bottom or your face hitting the dirt. It was an embarrassment.

Whenever that happened, which it did a lot here at Grandma's and at home too, Daddy would laugh at me while Mama'd tell me I wasn't being very lady-like. But I'd get off the ground, dust myself off, and try again. I liked the way Daddy looked at me when I did that, like he was proud of me or something for not giving up. Sometimes, though, he looked like he was ready to cry. When that happened he usually decided to go for a walk around town, and I'd be in bed long before he ever came home.

Holding onto the rope now, I jumped and leaned backward into the breeze as the swing rocked to and fro. The twine scratched my palms, and I could feel little bits of thistle embedding themselves into my skin. I loosened my grip a bit. Otis had set up the best swing in the world. Far enough out on a limb that you didn't have to worry about hitting the trunk, yet low enough to the ground that you didn't need help getting on. Self-sufficient.

I made it eight times. I tried pumping my body like I had seen Otis do with his arms to bring water up from the outside well. It gave me eight and a half before I jumped off. I peeked over my shoulder, making sure Grandma hadn't come out on the porch when I wasn't looking. My jacket was weighing me down, but she'd be upset if I didn't keep it on. In her mind it didn't matter what the thermometer said. If the calendar claimed it was November, that meant winter, and you were to dress accordingly. She and Mama were the same that way. I took a moment to pull out a tiny splinter from the inside of my pinky finger, wincing as the sliver bit down before it relaxed and let me slide it out. It made me think of that story about the lion and the mouse. It was funny how something so small could hurt so much.

Grandma wasn't anywhere in sight, so I took my coat off and threw it on the ground behind me and hopped back up for another swing.

In the distance I heard a sweet whistle making its way up the drive-way. At Grandma's there was really no need for a clock. The postman walked up the long drive every day 'round noon; you could set your watch by him. He'd park the truck down on the street. He told me before that he liked walking up among the promenade of trees, especially in the spring when the magnolias were in full bloom, but even in the fall when they were empty like they were now, and that in his mind's eye, they still erupted in mauves and soft pinks. "Hey there, miss."

"Hi, Mr. King." I jumped off the tire swing and grabbed my jacket. I didn't want to be told on for not obeying. Adults seemed to sense when kids were breaking their rules. "Enjoying your morning?"

"Sure am. The sun is out, the wind is down. I think winter has decided not to come after all. Yes, it's a fine day. Couldn't be better. How many swings you get so far?" He nodded toward the tree.

"Eight and a half. But I cheated to get the half."

"It's all about the take-off," he said and laughed.

"Don't I know it. Can't hitch myself any higher, though."

He looked at the tree and walked underneath it, tracing with his feet the path the swing took. "Seems to me that the ground is slightly higher from the other side. Try swinging from the opposite direction. The extra elevation may be just what you need."

I thought about it for a minute. "Wouldn't that be cheating?"

He shook his head. "Nah—Mother Nature put it there for a reason. Think of it as her little push."

I liked Mr. King. Always had. He reminded me a bit of Mr. Cotton, and I wondered if they had played together as children. "Mr. King," I said. "Do you know Mr. Cotton who runs the bus into town?"

Mr. King scratched his head as if he were thinking. "Don't think I do."

I shrugged and walked the rope swing over to the other side. "No matter."

"Is your grandma in the house or the barn?"

"House."

The weather had shifted from the other day when Mama had me wrapped up in winter boots, hats and mittens. Today was regular Georgia weather and the man on the radio this morning said it was going to get to the high sixties, maybe even low seventies. Mr. King already looked uncomfortable in his blue wool pants and jacket. I could even see some sweat gathering around his hairline. "You like a drink of water?"

"Oh, no thanks, miss. I'll be dropping this jacket off in the truck as soon as I get back there. Mother Nature can't seem to make up her mind none, now can she?"

I pulled the rope back as far as possible, stepped into the rubber tube with my left foot, bent my right knee as much as I could, and pushed off into the air. One, two, three, four, five, six, seven, eight, nine, ten.

Mr. King was a good sport and clapped as he watched me swing back and forth. "Ten! See, I told you the other way would work."

I was out of breath with excitement. Otis had promised me a quarter this morning if I could get to ten. Even though I think he said it to get me out of his hair, I knew he was good for it. He hadn't counted on Mr. King coming and giving away the hill's secret. Now I had an official eyewitness who could corroborate my success. I put my foot down in the dirt to slow my rocking, jumped off the swing and walked on over to Mr. King. "Grandma's down in the basement doing laundry. Otis is in the barn office adding the books. I've been told to stay outside for at least an hour so they can get their work done."

"I don't want to bother them none. Would you mind taking this mail from me? Only a few letters and this one package. Think you can carry them all, or should I place them on the porch?" He reached into his bag and handled me the bundle.

"No, Mr. King. I can carry 'em." I held my arms out like a hammock and then curled them in, the letters pressed tightly against my chest.

106

"What's in the box?" I asked.

He winked at me. "Wouldn't know. My job is to deliver them, not to look in them. Are you going to be able to open the door?"

I wriggled my right hand free and twisted it around in the air so he could see. "I've got it. You sure you wouldn't like something to drink? I thought it was proper of me to offer and that you're supposed to accept?" Mama was always offering people things to drink or eat, so was Miss Eunice, and people were always taking them up on it.

Back home our mailman was Mr. Byrd. I never understood how he managed to get his route finished for all the time he spent sitting on people's porches. He'd sit with Miss Eunice drinking sweet tea and eating gingersnaps for what seemed like hours. Then he'd stop across the street at Mr. Watkins's and take some chew with him, both of them spitting into paper cups that Mr. Watkins would leave out on his porch rail, lined up like some mini parade. I guess that's why I still saw Mr. Byrd walking the streets long after the porch lights came on, his post bag hanging under his arm, him humming some tune to the dark night sky.

Mama said he was a widower, his wife having died before I was born. Seemed to me a lot of people died before I was born. World must have been a crowded place then. Mr. Byrd could have retired a few years ago, but no one was quite sure what he'd do all alone in his house on the corner, so the post office kept him on, not forcing him out or anything. Maybe that's why no one seemed to mind if their mail got delivered around supper time or long after.

I'd even heard that people on the later route over on the other streets set an extra place just for Mr. Byrd, in case he arrived on their doorstep, mail in hand, about the time the roast was being placed on the table. Mama said she wished that he'd spend some special time with Miss Eunice, take her out for dinner. I supposed he could ask one of those families to set two extra plates, and he could pick her up along the way.

"Macey May," Mr. King chuckled, his eyes crinkling up, "you are being mighty kind, and you're right. It is getting warm, and I've got a long walk down the drive back to my truck. A glass of water would be quite refreshing." He took his cap off. "I'll just sit up there on the porch and wait. Don't want to be bothering your grandma by walking uninvited into her house."

"But I'm inviting you."

He smiled. "Just the same, my shoes are covered in dirt. Wouldn't want to make any more cleaning for anyone."

"Suit yourself."

Mr. King settled himself on the red rocker while I went in and put the mail and package on the hallway credenza. Out the window he had taken a handkerchief from his pocket and was wiping the back of his neck with it. I'd give him extra ice.

"Macey May? Is that you?" Grandma's voice lofted up from the open door to the basement.

"Yes'm. I'm getting Mr. King a glass of water."

The stairs creaked under her feet. "A glass of water? Is he all right?" Her full figure stood in the doorway, a basket of wet clothes in her hands ready to dry on the clothesline.

"He's fine. A little hot in those wool pants is all." I looked down at my shoes. "Thought it was polite to ask people up on the porch. Miss Eunice and Mama do it all the time."

"Oh, sugar, of course it is. You've accomplished a big feat is all. I've asked Mr. King up for a glass every time I catch him, and he always tells me no. You must have some sort of knack." She put the laundry hamper on the table and squeezed my cheek. I smiled.

I held out the glass of water. "Do you want to take it to him?"

Grandma shook her head. "No. He's your guest. I'll stay inside and look through the post so as not to bother you both, then I'll go put these clothes out to dry."

We walked down the hallway together. "All there," I said, pointing to the pile. "There's a package, too."

"A package? I wonder who'd be sending us something." Grandma picked up the parcel and arched her neck toward the front door. "Afternoon, Mr. King."

"Afternoon, Cora Lee."

I left Grandma inside and offered the water to Mr. King. He took a long, exaggerated sip, for my pleasure I was sure, and ended with a drawn-out *ahhh* as if he was on death's door and I had saved him. "Thank you, Macey May. Hadn't even known how much I needed that, but it sure hit the spot." He stood up and put his hands behind his back, bending to stretch out the kinks like I had seen Otis do after rising from milking the cows. "I best be going now. Thanks again for the hospitality."

I couldn't even get words out of my mouth before we both heard the shriek from the kitchen. The only yelling I had ever heard come from an adult was yelling for kids to get out of the road before they got hit by a car, or yelling for kids to not climb so high in the tree or they'd break their necks, or yelling for kids to get to sleep before they got a whooping so hard they wouldn't be able to sleep even if they wanted to. I had never heard an adult scream out of their own fear. And that's what I heard. Outright terror.

Mr. King was gripping the screen door before I could even move an inch, his legs running him down the hallway toward my grandma's cry, no longer worried about what dirt he might be bringing in. My feet turned on their own and carried me out back toward the barn. Otis was already out, halfway across the yard on his way to the kitchen. I had never seen him move so fast. I don't know if he saw me or not, but he didn't stop, just kept running until the wooden door gaped open, swallowing him up whole. "Cora Lee, Cora Lee." His deep voice traveled along the dirt ground and wrangled its way up my legs and into my ears, stopping me in my tracks. Every vein in my body pulsed.

I'm not sure how long I stood there in the yard before Mr. King was next to me. "Everything's all right. Seems like a snake slithered right across your grandma's foot and down the stairs into the basement. It scared her something fierce, though, and Otis has taken her into her bedroom to lie down for a time." He ruffled the top of my head with his hand. I wondered if he could feel my heartbeat all the way up there. "They come in sometimes when the nights get cold. Probably found a space to squeeze through in the foundation and made its way up to the kitchen where it was warmer. Wouldn't hurt her none, though. These snakes around here don't do much to anyone."

I must have looked worried because he bent down like Mama did getting ready for me to board the bus and looked me in the eyes. "Nothing to worry about. That snake is long gone. Sure he slithered himself out the same way he came in. Why don't you go inside now and see if Otis needs your help with anything. I saw a laundry basket on the table. Perhaps you could put the towels up on the line. Be a nice surprise for your grandma."

I nodded mutely and turned and watched as Mr. King made his way down the drive. I don't know what I expected to see when I walked into the kitchen—chaos, perhaps. But everything was right where it always was. The wicker laundry basket was placed on top of the table next to two opened letters tucked neatly back into their envelopes, the gold letter opener with the pearl handle beside them. The brown wrapping from the package was folded up neatly into a tight even square, and next to it was an open shoe box. A brown leather oxford, slightly scuffed around the bottom edges, sat snugly inside white tissue paper. One shoe. I didn't bother to look for its pair, the box being too small to hold more than the solitary one. I looked down and saw the cover peeking out from under the kitchen chair. I knelt down and picked it up.

From an upstairs room I heard the muffled sounds of adults talking and a closet being opened and rummaged through, a chair being drawn along the floor and *thunked* in place above my head. They were in the guest room. It used to be my grandma and Pap's bedroom, but she had moved down to the room on the first floor a few years ago. Said her knees weren't what they used to be, and if she didn't need to be climbing the stairs two times a day, she'd live longer. I wondered why she was up there now.

I grabbed an apple from the bowl on the counter and left the kitchen. Otis said I could help him later with the cows, so I figured I had better get over there. I figured too that if my grandma or Otis wanted to tell me what was really going on, they would. If they wanted to tell me whatever secrets they were hiding, I'd be more than happy to listen.

More than once I had witnessed my grandma picking up a snake barehanded from behind her rose bushes and carrying it across the back yard to let it go among the hickory trees, all the while talking to it as if it was some sort of dear friend.

Cora Lee Jenkins did not scream over snakes.

"Macey May, you in here?" Otis's voice carried through the barn all the way to the far end where I was sitting on a hay bale.

"Back here with Mabel," I said. Mabel was the prettiest cow I had ever seen. She was a Guernsey with big brown eyes and long eyelashes. I'd almost call her beautiful, if you could ever call a cow that. If we came back as animals, *carnation* people called it, I think, I'd want to come back as her.

"How's my girl?" Otis asked.

I cocked my head.

He smiled, understanding my unspoken question. "You."

111

I shrugged and picked up a stray piece of hay and put it in my mouth between my teeth. "Okay, I guess."

"Did Grandma's scream scare you?"

"Did it scare you?"

He nodded. "Sure did. Your grandma could raise the dead with her hollering."

"She's loud." I pulled the straw out and looked at the wet end, rubbing it between my fingers, thinking. "Otis, Grandma doesn't scream over snakes, you know that."

He picked a pail off of the wall and ran the hose into it. "Well, this time it skirted right over her foot. She wasn't expecting it in her own house. It's different when you come across them in the garden. They're supposed to be there. They're not supposed to be slithering over the linoleum of your kitchen floor." He continued to busy himself with the pail.

I shook my head and stood up. It seemed to me sometimes that all adults did was lie, although Mr. King had been truthful in the hint about the tree swing. Maybe it was the adults in my family who lied. I knew my mama was lying to me about my daddy. He wasn't away on some job in California, and I had a feeling deep down in those places inside you where you know things, those true places, that Daddy wasn't coming back. I put my feelings about Mr. Junior in that place. Now Otis was lying to me. I never imagined he'd lie to me.

Mabel "mooed," her neck stretching with the sound, her lashes blinking as if she had a question herself about the snake. I put my arms around her neck and kissed her. "Why would someone send one old shoe?" I asked more to the air and Mabel and myself than anyone else.

Behind me the pail dropped to the ground, the water sloshing up and hitting the backs of my pants.

"Darnit! Sorry, honey. Looks like I got you wet. Why don't you run into the house and change, then come back out. You can stay here with me until lunch, give Cora Lee some time to rest without having to worry about you."

I patted Mabel one last time on the head. "Do they think Grandma lost it?"

"Lost what?"

"The shoe. It's not even new. I looked at it. It's shiny but there are scuff marks like it scratched up against something all across the toe and side. Seems old in a way. Not like worn out old, more like…just old. What does Grandma want with an old shoe?"

"You know what? How about a burger from Chuck's for lunch instead? I've got some things I need in town anyway."

"Chuck's? Yippee!" I jumped up and clapped my hands together.

"Now, hurry and change out of those play clothes, but don't bother your grandma. Come right back here and you can help me with brushing down the cows before we go."

I was in and out of the house fantasizing about fries and ketchup and back to Mabel before I realized that Otis hadn't answered my question.

After Chuck's, Otis splurged and bought us ice cream cones from Bennie's. I got vanilla with colored sprinkles in a sugar cone. Otis picked chocolate. We walked down Main Street looking in the store windows waiting for our treats to be finished. He didn't seem to be in a rush to head home, and since it seemed like Grandma wouldn't be getting up any time soon, I took my time, It was like Mama and I did sometimes in downtown Harrison during the holidays when the trees were all lit up, and we wanted to soak in all the sights.

"Will they be decorating soon for Christmas?" I asked as we walked past the Five and Dime. "Mama says that Aunt Ruby says that Macy's puts a different display in every window of the store. You can walk outside for hours just looking in at them. Some even move. The one I want to see is the ballerinas in Candy Land. Aunt Ruby says they are dressed up like gumdrops and candy canes, and they spin and spin and spin around a Christmas tree with blinking lights! Must be beautiful." I spun around for effect and Otis laughed.

"Maybe you will." I felt the hot, deep voice on my neck before I heard the words in my ear.

My ice cream fell to the pavement between my feet. "Oh!"

Otis turned around. "Junior—hey."

Mr. Junior nodded at Otis and looked at me. "My goodness. I do apologize. It seems like I startled your ice cream right out of your hand. Didn't mean to. Let me buy you a new one."

"No. Th-that's all right." I shook my head and put my trembling hand inside my pocket. "I was almost done."

Otis looked at me. "You okay, Macey May? You've gone as pale as that vanilla. You're not going to be sick, are you?"

I thought for minute. It wouldn't be fibbing to say I was. Mr. Junior's voice set my heart pounding and my stomach into somersaults. Otis motioned me toward a bench. "Why don't you sit down there for a minute. Let me talk to Junior and then I'll get you right home."

I could feel Mr. Junior's eyes on me as I walked away. Their voices were too far for me to hear anything. The deep tone of Mr. Junior and the lighter rasp of Otis bantered back and forth. It wasn't one-sided, and it wasn't angry. Otis even put his head back once and laughed at something Mr. Junior said. Mr. Junior looked at me then and winked.

He hadn't lied.

"They like me," he had said.

"They trust me," he had smiled.

"They'll never believe you."

Chapter 10

CRAWFORD, GEORGIA
CORA LEE JENKINS
1937

"HI, do you really have to go?" Cora Lee reached across the bed and touched Hi's bare back as he sat on the edge, allowing her nails to follow the curvature of his spine.

It was a hot and lazy afternoon, the kind where no one thinks about moving. Where limbs fall limp and heavy and sweat evaporates before it has a chance to pool on your skin. Two o'clock with the sun blazing high overhead, there wasn't a brush of wind been felt all day. The heat was affecting everyone. Even the birds had put a hush to their music; instead, they had taken to sitting on the tree branches in the shade, quiet in their melodious intermission. All the cows had sauntered into the stillness of the barn, lying down in the coolness of the hay, and the bumblebees had left their job of harvesting the nectar from the rhododendrons to mull low on the ground under the cover of the leaves.

Cora Lee couldn't remember the last time she heard a car pass by the farm other than the mail truck earlier that morning. The magnolias they'd planted up the driveway a few years before hadn't yet grown high enough to produce any shade. No kids biked down the dirt path that followed along the creek, leading to the low-lying pool where they gathered to swim when the days became unbearable or the starry night sky called to them. It was too hot to move.

A heat wave, they announced on the radio last night. One like Georgia hadn't seen in over a hundred years. The heat, each day, increasing above the previous day's record. If it reached 99 tomorrow, Cora Lee felt she'd catch on fire just by breathing. The weekend forecast was for rain coming in from the west, a promise of a ten-degree cool-down, but that was two days away. She was sure they'd all be melted by then.

"Who's going to do business with you today, anyway? Too darn hot for anything. Can't believe anyone would want to open their mouths and talk, never mind sit behind a desk and discuss anything of any importance. Can't you take care of it over the phone or at least wait a few days?"

Hi stood up and stretched. "Not this. I've got to see Mr. Callahan at the bank; the appointment's already been made, and he'll be waiting on me. Besides, they just installed that new air conditioning system last month. It's sure getting broken in this week." He leaned over the bed and kissed her lips. "I bet you it's so cold in there that I might not even come home. Just stay there until I turn into ice. Might not be such a bad way to go." He smiled at her and grabbed his shirt from the back of the chair.

Watching Hi get dressed was like watching a magician transform right in front of her eyes or a caterpillar emerging from its cocoon to become a magnificent butterfly. She loved how his muscles flexed, the black skin taut and smooth. The graceful way his fingers moved on the buttons. In the mornings before dawn, when the pale light of the retreating moon threw its last rays of light across the bedroom floor, she would watch Hi become the farmer who worked the soil wearing overalls splattered with years of paint and grease, cotton shirts tried and true, and boots with steel toes. Her husband, a father, with strong arms that held his babies gently and dared the world to harm them.

Now, this morning, he became another man. Lehigh. The crisp,

116

ironed white shirt over his arms, the black tie, the belt with the polished buckle, the shined shoes still kept in the box at the top of the closet taken out only on Sundays and bank meetings, the hat, and suit jacket thrown over his shoulder. A man of business who knew how to hold an opinion, who wasn't going to be taken for a ride by anyone. A man who knew the obstacle of color in a white man's world and had successfully navigated through it.

She thought about later that night, when their clothes came off again, and they lay there skin to skin. She would trace the scar across his stomach from when his appendix burst, and she thought she was going to lose him. She would run her toes up against his formed calf muscles, feel their strength press against her, and he would become her lover. Another facet of whom he was.

"I'll be back by dinner. I told Otis not to bother with any fields today, told him to work on paperwork inside instead. No use trying to water the crops during the day in this heat. I think it would evaporate before it run out of the hose, or come out so hot that it would cook the sweet potatoes right there in the dirt. I told him we'd do the watering tonight after the sun went down. I doubt the mosquitoes will make any trouble then. Not a soul's been out for them to feed on. I wouldn't be surprised if they all haven't shriveled up and died these past days."

Hi laughed as he straightened his tie and looked in the mirror above the bureau. "Could be that this heat wave is the best thing to happen in Georgia in our lifetimes! I wouldn't mind a few less pesky insects. Why don't we plan on having some sweet tea and peaches with cream on the porch when Otis and I are finished? Maybe we should set up the cots out there tonight for the girls?"

Cora Lee shook her head. "Their room stays cool enough for them at night. But I'll put blankets out and tell them we're having a picnic when Daddy gets home. They've been cramped in this house for five days straight. Might give them something to look forward to. If it's cooled off enough, maybe we can take them down to the creek for a swim."

"I wouldn't get your hopes up about that. Without any wind, they say we'll be lucky to dip into the eighties during the night. You're better off filling the tub with water and giving them some toys."

She threw the thin bed sheet off of her body and waited for the movement from the ceiling fan to cool her off. She had put Rose and Ruby down for naps an hour earlier right after lunch. They were irritated and tired, their little bodies fighting against the warmth until they collapsed beaten on the living room floor. One by one she placed them in their beds, their dark hair matted around the sides of their faces, curls down their foreheads like you see pasted on kewpie dolls. She had kept the shades drawn all day, and with the fan on, their room was bearable. But they were antsy.

"That's a good idea. Poor babies, hotter than fever."

Hi turned and winked at her. "Save some of the cold water for us, and I'll join you later."

Cora Lee sat at the kitchen table, a bowl of summer succotash in the center. If the weather didn't turn soon, she'd run out of food. She couldn't bear to turn on the stove the past few days, the thought of the house getting hotter too distressing. She'd about cleaned out the refrigerator, and there wasn't much left in the pantry that didn't necessitate starting the oven. Cora Lee took a spoonful of the cold succotash to taste. The baby butter beans, sweet onion and tomato erupted like little bursts of flavorful ice in her mouth. Hi liked lima beans and okra in it too and as much corn as the bowl would hold.

Rose bounced her bare feet up and down against the bottom rungs of the chair and wrapped her fists around slices of green pepper while chewing on bits of cold ham. Earlier that evening after their baths, Ruby had fallen asleep sitting on the floor with her blocks. Fell right over into the tower she had made and didn't even wake up when it crashed down to the ground. Cora Lee had put her down in her bed again and didn't have the heart to wake her, deciding instead to wait until Hi got home.

She looked at the clock on the wall. Hi should have been home fifteen minutes ago. She shifted in her seat and added some butter beans on Rose's plate along with a heel from a loaf of bread. If she let Ruby sleep much longer, it would be a long night for everyone.

"Hey, Cora Lee." Otis stood outside the kitchen door, his face checkered in the shadow of the screen.

"Hey there, Otis. Come on in, and sit down at the table."

"Sorry I'm late. Was getting the hoses ready for watering after dinner. Shouldn't take me and Hi more than a few hours to get it all done."

"Don't worry none. He's not back from town yet. Wish I knew what was keeping him so long. The bank's been closed now for almost half an hour. Did he tell you what it was about?"

Otis took his hat off and wiped his forehead with a rag from his back pocket. "Sorry, Cora Lee. He didn't say anything other than needing to go in to talk to Mr. Callahan."

"Well, I was planning on waiting for him, but Rose was too hungry. I might as well get Ruby up and feed her too. No need making them or you, for that matter, wait. Take a plate from the table and help yourself. Sweet tea's in the fridge unless you'd like a grape Nehi. Some of those are in there along the door."

Otis had two helpings while Cora Lee pushed the ham around her plate. The girls didn't have much appetite in the heat and more of the succotash landed on the floor than in their mouths. She cut up some bananas, cold from the fridge, but even those didn't seem to interest them. Cora Lee cleared off the table and looked at the clock again. It was almost seven. Hi had never been an hour late to dinner in all the years they'd been married. Even when they were dating and he'd come over to her parents' house for Sunday dinner, he always arrived right on time. Lateness was not part of Hi's makeup.

She stood on the porch with Otis watching the drive. Rose and Ruby were spread out on blankets with paper and crayons, remnants of peaches and cream in bowls scattered around them. "Where is he, Otis?"

Otis took a toothpick out of his mouth and bit the inside of his bottom lip. "Not sure. Engine in the truck causing any trouble lately?"

"Not that I know of."

"Why don't I take a run up the road a little, see if I can find him walking. Once he left town, there wouldn't be any way of getting a hold of us to let us know if something had happened on his way back."

Cora Lee thought of Hi walking down the darkening streets, his sweat coming through his shirt, his jacket over his shoulder and his sleeves rolled up. He'd be exhausted by the time he got home, and he still had the fields to water. She thought about what it meant for a black man to be walking alone at night. A well-dressed black man often only made it worse.

She ran her fingers up her arms, a chill settling in on her. "Would you, Otis? I'd appreciate that. It's almost the girls' bedtimes. I'll get them settled. That way I can help both of you with the fields, get them done faster."

"I think I'll swing by and pick up Denim. I know he wouldn't mind lending us a hand."

Cora Lee thought for a minute and looked at Otis. "Are you worried?"

"Worried about Hi? In the twenty years he and I have been friends, I don't think I've ever worried about him. If there's one thing I know, it's that Hi can take care of himself. He's got a good head on his shoulders. Now don't you go distressing yourself. It will all be fine, I'm sure."

Instead of taking the girls directly up to bed, Cora Lee settled them around her on the double rocker on the porch. With her arms one around each, she began to sing.

I got-a wings, you got-a wings
All o' God's chillun got-a wings
When I get to heav'n I'm goin' to put on my wings
I'm goin' to fly all ovah God's Heav'n

"Mama, you have wings?" Rose rubbed her eyes with her fists and tried to look behind Cora Lee. "Where are they?"

"No, sugar. We all going to have wings some day when we get to heaven."

Ruby squirmed out of Cora Lee's arm and sidled off of the rocker. "I want wings! I want wings!" Her little body jumped up and down.

"You don't get them now. You have to wait." Rose shot Ruby an irritated glance, and Cora Lee smiled.

Ruby crossed her arms and stomped her food. "Want wings now!"

"What would you do with them if you had them, baby?" Cora Lee loved listening to her girls talk. She was always amazed as she watched them grow, at their ability to become themselves. To take on such distinctive traits. To know who they were. She was twenty-six, and she was more unsure of herself than she had ever been. Ruby wanted wings and darling red shoes that looked like bright garnet apples hanging from the trees. She wanted a white horse with pink ribbons in its mane and a dancing bear. She wanted a diamond tiara and bells on the underskirts of her dresses. She wanted to be a princess in a castle with a frog who turned into a prince when she kissed him.

Rose, at the age of only five, wanted justice. She wanted the stray dogs and cats that wandered onto the farm to be brought in and fed. She wanted the cows to never be put down, and she didn't want to sell any of the pigs for slaughter. She wanted to sit at the front of the bus so she could see everything from the big window. She wanted to be able to go into any store she chose and order ice cream from the counter at the Five and Dime. A double scoop in a sugar cone with rainbow sprinkles. She wanted her own farm one day where she could do all of this. When Cora Lee would tell her that maybe she'd find a husband who was a farmer, Rose would put her hands on her hips and say, "I don't need a husband. I'll do it myself."

Cora Lee worried most about Rose.

"Wings are in heaven, right Mama?" Rose looked at Cora Lee in earnest, the skin between her eyebrows furrowed in concentration. "Then we can fly around anywhere we want. Does Mammaw have wings? Is she flying with Jesus?"

Cora Lee looked at her oldest daughter. "Yes, I assume she is."

Ruby opened her mouth wide and yawned.

Cora Lee stood up and scooped Ruby into her arms. "She's flying around like a bird up there over the clouds looking down on us. Come now. I think it's bedtime for both of you. Daddy will be sure to kiss you goodnight when he gets home."

Rose squeezed Cora Lee's hand as they walked up the stairs. "But I won't know he kissed me if I'm sleeping."

"Sure you will. It will feel like a breeze passed by your cheek, and it will make you smile. It's what gives you happy dreams."

The girls snuggled down into their beds and Cora Lee said prayers over them. She shut the light off and left the room, leaving the door open a smidge.

"Mama?" Rose's voice spoke in the dark, a hardness to it.

"Yes, Rose? What is it?"

"I don't want no wings."

"Why is that, honey?"

"I don't want to be dead to get them."

Cora Lee walked outside and stood next to the chinaberry tree. The moon was full out now, the driveway appearing lit up as if the moon were a flashlight searching down on the world below. Her heart and head told her something was wrong. The still air increased around her. Mourning air. She had never felt it until now.

For years she had listened to her mother and grandmother sit on the porch and talk into the dark about haints and restless spirits, about mourning air and what it meant. She never could quite grasp what they were saying, and more often than not she'd fall asleep between them, her head on one's lap and her feet on another. Her daddy would come out and gather her up and put her to bed. Hi was like him. The thought made her happy. The girls were lucky to have a father like Hi, one who wasn't afraid to show them love, who got down on the floor and played with them. Yes, her girls were fortunate.

Truck lights turned off the road and made their way down the dirt drive. Cora Lee shielded her eyes from the brightness, and the tenseness released from her shoulders. Hi was home.

"Hi?" She ran to meet the truck.

"Sorry, Cora Lee. It's just me and Denim." Otis put the truck into park and shut it off. His elbow hung out the window, and Cora Lee walked over and grabbed on to the side view mirror for support.

"You didn't find him?"

Otis looked at Denim and back at Cora Lee.

"Otis, what is it?" The relief that Cora Lee felt a moment ago began to choke her.

"We found his truck off Sugar Mill Road. It was pulled off to the side underneath some of those big heavy trees. We almost didn't see it. Doors were unlocked but the keys weren't in it. Nothing was broken, though. Glass was fine. It didn't look like there had been an accident." Otis touched Cora Lee's arm. "There wasn't any blood or anything like that. Another set of tire prints a bit ahead in the dirt, but those could have been made any time."

She backed away. She needed to think. He was hurt; she was sure of it. Hi never would have let her worry like this. "Maybe his car broke down, and he tried a short cut through those woods between the roads. It would bring him out closer to the house than following Sugar Mill until it meets up with Bowditch."

Otis and Denim got out of the truck and leaned against it. "We thought of that," Denim said. "Took a flashlight and walked in a bit. It's too overgrown in there for him to get through, especially at night. Even by day you'd get lost."

She looked back at the house. The lights blazed through the windows. It was silly of her to have done it, to leave every light on in the downstairs after she put the girls to bed, but she wanted Hi to be able to see their home. Their babies. "Maybe another car needed help, those tracks. Maybe he stopped to help them and something happened."

"I think we need to call the sheriff," Otis said.

Cora Lee's shoulders went back, and she stared at him. "You think a white man's going to care about where Hi has gone? No. We need to go get his truck and bring it back here. There's a spare key in the barn."

"I know where it is." Denim started walking toward the barn. "Don't worry, Cora Lee, we'll find him."

Cora Lee looked at her watch. It was almost eleven. "Otis, when you get back with the truck, I'm going out to look again. If you want to come with me you can. If you don't, you don't have to. But I'll need someone to stay with the girls."

"You're not going anywhere alone. It's late and dark. It's bad enough

Hi is gone. I don't need to try to find you, too."

"I've got the keys," Denim said, running from the barn. "Otis and I won't be long."

Cora Lee's heart sped up. She didn't know how she could wait for them to bring the truck back. She needed to be doing something to find Hi. "Denim, the girls are sleeping. I don't expect them to wake. The fan's giving them a breeze and the noise from it keeps them under. Could you stay and watch them when you get back? I need to go try to look for Hi myself."

Denim looked at Otis who nodded. "Sure thing, Cora. You know I'll do anything." Denim reached his hand out and squeezed her shoulder.

Sitting on the porch waiting for them to return with the truck, she wished she knew more about the business of the farm. Perhaps there was a clue in that. She didn't even know why Hi needed to talk to Mr. Callahan that day. There was nothing unusual in it, though. He had monthly meetings with the bank and his buyers. Sometimes they came out to the farm, sometimes he went into town to meet them. The farm wasn't in any trouble; she was sure Hi wouldn't have kept that a secret.

She thought about Mavis Briggs, a woman from church whose husband left her and her three kids. They found his body a few months later back up in the hills surrounded by a dozen or so broken whiskey bottles and his shotgun. Mavis told her it didn't matter that he was officially dead; he had left her the minute the bottle had become more important to him than his family. Hi wasn't like that. He came from a good family and treated her right. Never got drunk, never raised a hand to her. Loved his girls so much it made her heart bust sometimes to see it. He was not a man to run away or look for answers somewhere else.

Tires on gravel broke through her thoughts. Denim and Otis drove in one after the other, Denim behind in Hi's truck. Cora Lee walked out to the drive to meet them.

"Denim, pull it up next to the barn where he usually parks it. Don't want it looking any different than usual," Cora Lee told him.

It was past midnight now and clouds had drifted in and out, covering the stars until there was only a sliver of moon, the darkness like a shade being pulled over the window of the sky. Otis turned his truck around and Cora Lee jumped in. "Keep the lights on in the house, Denim." She paused. "Please."

A half an hour later they passed through downtown for the second time. The windows on the Five and Dime reflected the light from the streetlamps, and she could see that potting soil and fertilizer were on sale that week for only forty cents. Across the way Chuck's Luncheonette looked gay with caricatures of ice cream cones and root beer floats painted on the windows. The town was sleeping. All was normal and at rest. Except Hi was gone.

"Cora Lee. I don't know where to go anymore, and I don't think it's the safest thing for us to be driving out this late at night."

She understood. Only last week a black boy had been beaten by a group of white teenagers. They said he was up to no good, walking around town at ten o'clock. All the stores were closed, nothing was open. Surely he was planning on robbing something. They were doing their "civic duty" protecting the streets, they said. It didn't seem to matter none to anyone when the news came out that he had been at the Reverend Wheeldin's asking him to go over to his house and pray for his ailing grandmother who was hours away from passing or that the white boys were out that late, too. It was the reverend who discovered him not fifteen minutes later on the ground, those boys kicking him like they were rabid dogs.

"I know. I need to think. Would you take me to our tree?" Tears welled in her eyes and she clenched her fists to fight them back.

"Are you sure?"

"Hi asked me to marry him there, and that's where I told him I was pregnant every time. If something big happens, that's where we go. I feel him there."

Otis turned the truck around and bore right. The cypress was a short way back up on a hill off an old dirt road. In the winter when all the trees were bare, the cypress could be seen in the distance, its gangly branches stretched out as if reaching for them to come to it. In the spring when everything was in bloom, it hid invisible behind a realm of petals and leaves. You'd drive all the way up the top of the hill and there it would be, splendid and majestic, a grand madam covered in necklaces of Spanish moss. It was so beautiful sometimes Cora Lee would find herself crying just looking at it.

The truck rattled up the hard dirt. Even at night the earth whirled up, handfuls blown in front of the headlights like some upside-down ticker tape parade.

Rose saw him first. The outline of a foot, a shadow against the night sky. She opened the door and jumped out before Otis even knew he should be stopping the car.

"Hi!" she screamed.

Her feet touched the ground and she tumbled, rolling over herself. Her head hit the hard ground and dirt stung her eyes. She landed on the grass and could hear Otis yelling her name, the brakes sliding in the gravel. Her shoulder hurt and her leg throbbed. She looked down and saw blood from her thigh soiling her house dress while bits of rock and sand embedded themselves into her palms. She tried to stand, but a sharp pain in her ankle made her collapse. On hands and knees she dragged herself over to the tree.

"Dear God, no!" Using the trunk to stabilize herself, she stood under the shadow of Hi's body, her hands barely touching his dangling feet. "Oh God, please!" She jumped to try to grab hold of him, and her arms scratched against the tree bark.

"Heaven have mercy!" Otis was behind her now, looking up at Hi.

Cora Lee grabbed onto Otis's shirt. "He'll be all right. He'll be all right. Go get the ladder from the truck. We've got to get him down." She reached up with her hands in supplication. "Hi, baby, I'm here. You'll be all right."

Otis ran to the truck and carried the ladder back, set it against the tree as quickly as he could and climbed up.

Time stopped. Cora Lee watched as Otis reached out to touch Hi's neck. Watched the slowness in which his hand then fell to his side. Watched his eyes look down on her. The wordless sorrow they held.

"Cora Lee, listen. Can you hear me?"

She tried to focus in on him. Her eyes couldn't see. Wherever she looked she saw only Hi's foot suspended in air. One shoeless foot. Even with her eyes closed, the foot swung before her.

"Cora Lee. Listen to me. I've got to cut him down, and you won't be able to catch him. I'm going to have to let him fall."

A strangled sound escaped her lips.

"Turn around, Cora Lee. I don't want you seeing this."

She didn't move. Otis walked back down the rungs, placed his hands gently on her shoulders, and twisted her away.

A foot. All she had seen from the car window was a dangling foot, and she had known it was him. Hi's foot.

Behind her the ladder creaked. The soft sandpaper sound of knife cutting through rope and then a thump as Hi's body hit the ground.

Cora Lee turned around and ran over to Hi. His eyes had been covered with cloth and his arms bound at the wrists behind his back. There

128

was a bullet hole straight through his heart. Frantically she untied him and took the blindfold off. Her fingers touched the blood, dry on his shirt, pressed down on the wound as if that would somehow do something to save him. "No…no…no."

"Shhh…Cora Lee." Otis was next to her pulling her away from Hi. She slapped at his hands and hissed. "Leave me be!" She wanted to stay, to sleep there with Hi, to go wherever he had gone. "Cora Lee, we've got to go. We can't stay here. Whoever did this might come back."

It was a minute before she spoke again, her voice changed. "They can't do this, Otis."

"I know. We'll go get the sheriff."

"No." Even in the dark he could see the resolution in her eyes, hear it in her voice. He touched her arm, and she threw it off. "I said leave me be!"

Otis stepped back and took his hat off, twisting it in his hands. "Cora——." His voice faltered. "Cora Lee, this is different. Hi was dead before they put him up there. He was shot. I don't know of the Klan killing like that."

"Didn't you listen to me before? The sheriff won't care. What's another dead black man to him?" She stood up and faced him. "We are taking Hi home. His life will not end like this."

Otis took down the rope from the tree and threw it with the ladder in the back of the truck. He took a branch and wiped out where the ladder legs had dug into the dirt, swept away where Hi's body had disturbed the ground. If anyone went up there, there would be no sign that anything had been amiss. With Cora Lee's help, he managed to put Hi's body between them in the front seat, his body bent over in her lap. As Otis turned the truck around and drove back down the dirt road, she looked away, their spot now changed forever.

By the time they returned to the farm, Cora Lee had her plan figured out. The KKK had been burning crosses and throwing Molotov cocktails through living room windows all over Montgomery. It appeared they had made their way to Crawford. Maybe Hi had fought them, maybe he had run. Maybe they knew they wouldn't be able to hang him unless he was already dead because he would fight, oh, she knew he would fight. He would fight with every bit of strength he had in him for her and for his girls. He could fight men, but he wouldn't be able to fight a bullet. They may have killed him to show their power, to scare others into submission, but she would make sure they didn't have that chance.

Denim was standing on the porch when they pulled up. Otis got out of the truck and met him halfway. Their voices were soft and deep against the night air. Otis turned and pointed back to Cora Lee in the truck in way of explanation.

"Damn it!" Denim said, his steel toe boots kicking up dirt. "Is this ever going to stop?"

Denim went to the driver's side and opened the door. Otis stood beside him. "Cora Lee. I'm going to sit in the car with you and check over Hi. Is that okay?"

Cora Lee nodded almost imperceptibly.

Denim lifted his arm and felt for a pulse. "Rigor mortis hasn't set in yet. He can't have been killed more than an hour or two ago. By the looks of his face, he was dead from the gunshot before they hanged him. Otis said there was no blood there, so they must have shot him somewhere else. I know this doesn't help, Cora Lee, but it would have been instantaneous. He didn't suffer."

Otis came around the truck. "What do you want us to do now, Cora Lee?"

She looked straight ahead out the windshield and spoke. Her voice was even and controlled as if she had been thinking long and hard about what she had to say and was determined they wouldn't misunderstand her. "Otis and Denim. I can't do this on my own. I need your help. Carry Hi up to our bedroom and place him in our bed. At five this morning, Otis, I need you to call Reverend Wheeldin's and tell him you came out to the farm for the early feeding and found me weeping on the porch over the fact that Hi had died in the night."

She turned and looked at them. In Otis's eyes she saw the pain over a loss of a friend, in Denim's the anger at the injustice of their time. In both of them she saw their undeniable allegiance to her. She cleared her throat and continued. "Otis, you tell him I don't want to see him none, and I don't want any visitors. I need to do my grieving alone. Tell him that we'll do the funeral here the next morning at eleven. The ladies from the church can bring by food starting at nine. The service will be in the parlor, and we'll bury him down by the water's edge. Think you can make him a coffin?"

Denim broke in. "I can do that for him, Cora Lee."

She bent over and kissed Hi's forehead. "No. I want Otis to. Hi would have liked that. Denim, I'm going to need you to do something else."

"Anything, Cora Lee. You know that."

She took a deep breath and exhaled. "Denim, I need you to fill out the death certificate saying he died of natural causes."

Denim leaned into the seat. She could hear his fist softly beating against the steering wheel.

"Denim?" Otis's voice was soft but strong.

Cora Lee continued. "I know I'm asking you to break the law, to break your oath as coroner, but it's the only way."

Denim twisted and looked at her. "I don't understand."

"If people hear that Hi died in his sleep, then whoever did this gains nothing from his death. They can't go around saying he died some other way because that would implicate them. Hi's death will not be used to make people live in fear, and his babies are not going to sleep every night with visions of their father swinging from a tree with a bullet through his heart. They will see him in his bed, peaceful, and I'll tell them he fell asleep talking about them. And maybe whoever did this will leave us alone." Cora Lee's voice was rising.

Otis looked over at Denim and opened up the passenger door. "Of course he will, Cora Lee."

Denim took a deep breath and nodded.

After the men left, Cora Lee closed the bedroom door behind her and locked it. She didn't want to run the risk of one of the girls getting out of their beds and coming in. Rose had a habit some nights, especially during thunderstorms, to crawl in between her and Hi. Like a stealth cat, she'd work her way up from the bottom and be snug in their arms before either one knew she was there. Otis and Denim had laid Hi out in the bed for her, bowed their heads in prayer before they walked out, and assured her they knew the plan. Otis would be back in a few hours, and Denim would be over by seven to fill out the coroner's report. It would be okay.

Cora stood at the foot of the bed and looked at Hi. Laying on his back, his hands softly folded on his chest, she imagined for a moment that he had only fallen asleep reading a book. The light on the side table shone on his face, his eyes closed, his lips slightly turned up in a smile.

She reached out and took off his one remaining shoe, delicately unlacing the strings. She lifted its box out of the closet and placed the shoe inside and replaced it back onto the shelf above his shirts. His socks came off next. She laid them on the chair as if they were made of imported silk. Her fingers lingered on the bones of his ankles, graced over the hair on his toes. Undoing his belt, her hands stopped. She had given him the belt buckle for a wedding present. "Cora Lee," he had said to her, "it's the nicest thing I've ever seen." And he had meant it, she was sure. The zipper was next, and she slipped his pants down over his ankles, carefully placing them in the hamper; they'd need to be washed. Each button on his shirt was a memory of their lovemaking, his slowness, his caring.

Holding the fabric up to her nose, she inhaled, hoping to breathe in his scent. But all that was there was acrid sweat of organic earth and the iron of blood. They had taken even that away.

She unlocked the door and walked across the hall to the bathroom. Filling a jug with warm water, she took a face cloth and hand towel from the linen closet along with the basin and walked back into the bedroom. She would clean him like she had done Rose and Ruby when they were babies.

She lifted his arm and dried it off. It was like seeing his body for the first time, the way the indentation of his biceps curled around the back of his arm, the freckles that speckled themselves across his forearms where the sun kissed his skin every day in the summer. The bullet wound was puckered, blood crusted around it, and Cora Lee delicately wiped it with the cloth, turning the water in the basin red. She thought of all the times she had wet a cloth, filled a basin to cleanse away the hurt of a skinned knee or a cut elbow. This hurt couldn't be cleansed.

His wedding ring shone in the light, and she wondered if she should take it off and keep it or bury it with him. They had never discussed such things. Why did they need to? Death was so far off. She felt her own ring, the gold band that had thinned against her finger on the inside. Hi hadn't given her an engagement ring when he proposed, a decision that suited her fine. She'd rather the money be spent on the farm, buying the things they needed to get it up off of the ground to make it their home.

She traced his fingers with her own. His fingernails were trimmed, the cuticles pushed back. For a man who worked the fields and milked cows and delivered pigs, his skin didn't show it. His hands remained soft and supple. *They'll never touch me again*, she thought.

Images of the tree, his dangling shadow, attempted to overtake her as her hand swept the warm cloth across his face, clearing away the dirt from where he fell.

A deep breath.

A glance at the nightstand where their wedding picture stood.

His reading glasses propped up against his glass of unfinished water.

Cora Lee picked it up and drank the remains.

She piled his clothes together and brought them down to the cellar wringer. Opening up the wood burning stove, she threw in the shirt and undershirt. There needed to be no evidence. She'd wash the rest in the early hours of the morning, as was her routine. The stairs were harder to climb on the way back up. Her legs were leaden, her heart heavy. Back in the bedroom, she took off her clothes, slipped on her thin nightgown, and eased her body into the bed. His skin was cold. Her mind was finding it more difficult to accept the fiction she had created. Bringing the sheet up over the both of them, she placed her hand on Hi's chest and rested her head in the curvature of his neck.

She had never had to be so strong.

Hi had been her strength.

By the time the sun rose, she was on the porch waiting for Otis. Hi's clothes had been washed and were hung on the clothesline, the early morning heat already beginning to dry them. Otis's truck rattled up the road, and he was quiet with the door when he shut it.

"How you doing, Cora Lee?"

"I'll be all right, Otis." She didn't look at him as they spoke, instead she stared out over the mass of trees in the front yard and rocked away in the chair.

"Are you ready for me to call Reverend Wheeldin?" Otis asked.

"Gonna be another hot one today, I'm sure."

"We can't wait too long. Don't know when someone will discover he's not up on that tree where they left him, but I suspect it will be sometime soon. This news has to be out before anyone even thinks of looking for him."

Cora Lee nodded her head. "I know. I know. You go call him. Let's do what needs to be done."

Otis went inside. She hadn't thought fully what to tell the girls. Ruby was so little that she doubted she'd understand what it even meant that Hi had died. Rose would cry and need to be by her all day, squirming into her arms, wrapping her limbs around her neck, asking to be rocked. Rose dealt with grief by wanting to crawl inside you. When a kitten hadn't made it in last year's litter, Rose attached herself to Cora Lee's leg for three whole days. Even when she needed to use the bathroom, Rose would sit out in the hall waiting for her, her little face pressed against the door jamb trying to look in through the small space.

Otis came outside and wiped the sweat from his neck with a rag from his back pocket. Barely five-thirty and already the thermometer read seventy-eight. "It's done," he said. "Woke him up and then had to convince him that you meant it when you said you didn't want him here. He said he'd let the ladies know and that he'd call back later tonight and see how you were faring and what Denim had to say."

Cora Lee raised an eyebrow.

"I told him looked like a heart attack to me. Don't worry yourself, none. He trusts Denim, and Denim's agreed."

135

Cora Lee walked across the lawn and felt Hi's pants. He had one other fancy shirt, his Easter one that she'd put on him to be buried in, but this was his only suit. She hated the thought that she'd have to put him back in the clothes he was wearing when they killed him. Killed him. The words felt hollow in her head. What did it mean, killed? Someone had taken the man she loved and shot him, and then to make sure he was good and dead, strangled the life out of him. The thought was so fierce that it knocked her down, and she found herself crying into the grass, the blue sky erupting overhead.

Otis was next to her. "Hush, hush. I'm here for you and so is Denim."

"They murdered him, Otis. Why did they do that, why?" Her cheeks were wet, bits of dried grass and dirt stuck to them. "Who did it?"

"Don't think we'll ever know that…unless whoever they are care to tell you."

"You know, Hi supposed that people would change. That someday the color of our skin wouldn't make a difference. He told me our girls would be able to fall in love with a white man if they wanted. I don't know if I believed him or not, but I listened to him paint fantasies in the air. I think I did believe, a little. He was wrong, Otis. The color of my skin will always matter. There may come a time when I'm told it doesn't, but that won't be any more than platitudes to quiet down the masses. My girls have to learn that. They have to know how to walk in town without being seen, to keep their eyes covered and their heads down, to not call any attention to themselves."

"Cora Lee, don't you think—"

Cora Lee closed her eyes and saw the image of Hi's foot dangling out of reach above her head. "I won't lose anyone else. They win, Otis. They win."

"You don't need to think about this right now. Do you want me to help you dress him? Denim should be here shortly, and won't the girls be waking up?"

Cora Lee looked back at the house. She didn't want Rose and Ruby to call for Hi and him not go get them. "I'm going to wake them up now and let them say their goodbyes."

She had made sure that the blankets were covering Hi's neck when she let the girls go in and see him. Ruby put her thumb in her mouth and inched herself behind Cora Lee's leg. Rose stood at the end of the bed and scrunched her face up in concentration. "It's okay. Go ahead. You can kiss him on the cheek." Cora Lee nudged Rose forward.

Rose dragged her fingers along the bedsheet until she was up by Hi's face. "Come here, Ruby," she said and motioned for sister. Taking Ruby's hand, Rose bowed her head. "Dear God, please take care of our daddy."

Ruby lowered her head as told but peeked out with one eye to look at Cora Lee.

Cora Lee held a finger over her lips.

"Now, go ahead. Pat him." Rose stared Ruby down as she said it.

Ruby looked at her sister and then at her mother. She shook her head and took a step back.

"Go ahead, I said." Rose was adamant.

"Rose, honey. Ruby doesn't need to pat him. Kiss him if you want, and then I'll let you both have popsicles."

Ruby's face brightened at hearing popsicles were to be served for breakfast. Quickly she bent over and kissed Hi on his cheek.

Rose's mouth twisted in a grimace as she leaned in to her father. "I hate you, Daddy!" she screamed and ran out of the room.

Cora Lee found her on the tire swing out back. Denim had arrived a few minutes earlier and was in the kitchen filling out the forms that needed to be recorded. Everyone in town would know by now. If Reverend Wheeldin hadn't spread the news, she was sure either Doris or Eugena would have the minute he called and asked them to organize the collation.

For this to work, everything had to follow the correct timeline. There couldn't be one minute when someone would be allowed to say that they saw his truck pulled over or heard how the Klan had been in the area looking to stir up trouble and that hopefully no one was where they weren't supposed to be. Hi had come home after meeting with Mr. Callahan, had eaten dinner and turned in early, the heat exhausting him. In the morning he lay cold next to her. That simple. Otis and Denim promised to corroborate if anyone inquired on the specifics.

Cora Lee grabbed onto the ropes of the tire swing, pulled them back and let go. "Your daddy loves you, you know."

Rose's little voice swung in rhythm with the swing. "Then why did he die?"

"It was just his time." Cora Lee felt the lie plant itself in her chest, spread out, and take root.

She stopped the swing. "Come here, baby." Lifting Rose up, she cradled her in her arms. "It will be all right. I promise you. Daddy's always going to be here with us, watching over us, making sure we're safe."

"Like an angel?" Her little head dropped against Cora Lee's shoulder, and she sniffled.

"Just like an angel."

"Does Daddy have wings now?" Rose asked, picking at the scab on her knee. She had given the girls orange popsicles, and they were now sitting outside on a blanket, a line of orange sticky sugar trailing down their arms.

"Wings!" Ruby said, jumping up and flapping her arms.

Cora Lee stretched out on her back and looked up at the blue cloudless sky. "Yes, baby. Your daddy's gone and flown away."

"Want Daddy back!" Ruby continued to jump, her arms flailing more and more with the increasing strength of her voice. "Daddy! Daddy! Fly back down here!"

Rose stood and pointed the empty popsicle stick at her sister. "Stop it, Ruby. You hear. Daddy's not coming back ever." She plopped down next to Cora Lee and put her head on her stomach.

"Oh, baby...shhh..." Cora Lee caressed her back. "My, how he loved you both. All last night, before he fell asleep, he was talking about how proud he was to be your daddy. How he knew you were going to do great things in this world."

Rose sniffled quietly. Her little head lifted. "Really?"

"I'm going to be a princess," Ruby hollered and began twirling around.

Rose sat up and shook her head as if wondering if her sister would ever come down to earth. "He talked about us?"

"Sure did. Every night, in fact. He'd lie there in bed, listing off what amazing thing he saw you both do that day, making me tell him everything he missed when he was off in the fields. I don't think any two girls were ever loved by their father as much as you are loved by him."

"Can he still love us from heaven?" Rose's eyes squinted against the sun.

Cora Lee embraced her in her arms. "He most certainly can. Now, it's okay to be sad, but I know your daddy wouldn't want you being downcast so that you didn't run around and play. That would make him sadder than having to leave you. Go take Ruby into the barn and see if Otis will let you help feed the cows."

Rose ran and grabbed Ruby's hand, and together they skipped off to find Otis. It amazed Cora Lee how easy it was to accept death when you were young, how believing in angel wings and heaven and all those other things seemed to happen naturally. She didn't know what to accept or believe now. She smiled as she watched them, though, knowing that she had protected them. If she reminded them enough about Hi's love for them, then they would never have occasion to second guess how he died. Even when they were older, if she did it right, the explanation of his death would be firmly established in their memory, with all of the other memories of Hi they'd either remember or fabricate. Maybe even in her own heart, she could come to believe it.

Denim came out carrying two cups of coffee and handed one to her. "It's done. Signed and sealed. Cause of death—natural. I wrote heart attack next to it, in case anyone cares to look."

Cora Lee took the cup coffee from him and took a sip. "Cares? If he were white, this would be a lot harder, you know. People would care and wonder." She took another sip of coffee and felt the warmth down her throat. "I can't break. My girls need me."

"Are you sure you don't want to bring this to the authorities? We could go over to Lincoln, talk to someone outside of Crawford who would listen?"

She shook her head. "No. It's ended. They killed him, but they won't get anything else from it. And so now we finish this day out."

"I think it's best if you do a closed casket. The shirt and tie will cover up the neck burns but if something slipped down, someone bumps into the casket and the collar shifts, they'd see it."

"That's a good idea. That way I don't have to put that suit back on him. I'll tell Reverend Wheeldin that's what Hi would have wanted." She cleared her throat. "Thank you, Denim. I need you to know that I understand what you have done for me, for Hi, and the girls. I'll never be able to repay you."

Denim leaned in and kissed Cora Lee on the cheek then wandered off to the barn.

The next morning, Cora Lee woke early enough to walk the property before the girls would be ready to wake, one last time, pretending Hi was there with her. Back when they were first married before any children came, they'd take their coffee and biscuits and walk along with the rising sun. Her favorite path was the one that ran along the creek. Covered by the shady branches of hickory trees, it was a straight line of acres, a shelter out of the prickly heat. The grass was green along there before the ground turned up for rows of vegetables. Cora Lee loved mostly to walk it barefoot and let the coolness of the grass work its way up from her toes to her fingertips.

"Hi." She stooped and picked up a stick. "Hi. This is crazy. I feel like I'm living in some sort of nightmare. I wish I knew what it was all about—who did this to you, why they did this to you." She raised her arm and threw the stick into the water, watching it hit off a rock and cascade its way along with the current. "I promise you, though, that I'll protect the girls. They'll never know, and I'll make sure they're safe."

She got to the far end where Otis had dug the grave the night before. It had been at least a year since she had attended a funeral and that was for Hi's Uncle Saul who was eighty-six and had truly died in his sleep. The family did it up in a funeral home with hand fans covered with colored pictures of waterfalls in Hawaii and the address and name of a lawyer who thought a donation of fans might drum up some business. Cora Lee remembered thinking how strange they were in their festiveness, but they did keep the air circulating. Uncle Saul had been buried in the town's designated Negro cemetery next to his wife who had passed on a few years before.

It probably wasn't lawful that she was burying Hi on their property, but she didn't care. Blacks had been doing it with their kin for a long time, and no one seemed bothered by it. Crawford didn't even have a designated Negro burial ground. A section of the town's cemetery was used for that purpose, but the groundskeeper didn't mow it or keep it up, simply let it get run over with weeds and broken tree branches. Kids in town ripped up any flowers there that families may have planted, and only last year four headstones were toppled. None had been replaced. The city refused to pay for them, saying they were the families' property. They knew that most of the families couldn't afford new ones. Those graves, headless memories, were the saddest she had ever seen.

Cora Lee picked up a handful of dirt and threw it into the gaping hole, turned around, and started walking back.

Three hours later the house was bursting at the seams with people. Doris and Eugena had outdone themselves and, by the looks of it, had managed to get ahold of every woman who was ever on the rolls of First County Baptist Church to whip something up fast that morning and get it straight over. There were ribs and eight bean barbeque, fried chicken and biscuits, coleslaw and mini chicken salad sandwiches, and enough cornbread and chili to keep feeding the place long after people had left.

The dining room table was covered with pecan pies, peach pies, strawberry pies, rhubarb tarts, sandies, blondies, brownies, black and whites, triple chocolate delight made special by Eugena, and a punch bowl trifle. Someone had even made a Lane Cake, although Cora Lee had no idea how one would have found the time. Perhaps they had made it in advance waiting for someone to die so they'd have the occasion to gift it.

People gathered in the front parlor where Hi's coffin was laid out on a makeshift table that Otis had put together using two sawhorses and a few pieces of scrap maple from the barn. They had covered it with a white bedsheet; it looked respectable enough. On top of the casket was a small picture of Hi, one of the only ones she had of him alone. It was about six years old. In it he was standing next to the new tractor he had bought, work clothes on, hat covering his head, his eyes squinting into the sun. He was smiling, and that made it her favorite. Hi had such a big smile, it took everyone and everything around it in. You couldn't help but smile back when he flashed it at you. Now she wished she could be swallowed up by it.

Cora Lee walked the girls up front with Otis by her side and sat them down in the only three chairs. Her black polyester dress itched her arms, and she prayed she'd make it through without perspiring too much. Reverend Wheeldin raised his hand and the entire room quieted down.

"Friends, congregants, souls on this journey we call life," he brought his eyes to Cora Lee and the girls and shook his head as if hearing something he knew to be true and agreeing with it, "children, wife, we come here today with heavy hearts, filled with a sadness beyond understanding. We have lost Lehigh Jenkins. A good man, a young man. A father to these two precious babies and husband to Cora Lee. He was part of our community. I don't think there's one of us here who can't say that when they called on Hi for help that he didn't come. No, sir. Hi was there before you even thought of asking. Love they neighbor, the good book tells us. Hi was living and loving God's word his entire life."

A few "Amens" circulated around the room and Cora Lee wished she had one of those fans with the pictures of Hawaiian waterfalls. Rose fidgeted in the seat next to her, pulling at the collar of her dress.

"Now, I don't need to tell anyone here that Hi is in a better place."

"Uh-huh," "Amen," "That's right, you don't," sounded from the back.

"We grieve his passing because we are left without him. But he doesn't want us to lament. No, I tell you, he wants us to be joyful, because he has made it to Glory! Glory, I tell you! Where streets are paved with gold and the sad will weep no more!"

Behind her Doris clapped her hands. "Hallelujah!"

"Beloved, we have lost him, but he has gained much!"

More hands clapped together and a chorus of "Soon and Very Soon" started until everyone had joined in.

Cora Lee looked around and wondered how different Hi's funeral would be if they knew the truth. What would Reverend Wheeldin say about a black man being shot through his heart and then a rope put around his neck, left hanging from a tree no better than some old coon hound who had met its last days. Would he still spit out words of *Glory* and *Hallelujah*? Would people still say *Amen*? She wiggled in her seat, droplets of sweat pooling around her stomach and dripping down the swell of her back. She had promised herself that she wouldn't cry. She didn't want her girls to see her sadness, afraid that if she let her emotions go, she might somehow give away the truth of Hi's death. She sat up straighter in the chair and stared ahead.

"Thank you, Doris," Cora Lee said, grasping her hand. Only a few ladies from church were left, and they were all in the kitchen organizing and freezing leftovers. She'd have to give some of the food to Otis and Denim to take home. There was no possibility that she and the girls would ever be able to eat it all.

"You're more than welcome, Cora Lee." Doris took a small step back. "You gonna be all right, here, without Hi? Who's gonna help you with the farming? It may be too early to say it, but maybe you need to think about selling this place."

Cora Lee fought back an urge to scream. Already? People were going to start on this with Hi dead going on two days? She forced a smile on her face. "Thank you for your concern, Doris, but we'll be fine. Otis isn't going anywhere, and our buyers don't care who sells them our crops and livestock as long as they get sold to. Besides, this is my home."

Eugena had taken to standing next to Doris, a container of opened barbecue beans in her hand. "Are you sure they won't mind? I've never heard of any of those buyers dealing with a black woman before. You better watch it, Cora Lee. They'll try to trick you." Eugena's eyes narrowed and she clicked her tongue.

Cora Lee breathed deeply and took the beans from Eugena. "Otis will do the dealings now, take over where Hi left off." She turned and set the container on the counter and started to cover it with tin foil. "Ladies, thank you again. Lord knows I wouldn't have been able to feed this crowd on my own, not with watching the girls. Now, I don't want to be keeping you. I've taken enough of your time." She hoped if she kept her back to them, they would take it as an emotional stand for them to leave.

Both were by her side, their hands on her shoulders. "Don't think this is over. No ma'am," Doris said as Eugena nodded. "We plan to check on you and help out whichever way we can."

"It's not going to be easy running this farm on your own and taking care of those beautiful babies of yours." Eugena's throat caught, and she held a tissue up to her mouth. "Those sweet, sweet babies."

Doris patted Cora Lee on the back one last time. "We'll stop over in a few days. See how you're doing for meals."

They were both good ladies, Cora Lee knew this. She'd watch them whip together church socials over the years with a vigor she imagined only heads of fancy restaurants did when they knew dignitaries would be coming to eat. Tables were set just right, the food stayed warm, there was enough sweet tea that the Israelites could cross it if need be. There was always plenty, and people were sent home with more than they came with. Their socials were loaves and fishes miracles. But she didn't want their niceness at the moment. Earlier, when she sat on her bed in her slip, her stockings resting beside her, she thought it would be easy to accept condolences for Hi's "death." Death was death, sadness was sadness, condolences for those lost were condolences. Why would the way he died affect the way she'd grieve or accept sympathy? She hadn't believed it would. Now, however, the lie was weighing on her. She had deceived all these wonderful people who loved her and Hi and her girls. Or she had spared them. She'd like to think the truth was the latter.

She saw Doris and Eugena off at the door, parted with hugs and kisses to their cheeks, and walked back into the sitting room. Reverend Wheeldin and his wife had taken Rose and Ruby back to their house for a few days to give Cora Lee "some time" to adjust. The house was quiet. The mantel clock chimed five. There was a feeling growing inside her, mounting a force that was filling her up. Emptiness. She was chock full with such a stark hollowness that she put her hand to her chest, certain her heart would explode from it.

"Cora Lee?"

Cora Lee spun around. "Oh!"

"Sorry, didn't mean to scare you." Otis took off his hat and bowed his head. "Just checking in before I head home to change. The animals are taken care of. I'll come back in a few hours for their last feeding and make sure they are set for the night. Denim said he'd come out with me tomorrow and help in the fields."

"I'll help. With the girls away, there's not much for me to do."

"We'll need to talk soon. You're going to need to figure out your next steps. What the buyers can expect. We've got a crop due out to Mr. Walsh by the end of the week. Shouldn't be a problem getting it in. I know some guys looking for a few days of work. They'll work cheap, extra cheap if you feed them and let them sleep up in the barn loft."

"No problem with feeding them. And we'll pay them the regular rate. Times are too hard right now for everyone. I'm not about to take advantage of anyone's misfortunes. Line them up and tell them room and board included if they can stay the full week."

Otis smiled. "That's exactly what Hi would have said."

"Yes, he would have."

Later that night the doorbell rang. Otis and Denim were back and out in the barn taking care of the animals and making sure everything was set for the morning. Cora Lee had finished putting away all of the leftover food that her refrigerator could store and was washing up the last of the good silverware and china they had used. Two boxes filled with servings of chicken and biscuits along with angel food cake for both of the men sat on the kitchen table ready for them to take home. They wouldn't have to worry about cooking dinner for themselves for at least a week, and with what little Rose and Ruby ate, she wouldn't have to cook for a week or longer.

Cora Lee wiped her hands on a dishtowel and shut the water off. Otis never used the front door and certainly wouldn't ever ring the bell. The sensation of an egg cracking over her head rushed down on her. Her heart sped up. Perspiration broke out on her hairline, and she wiped it away with the back of her hand. She had been waiting for this. It was foolish to think she could get away with it. The sheriff, men from town—white men—someone who knew something, had come "to pay her a visit." She said a silent prayer for the fact that her babies weren't there.

The back door of the kitchen was feet away, and her hand reached out in the vacant space for the doorknob like a baseball player preparing to steal third. If she ran fast enough, maybe she could get to the barn before the men out front got her. Would they have guns? Or a rope and a pillowcase for her head? The doorbell rang again, this time accompanied by two knocks and a muffled voice. "Cora Lee? You in there?"

Mr. Walsh.

Cora Lee put her hand to her chest and let her head fall down.

"Good gracious," she said. "Is this how it's going to be from now on? Me getting riled and worried every time someone stands on my porch?" She straightened her shoulders and walked to the front door. "Mr. Walsh?"

Thomas Walsh took off his hat and bowed his head. "Cora Lee. I've come to pay my respects."

She stepped back and brought him into the sitting room. "Now you sit right there, Mr. Walsh, and make yourself at home. The ladies of the church seemed fit to make enough food to feed all of Crawford and me for a year, so let me get you a plate and some sweet tea."

He sat down by the window. "Really, that's not necessary. Eugena left some chilled chicken salad that I had earlier. When she told me of Hi's passing, I gave her the day off…knew there'd be a lot of prepping she'd be helping with from the church." He cleared his throat. "Mrs. Walsh has been feeling a bit under the weather lately so Eugena's taking over most of the cooking, too."

"How about something sweet instead? I still have an entire pan of Eugena's chocolate delight?"

Mr. Walsh smiled. "Eugena's chocolate delight? That's hard to pass up. If you sure it's no trouble."

"No trouble at all. Gives me an excuse to have a second helping."

A few minutes later she was back with two plates of Eugena's longed-for recipe and two large glasses of sweet tea with lemon.

Mr. Walsh lifted a fork of it into his mouth. "Mmm…how does she do it?"

"Sure if I know."

He set his plate down on the small tray next to him and cleared his throat. "Cora Lee, I want you to know how sorry I am to hear about Hi. I thought about coming this morning, but then," he cleared his throat again, "I didn't know if it would be appropriate."

Cora Lee looked down at her plate.

He continued. "Hi was a great man. One of the finest colored men I had the pleasure of doing business with, and I hope you don't mind me saying this, but I can't help thinking that if times were different than they are, well, we might have been friends. Whenever I see colored men acting the way they do sometimes, I shake my head and say to myself 'if they'd just act like Hi, no one would have any problems with them.' "

Cora Lee gripped her fork, her nails digging into the palms of her hand.

"My, this is good, isn't it?" He motioned to the dessert on his plate and ate another spoonful. "You understand what I'm trying to say, don't you, Cora Lee? You and Hi are good folk, and what happened is tragic. I tell people all the time they need to watch themselves—you can never be too careful."

Cora Lee looked up. "What do you mean, 'watch themselves'?"

Mr. Walsh sipped his tea. "Huh? Oh, nothing." He shooed the comment away with the flip of his hand. "The Lord giveth and the Lord taketh away. So the Good Book says, right?"

Cora Lee stood and took his empty plate. "Mr. Walsh. I thank you for your stopping by. Your condolences mean a lot to me. Hi thought very highly of you and always said you were a fair man to work with. But, if you don't mind, I'm tuckered out and there's still some cleanup left to do and talking with Otis about getting next week's crops ready."

"Now, don't you worry. I've already spoken to someone over in Garreton, used to buy from him before you all moved here, and he says he can supply me with what I need until you get back up on your feet again. Of course, my business will come right back to you as soon as you are ready." He stood and took her hand. "You can count on me."

His hand was large and sweating from the heat. Cora Lee felt hers slip around within its grasp.

"You tell him that won't be necessary. Otis has men lined up to help. The farm will continue working as if nothing has happened. There will be no interruption. Hi would have wanted it that way."

"Well, Cora Lee, maybe you need to take some time and think about—"

She cut him off midsentence. "There's nothing to think about, Mr. Walsh. Otis will deliver your order on the scheduled day. Now, if after that you choose to take your business elsewhere, why, I can't prevent that."

"How are you going to run this farm all by yourself? You've got your daughters to raise." He took a sip of his tea. "I hadn't planned on mentioning this today, seeing it's so close to the time and all, but, Cora Lee, maybe you need to reconsider what I've asked Hi for years."

Outside the sky had darkened, and her reflection stared back at her from the sitting room window. Distorted and blurred, she saw herself and her new situation for the first time. A widow.

A black widow.

A black widow with two little girls.

A black widow with two little girls with a farm to run.

A black widow with two little girls with a farm to run in Georgia in 1937.

A black widow with two little girls with a farm to run in Georgia in 1937 because her husband had been shot and lynched.

And a white man stood in her house alone with her.

A white man.

In the kitchen the door sprang shut, and Otis and Denim's loud voices called out for her. "Cora Lee, you around?"

Her shoulders relaxed, and she smiled at Mr. Walsh. "Again, your kindness for coming by is greatly appreciated." She turned her head toward the hallway. "I'm in the sitting room with Mr. Walsh."

Denim and Otis appeared in the doorway. Both men nodded their heads in acknowledgment.

"Boys. Good to see you. I came by to pay my respects and tell Cora

Lee that if there's anything I can do to not hesitate to ask." He picked his hat off of the back of the chair. "Cora Lee, I'll see myself out. You get yourself some rest, now."

"Thank you, Mr. Walsh. Please tell Mrs. Walsh I hope she's feeling better."

He looked down at his hands. "Will do, Cora Lee."

The three stood frozen in the sitting room until the click of the front door and the echo of the engine going down the dirt driveway faded. Otis went to speak, but Cora Lee lifted her hand to stop him. Picking up the plates and the two glasses of tea, she walked back into the kitchen. Denim sat down at the kitchen table, and Otis leaned again the doorframe. Once she was done washing out the plates and glasses, wiping them down, and putting them away in the cupboard, she looked at the men.

"What did he want?" Denim asked.

"He said he came by with his respects. Couldn't come this morning because it wouldn't be proper."

"Proper." Denim rolled his eyes.

"Is that all?" Otis took a toothpick out of the metal holder on the wall and rolled it between his fingers before sticking it between his teeth and biting down.

Cora Lee shrugged. "It's just—"

"Just what?" His jaw was clenched as he asked it, and his eyes skirted over to Denim.

"He said something funny, is all." She opened the refrigerator door as if the answer lay on the shelf next to the mayonnaise jar.

Denim was on his feet. "Funny?"

"Strange, actually. Said people need to watch themselves, that you can't ever be too careful. I asked him to repeat himself, but he raised his hand like it was no matter."

Otis took the toothpick out of his mouth. "Warning, you think?"

Cora Lee knew the comment was for Denim not her, and she sat down at the kitchen table and poured a glass of water from the jug left from the afternoon. It was warm, but she didn't care. Her throat felt like it was closing up on her. She didn't like the looks on either Otis's or Denim's face.

Denim raised an eyebrow. "Reason?"

Otis shrugged his shoulders. "Not sure what the reason would be. Cora Lee, you tell him the crops will be ready next week like always?"

"Mmm-hmm. Told me his old distributor over in Garreton is more than happy to fill his order until we can get our feet back on the ground. I told him it was no problem, we're all set."

"Let me guess. Then he offered to buy those acres." Denim shook his head.

Cora Lee nodded. "Wouldn't be Mr. Walsh if he didn't."

"I don't like it," Otis said.

Cora Lee stood and set her glass in the sink. "Not much I can do about it, now can I? I've got bills to pay and customers who have dead-lines. Doesn't matter none to them who fills the orders. Hi, you, me, someone else. It's all business. Now, if you gentlemen don't mind, I think I'll turn in."

"Cora Lee, you want me to stay? I can sleep down here on the couch or over in the barn." Otis threw his toothpick in the trash.

"Otis, there's no need for that." Mr. Walsh's words crept back into her brain although they hadn't really left. *You can never be too careful.*

"I think I will anyway. The cot's made up in the office, and besides, I've got to be here by four-thirty to get things set for when the men come in at six. Makes sense for me to stay."

She tried not to show the relief she felt. "Stay on the couch then.

152

Don't want you out there in the barn breathing in hay dust all night. I'll get you some sheets and an extra pillow."

"I'd stay if I could, Cora Lee, you know that." Denim reached over and kissed her on the cheek. "Boomer's bringing Gus in tomorrow at seven. Poor old hound. He's so arthritic Boomer has to carry him in and out of the house all day. Says he lays him out under his favorite tree so he can see the squirrels running by, but he doesn't even lift his head anymore. Cataracts in both eyes. Boomer's asked for some cortisone shots in Gus's hips. Might ease the pain some, but Gus is fourteen. That's old for a dog. I'm pretty sure Gus would go of his own accord if Boomer'd let him."

"Poor Boomer," Cora Lee said. "Not sure how he'll make it without Gus. He's got no one." Her eyes saddened. Everyone knew Boomer felt animals were next to kin, and he'd prefer the animals rather than most of his folk.

It seemed like it was a season for losing.

Cora Lee rolled over in bed, her fingers caressing the emptiness next to her. There would never be anything there again. Her hand would continue to reach for something that was ungraspable. And because her girls were out of the house and Otis was far downstairs on the couch closed off by the heavy oak parlor door, and because her husband had been murdered, she opened wide the tears that had been hovering above her heart for days, and let her anguish pour forth.

Chapter 11

CRAWFORD, GEORGIA
ROSE JOHNSON
1962

EARLIER THAT MORNING the movers had come, a few local men, friends of Curtis who had worked with him years before making room for the railway. They were discreet about it, moving most things in through the back mudroom door and right down into Miss Eunice's basement. Unless neighbors were looking, it was doubtful anyone would realize a household was being transplanted. Rose was thankful for their help. She didn't need the whole town knowing or assuming her business right now. She figured that would come soon enough. The house had been mainly furnished when they moved in. Other than their personal items, little belonged to them.

With overseeing the transfer of her things from house to house that morning and working at the bakery until an hour and a half past closing, Rose was beyond exhausted when she walked through the door of Miss Eunice's house later that night.

"Pies don't make themselves," Adele always said to her.

Oh, how she wished they did!

"Now you sit right there, and eat some of this pot roast I put aside for you." Miss Eunice had been standing like a sentinel next to the kitchen table waiting for her. "You give me your purse and sit right down. You can't continue to burn the candle at both ends like you've been doing. Moving from the house, working late at the bakery. You'll run yourself ragged, and that won't be any help to you or Macey May."

Rose looked down at the plate and inhaled. She could smell the savory onions and potatoes, and her stomach reminded her that she hadn't eaten since lunch. "Miss Eunice, you are too good to me and to Macey May."

"Shush now," she said. "I haven't done anything. Now, you eat up, and then get yourself some rest." Miss Eunice pulled at the bottom of her nightgown sleeve that poked out from under her housecoat, splaying the white eyelet ruffle around her wrist. "We can talk tomorrow when you're rested or whenever you feel the time is right. And remember," Rose's heart almost broke to see the look of compassion on Miss Eunice's face, "my home is your home. You and Macey May are the only family I've got—only real family I ever had."

Miss Eunice nodded at the plate in front of Rose. "Eat. I'm turning in early. I'm almost done reading my book, and I want to see how it ends." She touched Rose on the shoulder and squeezed it as she walked by.

Rose picked up a fork and then lowered it. Her back ached, her feet were sore, even her fingers hurt from using the rolling pin all day. It seemed to her that the last two months hadn't given her one minute to catch her breath. Between the worrying over Curtis and the worrying over Macey May, she wasn't sure she was going to make it. She had never had to be this strong.

She ate a few carrots and mashed up a potato to mix in with part of the onion. Her mouth would only allow her a few bites of the roast, and she scraped the rest of her plate into the trash.

Rose didn't know how long she had been sitting in Miss Eunice's darkened living room next to the front window. Turning on lights seemed to require a strength she didn't have. The overhead oven light spewed a line across the floor, and she stuck her toe into it, pulling her foot back quickly, then tucking it up beneath her in the chair. Her head leaned against the chair's high back.

Their house next door would remain empty, which made her eviction even harder to bear. *Eviction.* There was a shame in her she didn't know possible when the notice had come in the mail and that word had looked back at her off of the paper. She would have to bear the embarrassment. There was no way of hiding her eviction from the town, no way of stopping more talk about Curtis behind her back, or in front of her, for that matter. Now he was a man who had abandoned his family.

Outside the streetlights buzzed low and blinked once or twice. She moved the curtain slightly with her finger. The road was empty save for a car parked here and there in front of a house, the blue haze of television behind drawn shades.

It was foolish, she knew, but a part of her was holding onto hope that a last-minute miracle would occur. That somehow wherever he was, Curtis would manage to fix what was broken inside of him, and he'd come home. If she closed her eyes she could picture him walking through her mama's kitchen door on Thanksgiving morning with a smile on his face and bag of the red licorice roll-ups that Macey May loved so much. She promised herself that if that happened, the lies would end. She would talk to him about his missing, what he did. She would tell the truth to her mama and Otis, even go to Willie to get him help. Anything to keep them a family.

The truth was she didn't expect Curtis to come back this time, not ever.

The reality of it all was enough to make her cry, and the night before she had called Cora Lee only to find out that Macey May wasn't feeling well. So there her little girl was far away from her, and Curtis was nowhere to be found, and she was weaving a web of such deceit that she doubted she'd ever be able to find her way out.

A light turned on overhead.

"Oh!" Rose jumped out of the chair.

Miss Eunice stood at the bottom of the stairs. "I'm sorry. Didn't mean to give you a fright. Thought I heard a noise and figured I'd come see for myself."

"Miss Eunice, you came down because you heard a noise? And tell me, please, what you would have done if you came across someone robbing your place?"

Miss Eunice shrugged. "Hadn't thought that far ahead. Lucky for me, it was only you. Well, I'm up. Why don't you put on some water for tea and tell me about what Willie had to say." She walked across the living room floor with her cane and sat herself down on the couch. "There's some nice chamomile in the canister next to the stove. I don't drink it very often, but they say it helps with rest. Check to see if I have those Lorna Doones left. I could eat something a little sweet."

Rose brought everything into the living room and set it on a table next to Miss Eunice.

"So, what did Willie tell you?"

"Gambling."

"Gambling? That doesn't make any sense. Men don't leave for gambling. They're met with cold beds and flying frying pans for staying out too late for a poker game, but leaving their family? I don't think so."

Rose stirred some sugar into her tea and took a sip. It was bland and tasted like flower petals. "He said he walked out of a game owing money and that now they could be after him. He's probably staying away so they don't trace him back here. Keeping us safe."

Miss Eunice dunked a shortbread cookie into the tea and ate it. "Ick," she said, staring into the teacup. "No wonder why I don't drink this. Tastes right awful. How about some coffee instead?"

"That's all right, Miss Eunice. I'm about ready for bed now. Coffee would keep me up. I promised Adele I'd be in by five and start on the cinnamon rolls."

"Curtis has your mama's address and phone, right?"

Rose nodded.

"Whatever it is, I know he has a good reason for keeping away. He wouldn't leave you or Macey May for anything in this world. I'll keep my eyes and ears open. See if anyone tries to snoop around next door looking for him. You should probably give Willie a number to reach you at."

"I did."

Miss Eunice stood up. "Good then. Let's leave this cleanup for the morning."

Rose rolled over. The clock next to the bed read 3:32. She couldn't sleep, had been counting sheep in her mind's eye until she felt like pulling out a shotgun and shooting them as they jumped over the fence. "Curtis, Curtis, Curtis," she said quietly into the darkness. "Where are you?"

The first time he had disappeared Macey May was six. He didn't come home after work one night. Two days later, filled with worry and anger that kept colliding with each other inside her breast, she had taken Macey May and gone to the farm. Told Adele she was needed at her mother's and didn't even leave him a note of explanation. She thought it would teach him a lesson when he returned to an empty house, no dinner waiting for him, no clean clothes. It was the first time she lied about the situation. She told her mama and Macey May that Curtis was working double shifts. She had no idea how long the lies would continue or how big she'd need to make them over the next years.

When they returned home Sunday night, there he was sitting on the couch listening to the radio. His eyes lit up, and he kissed her on the cheek and took her suitcase so she wouldn't have to carry it up the stairs. "Hope you had a fine time wherever you all went. I missed you, though," he said and proceeded to suggest that they all go out for ice cream, like her homecoming required celebration. It would be years before she could understand what was making him run or what demons were pulling at his soul. At that moment he had simply been another man who had left her. And she was livid. If Macey May hadn't looked at her longingly with the mention of ice cream, they wouldn't have gone.

Forgiveness came by the time Rose was done with one scoop of rocky road.

Since the day he followed her into the bakery, Curtis, it turned out, had been easy to love.

A year later he gave her a black eye when she came up behind him in the bedroom. It was morning. Macey May had left for school, and he was getting ready for work. "Curtis," she said. "Macey May needs new shoes, and she's about grown out of all of her clothes. Do you think you could ask for a few extra shifts this week? It would be nice if she didn't have to wait." She reached her hand out to touch his shoulder. She didn't want him to think he wasn't a good provider.

As soon as her fingers grazed his shirt, a grunt emanated from him, and he turned so quickly that she lost her balance. His fist was in her face before she could even raise her arms to protect herself, and then she was on the ground, belly down, his knee in her back, her arm twisted behind. His army training. He mumbled coordinates in her ear and said something about taking a hill that she didn't understand. She understood one thing, though, and that was that she may have been in their bedroom, but Curtis was not.

Miss Eunice accepted something about a loose slip rug and the door to the refrigerator along with a half-gallon of orange juice all over the kitchen floor. The lie had slid off Rose's tongue like a muskrat gliding into the cool water of the creek. It slid off just as smoothly later that afternoon when Macey May came home from school and later that night when Curtis walked through the kitchen door after work. His concern for her black eye was so genuine it made her cry. He left before dinner was even on the table to buy double-sided tape at the hardware store and spent the next hour securing down all of the slip rugs throughout the kitchen, hallway, and bathroom.

Later that night, he snuggled up to her in bed and kissed her neck. "I thought I'd ask for some extra shifts tomorrow. I noticed Macey May's clothes are getting small for her. Don't want our daughter to not measure up to the other kids. I used to hate waiting for new pants once mine hit the flood stage." It was then she started to worry. An abusive husband made sense, a woman could understand that; one who hit but didn't remember, that was altogether different.

After the eviction notice had come in the mail, Rose had spent her hours between work and Macey May's return from school looking in every nook and cranny of the house, under mattresses, behind cabinets for anything, something that she may have missed that would tell her where Curtis had gone. She had even tapped the walls with her knuckle, listening for hollow spots where Curtis might have squirreled away more money. Nothing.

But what if she had missed something? During the past few months

Curtis's behavior had become more erratic. She found him once locked in the bathroom, the shower running for two hours. Another time she went to go to bed only to find he had barricaded himself in the bedroom, and there he had stayed whispering behind the door until early in the morning. If he kept money in a sock drawer, he may have kept some elsewhere.

The wooden floors were cold on her feet. She grabbed her slippers and tied her bathrobe tight around her waist. Miss Eunice kept a flashlight in the drawer by the side door. She'd take it and go back to the house for one last look. The spare key was around back in the shed taped to the bottom of a rusted Chock full o'Nuts can. The stairs creaked with every step, and Rose held her breath as if that would someway make her feet lighter.

Outside the moon was full, its light casting everything in an alabaster blue. She looked up in the sky and saw the brown lakes or whatever they were on its surface. So clear, so far away, up there so high. For a minute she forgot her plan and stood gazing at it. Just two months before President Kennedy said that someday America would get there. Tonight, it looked like if she jumped high enough she might be able to latch onto the moon and sit, her legs dangling over the edge. If she had a fishing pole, she could cast down and try to reel in the earth. Maybe she'd be able to find Curtis from way up there.

Cora Lee had superstition about nights like these. "There'll be mourning air come sunup, Rose. You mark my words." Rose never understood about mourning air, but she knew it required that all the windows be opened, while her mama would spend most of the day telling people to "shoo" and "get" even though there was nobody there. Sometimes the mourning air would stay around for days.

Rose retrieved the key and opened the cellar door. She turned on the flashlight. It was a root cellar, stone walls and a dirt floor with shelves built along the sides. She picked up a can of peaches. She had forgotten about these. Beets and sugared beans, pickled tomatoes, even some whiskey marmalade. It was a shame for them to go to waste. Her mama's cellar in Crawford was lined with her own stock and certainly didn't need any of Rose's offering. She grabbed an empty bucket on the ground and loaded up the glass jars. Miss Eunice would enjoy them.

It was strange being down there, her cellar, or at least it had been for the nine and a half years they lived there. Rose shook her head, wanting the memories to leave, wanting them to stay. Her mama thought she was crazy for moving in with a white man. Cora Lee never told her that, but she could tell. Her mama didn't understand that times were changing.

She sat there back on her farm allowing the town to have Whites Only water fountains when most of the other states were fighting Jim Crow rather than inviting him in for a slice of peach pie. But not Cora Lee. *No*, Rose thought, *she'd be saying "yes'mm" and "no, sir" until they carted her off in a maple box and put her to rest next to her daddy down along the river. Even then she'd probably ask permission to be buried there, even though it was her land.*

In her mind her mama was always afraid, fretting over something happening to her girls. "Mama," Rose had said to her once when she and Curtis were out visiting, "no one's owned you for almost one hundred years. Stop acting like some massa going to turn the switch on me or hang Ruby from some tree if your cotton crop doesn't meet quota." Cora Lee had gone silent then, her face pale.

Even Otis told her she had said too much with those words, gone too far. Cora Lee hadn't spoken to her for the rest of the night; instead, she sat on the porch rocking away, barely sipping the sweet tea that Otis brought to her. "You have no idea what your mama has given up for you," he said to Rose in warm breeze of the early evening. "And then I see you treat her like that, like she's some stupid dog." He shook his head at her.

"No idea, at all."

Rose and Curtis had cut their time short and left the next morning, Cora Lee surrendering a hug with a vacant look in her eyes. "Take care," she had said and then went back in the house, not even waiting for them to close the car doors.

Rose turned the kitchen light on at the top of the stairs. It would be silly to use the flashlight and more likely to draw attention if anyone was passing. The electricity hadn't been shut off, and the kitchen erupted in fluorescent light. The brightness made her blink. She ran her hand across the Formica countertops, pink with bronze flecks, to match the brown wallpaper. How she hated them; how she'd miss them.

It was a Tuesday when he left. His birthday. She had been in the kitchen cleaning up and listening to *Suspense* on the radio. That half an hour a night was her time, that's why Macey May hadn't come in right away to tell her about Curtis. The show ended and she had started on the dishes, hearing the silence but assuming the two of them were sitting out front on the porch out of earshot.

By the time Rose realized he was gone, it was long over an hour. All Macey May could tell her was that Curtis had stood up, went on to the porch, came back in to tell her he'd finish his cake later, and walked out the front door. For days after, Rose wondered if he had planned it, the leaving them. Had he woken up that morning knowing it would be his last birthday with them? Had he been purposeful in not saying goodbye, thinking it would make it easier?

She opened a drawer next to the stove, a few ripped corners of a phone book and broken toothpick. Nothing. The cupboards were empty except for three juice glasses and a turkey platter that were there when they had moved in. She pulled out a chair and sat down at the table. She needed to think. It was hard, this lying. Harder than she imagined it would be.

Her mind went back to *that* night. His birthday. When he still wasn't home by Macey May's bedtime, her suspicion was gambling. It was to the point by then that she wished it was gambling. Gambling meant gaining or losing money but a sane Curtis. She shuddered to think if it wasn't. There had been talk around town of back-room poker with big winners. The women whispered about them over the chicken thighs in the grocery. *Did you hear who won last night? I heard the cops had to go out to Denny's and break it up...fight broke out over someone playing two of the same aces...* She pretended to pay no mind, but she listened. Like her mama, she knew enough to keep her ears open wherever she was.

Every man had his vices; gambling was something she could overlook. Her heart was broken after Willie left, her life on the cusp of crumbling down on top of her. And then she had caught Curtis's eye. He seemed lost, like he needed someone to take his hand and walk him out of wherever he was. And she had needed someone's hand to hold. Her timeline allowed little choice in the decision, and his gambling was a small price to pay for the security Curtis offered.

Sometimes when she thought about it, all of it, what she had done to him at the beginning, the secret she had kept from him, it made her ashamed. Even though she had come to love him, truly and whole-heartedly love him, she knew she had been selfish. That's what it was. She had been selfish and scared, more scared than she had ever been.

From the beginning, he willingly gave her whatever she needed. Never even had to ask. If she admired a new set of pots and pans, they were in her kitchen the next day, and he was working extra hours at the site to pay for them. When Macey May was born he surprised her one day by renting a house. "Can't raise our daughter in a one-bedroom apartment," he had said.

"She needs a lawn to play on." They had moved into the house next to Miss Eunice's then and stayed there. The compromise for all of this, in the beginning, was his gambling and her pretending. She played the hand well. Rose continued to pretend her way through what it became, what it was now.

She got up from the kitchen table and walked slowly up the stairs to the bedroom. The mattress was moved out from the wall, the brass headboard safely tucked away in Miss Eunice's cellar. An empty bureau stood between the two windows. Rose looked around at the emptiness. It was like they had never been there at all. Their life together a shadow waiting to disappear completely in the light of day. She leaned against the doorframe. Some of this was her fault, and she knew it. There had been a chance, there in the bedroom, a chance for all of this to be different, yet she hadn't taken it. She had let him go.

A few nights after his birthday, Curtis had come back. Thinking about it made her gut turn over at the secret, her deception to Macey May, to Miss Eunice, to her mama. She had never told them. Around one in the morning, he had opened the door to the bedroom. She hadn't been sleeping. Instead she was lying in bed, the covers propped up under her chin, deciding what she'd say to him when he walked through the door. It had to stop—his leaving them, her, without notice.

Before she could speak, he sat down at the edge of the bed and put his head in his hands.

"Rose," he said, his shoulders rounding. "I have to leave for a while. I'm not right, and you know it. My head's all messed up."

A thousand thoughts flooded her mind, and Rose was scared. There weren't words for this conversation. "Can't you find help?"

Curtis shook his head. "Maybe, I don't know."

"But what about work? What will I tell them when you don't show up?"

"No one will ask. I already quit. Last week actually. I told them I was taking a job in California that paid good money, double what I was making." He got up from the bed and walked over to the dresser, opening the drawers and filling a bag with belongings.

She could see sweat forming down the back of his shirt and noticed dirt along the bottom cuffs of his pants. His face was scruffy and unkempt, and she wondered where he had been sleeping the past few nights. Rose got out of bed and stood behind him. She lifted her hand to touch him, but then let it fall back down to her side. "But how will Macey May and I live? Curtis, we've got bills…food…my salary can't do this alone."

He kept his back to her and his voice lowered. "The rent is paid up for this month. I'll send more when I can. I promise. Don't worry, Rose, I'll take care of you."

Her hand went to her belly. Her one chance to convince him to stay. Her mouth opened to say the words, to let him know what she'd only just discovered, the swell barely noticeable, but he turned and looked at her. The fear and pain she saw reflected in his eyes as he stood there ready to leave told her it wouldn't be fair to him, not now, not when he was doing everything in his power to hold on. "Are you coming back?" she asked.

He walked to the door, looking around the room one last time. "Tell Macey May I love her, and Rose, I'm sorry. For all of this. You and Macey May deserve so much more. Promise me that you'll only remember the good times. That you'll remind Macey May of those. I need you to promise."

She nodded.

She'd kept her promise to him and kept his secret. Mounted lies that spun around her so tightly she couldn't see straight. And in that promise, she kept hoping that he'd find his way out and back to her, to them. By the end of October, it was clear something else had happened. He would have known she'd run out of money, even scraping every nickel she could find. Rose imagined the memories had taken him over for good, and there wasn't anything she could do about it.

There was nothing in the house to find, no money squirreled away, no magic map that would tell her where he had gone. She knew that it had been a fruitless hope. He hadn't answered her when she had asked if he'd be back because he didn't know if he would be coming back. Hadn't known if he would make it.

And she hadn't told people the truth. Not one lick of it.

Her pride wouldn't let her.

She shut the light off in the bedroom and walked down the stairs. In the living room, she turned around, the walls now blank of everything except for a gold mirror above the couch. This had been their home, and now it wasn't. The storm door whined as she opened it. She placed the spare key under the welcome mat and walked around the side of Miss Eunice's house. The sun was still hours away from rising, the moon still holding the reins of the sky. She'd sleep. And then she'd go open the bakery.

That much she could do.

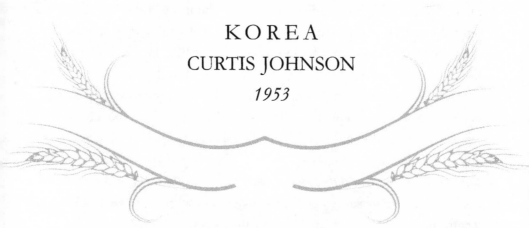

Chapter 12

KOREA
CURTIS JOHNSON
1953

THEY NEVER TELL YOU about the cold, or the boredom, or how the wet gets into your shoes and stays lodged in your socks. You can't ever get your feet dry after a rain, and you can't ever get your hands warm once the snow comes in. The army-issued boots don't seem to know what their job is, believing instead that we are boys on holiday hiking through a well cut-out brushway through the forest as birds sing a song for us to follow, a warm fireplace waiting for us back home. They don't know to be quiet when they sluck up from the mud, giving away our location to the enemy who appears to be everywhere we are and everywhere we haven't arrived yet.

The enemy.

I'm starting to realize they figured out a way to get into our heads too, but I wouldn't ever say that out loud.

Yesterday during breakfast, as we waited for the captain to give us orders, a guy next to me took his boots off and said he was sure that they were giving Morse code to the Koreans. It was the only reason he could come up with as to why the bombs would drop so close to us. The captain assigned him double night patrol and told him to stop trying to get a

Section 8. I know he wasn't trying, though. Sometimes in the quiet of the night, I've thought those same thoughts, not about my boots, but about our radio being intercepted or a spy on the inside. Anything to make sense of it. When patrol went out this morning to relieve him, he was dead. Cut his own feet off and bled to death while we slept. How does one do that?

The war doesn't seem to want to stop. The U.S. is supposed to be negotiating an armistice with the Koreans and Chinese. It's impossible to tell what they are doing. Maybe, behind closed doors, they are all playing a game of Mahjong and talking about us. *Those stupid boys. When do you think they'll realize that if they all put down their guns the war would have to end?* Maybe wars are some sort of psychological experiment to see to what lengths man will blindly follow. If that's the case, we are all lost.

We heard a bunch of our boys a few miles away have been holding a hill just in case the armistice doesn't come around. It's Hill 255 but some of the guys have nicknamed it Pork Chop Hill because that's what it looks like on the map. I know I shouldn't laugh about it, but sometimes I do. A pork chop. I'd give anything right now to have one of my grandma's pork chops with a side of apples and sauerkraut.

If those men in Washington would all come out here for a few hours, pick up a gun, and fight beside us, I'm sure they'd all sign on the dotted line to end this thing and be rushing to get the pen to do it. I guess it's easier to have a war if one doesn't have to be physically present in it while it's happening. The Great Oz behind the green curtain…the ultimate puppet master.

"Private Johnson!" The sergeant's voice is gruff from too many cigarettes and scotch bought on the black market—not the worst crime to commit over here. He's twenty-five, barely older than I am.

I stand up quickly from the end of my bed where I am looking at a magazine—*Life*—army-issued from this past December. In case we don't think we are living it, I guess. A picture of weird marionettes on the front, but no mention of the war on the cover or anywhere really. It's as if it's not happening to the rest of the world. This issue's got a new Sherlock Holmes story written by his son, though: *The Adventure of the Seven Clocks*. It's been forever since I've read anything. It might be nice to lose myself in somewhere else. I always favored Watson—his naiveté, his desire to not see the evil in man at every turn. Tonight after chow I'll read it.

The smell of nicotine pulls across my nostrils, and I remember the sergeant is waiting for an answer. "Yes sir." At attention, I puff out my chest, my response Pavlovian after all this time.

"I need you and Private Stone to take first watch. Look Out says it appears clear. The enemy retreated last night by fifty yards over on the hill. Let's keep 'em back there."

I almost laugh. Fifty yards. Less than a football field. Back at North High I've watched guys run more than that in less than ten seconds right through the end zone without losing anyone. I heard those fifty yards costed twenty-three lives and lasted eight hours. It was the longest game of pigskin in recorded history. That's where we are in this war, scrimmaging over a 150-foot patch of grass. I do the requisite salute and watch the screen door slam shut behind him.

I lay back down on my cot and lift *Life* high in the air, my arms straight up to the sky. The same way I would hold my Archie comics on my bed in my grandma's house. Nowhere in these glossy pages do I see men without arms, guys with legs severed, bodies blown apart, flesh covering an open field like a first snow in November. That only seems to be our lives.

There's a picture of a Whitman's chocolate sampler on the back cover…I miss those. Caramel are my favorite with coconut next. Black and white pages throughout the magazine show Lucky Cigarettes and Zippo lighters for Dad and a Hoover upright for $49.95 for the lady of the house. Ads for Post Cereal and Pillsbury Pancake mix, women with hair flipped up at the ends and men donning new hats on their way out the door. Maybe they are carrying their 9mm under their suits, the women a grenade taped under their bras.

I don't trust what I see with my own eyes anymore. I put the magazine down. There's a half an hour before chow and I need a nap. Maybe I'll dream about home, or better yet, maybe I'll dream of nothing.

"Come on, Johnny," I say, catching up with him at the mess hall. He is sitting in the corner, coffee cold in the cup in front of him, sketch book out on the table. He doesn't look up. "We are on in twenty. Better grab some chow."

He mumbles something.

"What?"

"Can't do it, Curtis. This place is making me batty. Not those trenches. We're sitting ducks, for Christ's sake."

I look around. Johnny's been off lately, and it's making me nervous. I'm also hungry, and the chow line is getting longer. The food isn't great, but I also don't want to be out all night on an empty stomach. "Johnny, we're not parading around in evening wear with diamond tiaras for bullseyes. We're hunkered down four feet below the ground level. All the fighting's going on over on that hill anyhow. We've got nothing to worry about. Just watch the skies and make sure they stay their distance. Anyway, it's not even that dark out yet. You know these bastards prefer to fight at night."

He takes a sip of his coffee and leaves the cup on the table. "This coffee sucks. First thing I'm doing when I get home is getting a good cup of Joe."

The harshest word Johnny ever used before the war was "jeez." It needs to end soon for all our sakes, but especially his. I'm not sure Johnny ever had the war in him in the first place, and now that he's here, I'm not sure it will really ever leave him. We've seen too much. We've done too much.

"Cheer up. Take your pencil," I tell him. "You'll have plenty of time to draw. I'll take the first watch." He nods and smiles a little. It's all he's able to give most days.

Our trench is one of the shorter ones, ten feet long, more of an ambush trench in case anyone makes it past the first line of defense. First line, second line, it's like a long drawn-out game of king of the mountain. I regret not playing more sports in high school, then I'd have more lingo to describe this shitty place. Luckily, though, I managed a good shot during training—number one in my infantry. Deer, rabbits, men...guess they are all the same through the end of a rifle.

We jump in, rearrange the sandbags above us, and hunker down. I light a cigarette. Johnny declines, a promise he made to his mother before he came over here. Instead, he takes out his small drawing pad that he keeps strapped to the inside of his helmet along with his pencil. They don't like us keeping things in our pockets, so most of the men stash things other places—a letter from their girl back home in their sock, a picture of their kids in the inside band of their helmet. Like Johnny with his drawing supplies.

I carry nothing.

"When I get home, I'm going to school." Johnny has been talking about college since a month after we signed up. "Forget the uniform. I'll get the girls through my wallet."

I raise an eyebrow and lighten my voice. "Johnny Stone...your mama would be ashamed of you. Paying for a woman. Well, I never." I nudge him with my elbow as I say it, hoping the gibe might be enough to calm him down, lighten his mood.

He cracks a smile. It almost seems genuine. "Shut up. You know what I mean. A job. I'm gonna get a good job in advertising. I figure I can draw the pictures for magazines, car dealerships…or maybe houses. How long does it take to become an architect, you think? I can draw all those nice, new houses you see going up everywhere. Maybe even on one of those billboards along the interstate. Welcome to Maple Estates." He spreads his arms wide while saying it as if he can see the words in front of him. "Mama said in her last letter that there's plans to build a whole new development a few towns over. Can't build what you don't have a picture of."

I crane my head to see what he is drawing now. He lifts his shoulder and turns away.

"Put your helmet back on," I say.

"In a second. Got to finish this shading while it's in my mind's eye."

"Johnny."

He puts it on haphazardly, the chin strap dangling from the sides. "Happy now, Mama?" he asks.

I draw on my cigarette and let my head rest against the cold earth behind me. I have no idea what I plan to do when I get home, wherever that is. No home is waiting for me. The world is my oyster, I have been told more than once. I assume I am to look on the bright side—I can go anywhere. Most days I just know that I have nowhere.

My eyes are closed, thinking about that big pearl that has to be somewhere in my life, when the bullet with barely the sound of a mosquito passes my ear. And then Johnny slumps onto my shoulder, a tiny stream of red flowing from a perfect round spot on his forehead right underneath the rim of his helmet. Instinctively I push him off. He slides, bent in an odd ninety-degree angle to the ground, the pencil still held between his fingers. A pause between shading.

I pull him back up to a sitting position, hoping, perhaps pretending, all is as it was only seconds ago and that he's only dozed off. Johnny's always been a sound sleeper. Once in high school I gave him a nice black marker moustache after he'd fallen asleep on the couch while we were watching television. I look at the blood. This isn't marker, no matter how much I wish it is.

When the enemy jumps down into the trench, I'm not expecting him. My mind is still on Johnny and the red line that now has snaked down his nose and waits, a droplet about to jump off. *Shouldn't there be time, a pause after someone dies, a minute for those of us left to come to terms with what we've lost?* He looks down at Johnny, and a grin spreads across his face. One tooth is missing on the left side. The black cavernous space seems to want to swallow me whole. My brain slows down, and for some reason I think that it isn't right that Johnny should be killed by such an ugly man. With all the injustice going on in the war, that is the one thing that doesn't settle right with me.

As if someone had a wire connected to my chest, I feel it pull and tug and then finally let go and ricochet back against me. When it does, the reverberations from it are so strong that a force comes up within me that I never knew could exist in someone. Before my mind can even register what I plan to do, my hands grasp his neck, which, like brittle chicken bones, twists and breaks under my fingers.

There is a short gasp from his mouth, a balloon leaking air, and then his body is limp in my arms.

They tell you not to count—how many you kill, that is. They say it won't do you any good in the long run. I'm not sure what my body count is in the months I have been here. I never knew when I fired my gun where the bullets went, off into the distance, the dark. Most of the time I was shooting toward sound, trying to make it stop. I knew I needed to make it stop.

Killing a man with my bare hands, looking him in the eyes, watching the last breath leave his body. Well, I have never done that before.

His skin is surprisingly warm.

It reminds me of my grandmother's when I would help clasp her necklace.

My hands know the crime they have committed. They push him away, and he falls on top of Johnny. There they lie together: Johnny, his back pressed up against the dirt trench; the Korean I have been trained to view as an enemy sleeping in his lap. I roll him off with the toe of my boot and his eyes stay open, looking up at me, the sky, or Johnny. I can't tell which. His smile, that stupid cavernous grin, is frozen on his face, and it angers me that he doesn't know better than to remove it after what he did to Johnny. My hand moves across his eyelids to close them, to erase his stare that I'm now sure I will see forever, but I can't figure out how to wipe the smile off of his face, so I leave it alone, a cemented grimace. And that's when I notice a corner of something sticking out from under the side of his helmet.

I pull it out. A photo. I'd seen ones like it before. Many guys carried them in my unit, guys much older than Johnny and me. Guys like Jones who lost a leg and was discharged (but he was *discharged)* or Garcia who took shrapnel to his face and won't ever see again (but he won't *ever* see again—small blessings). Or Thomas (A.K.A. Lucky) who wasn't lucky after all and was shipped home in a coffin (covered with an American flag because *that* made it better) to his wife and three kids only seven days after arriving here in hell (*only* seven days).

What does the enemy do when they find our pictures?

I look at it closely. A woman, young and plain, her head bent slightly in deference or because of the sun, it's hard to tell. A baby wrapped in a blanket, its head exposed, a smile playing across its face, one hand emerging and reaching toward the person behind the camera…uttering, "Dadda" or "*abeoji*" maybe.

176

The enemy without a tooth has a family. The war, my war, now has a face.

I write Johnny's mom a letter, although the official letter comes from the captain and mine is detained until his is sent. *Proper channels, Private Johnson.* I know the formalities his will render—*Dear Mrs. Stone...sacrifice...honor.* I want her to know that Johnny didn't suffer, that it was quick, and that he was doing what he loved (drawing) when it happened. I had planned on apologizing too, to confess, ask for absolution. I shouldn't have rested my eyes; I had said I would take the first look out. But as much as I try, my pen won't write the words, truth hides beneath my ink, and I find *sacrifice...honor...*slipping onto the paper. Benign and empty.

I sign the letter "Sincerely, Curtis."

I'm conscious of another letter. The one that will be sent to the baby in the picture, written in a language I don't understand. I wonder if the words will be as hollow as those I've written to Johnny's mother. I take the picture out of my wallet where it has stayed since I put it there, and I look at it. I want to feel something. Regret. Peace. Sadness. I have murdered someone's husband, someone's father. Johnny is dead. Everything that isn't supposed to happen has happened.

They say war makes you strong; this war has made me weak.

Chapter 13

CRAWFORD, GEORGIA
MACEY MAY JOHNSON
1962

OTIS LOOKED WARILY over at me, the truck bouncing along the road. "This too much for your stomach?"

"Nah, I'll be all right."

"Cora Lee will have my hide. You just coming off of some stomach bug only a few days ago, and here I am filling you with greasy burgers and ice cream to top it all off." Otis shook his head, upset with himself.

"Otis. Don't worry. I won't say nothing. It will be our secret. Besides, that burger sure did taste good going down." I hesitated. "What did Mr. Junior want? Was he talking to you about those acres again?"

We turned into the driveway. The farmhouse looked tired, as if it were taking a nap, closing its eyes for a few hours to rest itself. "Actually, not this time. Truth be told, he was asking about your mama…and your daddy. Was wondering when I thought they'd be coming in for the holiday."

I fidgeted in my seat. Otis had always been one adult whom I knew would talk to me straight up, which was one of the reasons I had never asked him about my daddy and where he thought he was. I guess I knew my truth was just that, my truth. But if Otis agreed, then it became *the* truth. Even though my head knew it, my nine-year-old heart wasn't as far along.

"Grandma says Mr. Junior used to be sweet on Mama."

Otis shut the car off and turned toward me. "She told you that, did she?"

I nodded.

"Yes, I guess that's about right. I think Rose broke his heart the day she left here with Willie, and then again when she came back here with your daddy." He looked out the window, talking more to himself than me. "More so when she came back with your daddy."

"Willie? You mean Dr. Price?"

Otis nodded. "Sure do. Your mama was all set to marry him. Followed him all the way to Harrison."

"What happened?"

"Korean War, and he went off to school. Sometimes distance doesn't make the heart grow fonder. But then she met your daddy and had you, so it all worked out for the best."

"Why was Mr. Junior mad when she came back here with Daddy?"

Otis peered at me over the rim of his glasses. "Why so many questions?"

I shrugged. "Don't know. Mama never mentioned him at home, ever, but he seems to know an awful lot about us. He says I look just like her, but I don't ever remember even meeting him until this visit." I paused and could feel the blood rush up my neck. "Do you think he still loves her?"

"Loves her? Those some big thoughts for a girl of nine." He narrowed his eyes. "What do you know about love? You got some young gentleman be whispering pretty words in your ears? You tell him to come back in about ten years." He patted me on the leg and opened his door. Otis must have thought I was disappointed because he looked back at me again when I didn't move. "Oh, Macey May. Slow down. You'll understand the ways of the world sooner than later. Boys will start paying attention to you before you know it. You've got your mama's beauty."

But he was wrong. My real feeling, the one he misunderstood, was fear. Because if Mr. Junior still loved Mama, I thought he'd do just about anything to get her…anything.

Otis motioned for me to get out of the car. I wiggled my way across the seat and jumped onto the ground. "Come on. Let's get you inside," he said. "Why don't you take a book out to the resting porch while I finish up in the barn."

"Can't I help?"

"No, I think it's better for you to relax. Not much to be done there right now anyway. Maybe after dinner, if you're feeling up to it."

I didn't really want to be alone on the porch. Junior's voice still resounded in my ear, his breath on the back of my neck, sticking like a hot cobweb. "Don't they say people will do crazy things for love?" My voice was louder than I intended. "My friend Biddy from school didn't like Emmett in that way either, and when he found out, he was right mean to her. Pushed her down so hard at recess one day that she skinned her knee. He had to go see the principal for that. Didn't seem to stop him, though. He'd call her names under his breath whenever he was close enough for her to hear, names that aren't right for a girl to be called. Junior won't do that to Mama when he sees her, will he?"

Otis ruffled my hair with his hand. "I'm sorry Biddy had to go through that. Sometimes children don't know any better. Junior's a grown-up. He knows how to behave. You have nothing to worry about."

I put the *Anne of Green Gables* book on the floor and stretched my legs out on the cot that was set up on the screened in. If it stayed this hot, Grandma might let me sleep out there. Mama told me she'd call every night at seven, but Otis asked me in the car not to say anything to her about today's delivery. Said Mama wouldn't understand and then there would be more explaining to do that was better to be done in person when she came home tomorrow night for Thanksgiving rather than over the phone with who knows who could be listening in. Another secret for me to keep.

"Macey May?"

I heard the whisper in the distance, coming from the tree line where it led into the woods. My name lilting over the grass.

"Macey May. Over here."

I perched myself up on my elbows and squinted to look through the dark of the screen searching for the voice. I blinked and swallowed hard. "Daddy?" My gut told me not to yell.

"Come to the side."

I looked over my shoulder at the open door into the main house. The hallway was deserted, the quiet looming high in the air. Otis would be in the barn for at least another hour, and from my vantage point I could see that Grandma's bedroom door was still shut.

Sliding my bare feet back into my Mary Janes, I sidled over to the far side of the porch and hid in the shadow that had settled in the corner, it seemed for this exact purpose. "Daddy? Is that you? What are you doing out there? Why don't you come in the house?"

I could make out the silhouette of his stance under the trees. If anyone was in the living room and looked out the window, they wouldn't be able to see him. It was as if he knew how far he could go and still be safe, still be hidden. "Can't right now, sugar, but I wanted to see you. Can you come out?"

I nodded and opened the door quietly, holding it till it closed with my hand. To my right, Daddy had crossed over down to the grouping of trees that bunched along the creek where Pap was buried. He waved for me to follow him. Soon we were both below the ridge, walking beside the water, apart from most everything. I wasn't supposed to be down there. Grandma had her rules and that was one of them. "Stay away from the water, Macey May," she told me. Always. Mama said it was because Grandma couldn't swim. Never learned. Her biggest fear was that I'd be swept away, and she'd be left on the shore watching me go by her, lost forever.

Mama says Grandma always seemed to be worried about losing people. When we had lots of rain, the creek would rise and the current would speed up. Grandma told me that a farm down the way lost a lamb once in the raging waters. Poor little thing drowned before anyone could get to it. It finally got hooked on a tree limb sticking out from the side. By the time the rain ended and the water stopped its pulsing, the lamb was two days dead and its bloated carcass had been picked apart by the crows.

Daddy could sense my hesitation, had heard Grandma's warnings every strawberry festival. "It's okay. I'm with you. She'd be fine with that."

I bit the inside of my lip. I had heard Otis earlier that day talking with Denim about a storm likely coming in Thanksgiving night. I looked out at the calm creek and thought about that lamb and how scared it must have been. How circumstances could change so quickly. "She doesn't know you're here, does she?"

He shook his head. "No one but you." Then he smiled. Big.

"Mama said you were in California. Are you back now?" Even though it wasn't mine, the lie tasted like a lie in my mouth, thick and sulfurous.

Daddy bent his head down. "Wasn't in California."

The bubble inside me burst, and I could feel tears welling up in my eyes. I had wanted to believe the lies, untruths, misleading details, whatever grown-ups called it when they chose dishonesty. I pressed the palms of my hands into my eyes. I didn't want him to see me cry.

"Come here, honey. Let me talk to you." He settled himself down on a log along the shore and patted the spot next to him. "Can't stay long."

So this was it, I thought. He'd come to say goodbye. Without ever

being told, I knew this had always been the truth. Those days he had disappeared and Mama said he was on a job, the times he wasn't home and
she said nothing. I spoke quickly. "You love me." It wasn't a question. I
didn't doubt his love for me. I wanted him to know that I knew. If this
was to be it, I needed for him to know that I had always felt his love for
me—couldn't stand if he thought bad about himself, if he thought he
hadn't been a good daddy.

"Honey, I love you more—" His eyes were on my arm. His fingers
reached out and lifted the corner of my short sleeve. Even under the can-
opy of trees the dark imprints were visible. "Macey May? What happened?
Has someone been hurting you?"

I pulled the fabric down and slouched, trying to make my arms
shorter, to cover up the purple-brown bruises that I had been trying to
forget about. He held my chin in his hand and lifted my head to look
him the eyes. "Macey May? I'm your father. Tell me who did this. I'll
protect you."

Beyond us I heard the sparrows' meager song and remembered in
Sunday school when Pastor would tell us the story about God looking out
for even the smallest sparrow. "But you aren't here," I said.

He looked away, and I felt bad. I hadn't meant to shame him. I simply wanted him to know my truth.

"I know, Macey May. I wish I could explain what is going on,
what happens to me sometimes, but I don't even know myself. But
I'm here now, and I promise I'll protect you. Now, tell me. Is someone
hurting you?"

I closed my eyes and nodded. A small nod, one you'd have to look
for. I figured if he saw it then, well, my secret would be shared; if he didn't
see it, then it would still be mine.

His jaw tightened. I knew he knew.

"Who, baby?"

My voice was soft. "Mr. Junior."

I saw Daddy's hands curl into fists. The vein on his neck became taut and his face reddened. I looked down at my feet, unsure if I had done right by telling. What if Daddy blamed me? Daddy stood up from the log and started pacing.

"Did you tell Grandma or Otis?"

I shook my head quickly. "He said they wouldn't believe me, that they'd call me a liar and the whole town would know I was no good, proving that Mama had done wrong by going with you. He said I was a double-bastard. First 'cause you and Mama ain't married and second 'cause I'm a mongrel. Why does he think I'm a dog?"

Daddy stopped in front of me and let out a long breath, his shoulders reaching up high to his ears and then stretching down as he exhaled. "I'm so sorry, Macey May."

"He said there were laws against what you both did…anti-misgeneration?"

"Anti-miscegenation."

"What does that mean?"

"Nothing. It means nothing. Laws made by men who have no place telling others who they can and cannot love." Daddy ran his hands across the top of his head and then down along his chin like I'd seen him do when he was struggling with fixing the radiator in the bathroom. He started pacing again.

I scratched my arm where the bruise was. Talking about it seemed to awaken the leftover hurt. Daddy stopped in front of me and knelt down, getting to my level. I knew he was going to ask me something serious because he always liked to look me in the eye when he was looking for truth from me. It was hard to lie when he did that.

"Macey May, did Junior—?"

Even at nine I knew what question he was asking. Mama had already talked to me about the birds and the bees, what happened sometimes between a man and a woman when they loved each other and sometimes when they didn't.

"He talked in my ear about Mama and how I looked like her. He put his hand on my leg. I don't think he knew how tight he had my arm, though. It was like he even forgot I was there for a moment, saying things about Mama I shouldn't be hearing." My words came out fast, and I had to catch my breath.

"Macey May?" Daddy stayed on his knees in front of me, his hand on my shoulders.

I think he knew I couldn't answer his question. Couldn't make those words come out of my mouth.

His arms enclosed me, tight. It felt good to let him hold me, and I leaned into him and rested my head against his shoulder.

"You don't have to worry about Junior anymore. I won't let him hurt you again."

I nodded into his chest.

We stayed that way for a while, his hug turning into a rocking in rhythm with the flowing water beside us. The air was changing and getting cooler, the light breeze moving across my cheek.

"Macey May?" Grandma's voice was in the distance. I looked at Daddy.

He pointed down the bank a bit. "Run down there and go up through the woods. You'll come out on the side of the house, but she won't see that you were by the water. Don't tell her I'm here, though, okay? It needs to be our secret." He hesitated. "Don't tell anyone."

He kissed the top of my head, and I scurried along the edge, my heart beating in my chest.

My knees got covered in dirt as I climbed up. I spit on my hand and tried to wipe it away but only proceeded in coloring in my skin.

"Good Lord, child. What have you done to yourself?"

Grandma was staring at me, mouth agape, arms crossed in front of her. I wiped my forehead with the back of my hand, and she shook her head and rolled her eyes. "Stop it. You are making it worse, smearing it all over yourself. You've been down by the water, haven't you?"

There was no reason to lie as the evidence was to the contrary, and while I knew I had the talent for fabrication, I wasn't sure my brain could hold one more story. I cast my eyes down and kicked the dirt with my toe. "Yes'm."

"Stop kicking. Just cause you're covered doesn't mean your shoes need to be, too. Come on. I'll pull you a bath."

I looked up at her. "You're not going to ask me what I was doing down there?"

"Nope. I figure you know my rule. Must have been something important for you to go ahead and break it. You'll tell me when the time needs."

Now I was starting to understand why Mama talked the way she did sometimes about Grandma. Just when you think you start to understand, to know her ways, she ups and changes on you, so you can never be quite sure—ever.

Chapter 14

CRAWFORD, GEORGIA
CORA LEE JENKINS
1962

A N D N O W she understood why she'd been feeling mourning air.

Cora Lee sat on the edge of the bed with a shoe box next to her. This one was worn, its corners sagging, the cardboard curled and frayed along the edges—signs of aging. Dust covered the discarded lid except where her fingers had hurriedly removed it, white tissue paper inside faded to a pale yellow over the years. The newly delivered brown oxford sat in her lap, her fingers wrapped lightly around it. A perfect match to the one in the box.

She had told Otis when he had followed her up to the bedroom that she'd be fine, and she'd go back downstairs in a minute to rest in her room, that she needed some time alone in the space that once belonged to her and Hi. Their marriage bed. Minutes had passed, hours, yet she hadn't moved. She felt more immobile now than she had all those years back sitting on the bed bathing her dead husband, their two sweet babies fast asleep in the room across the hall.

Hi's shoes. A pair again.

Twenty-five years. It had been almost twenty-five years since that night when she placed Hi's one shoe back into the box and put it up in the top of the closet to the space where he set them until he needed them for a meeting or church. Back then, in the darkness, under *their* tree, which would never be *their* tree again and had stopped being *theirs* the moment she saw him swinging from it, time hadn't allowed for her to search for the other one. It was all they could do, she and Otis, to get him down and into the truck.

She had wondered at the start, when life had quieted and fallen back into ordinary, if that would be the end of it, if whoever had killed Hi would be satisfied with her silence, her acquiescence. It didn't look that way. Her fingers touched the leather, dry and brittle. *No*, she thought, *they want to remind me again of their power to play with my life, to take away what I love most.*

Someone had kept Hi's shoe for as long as she had kept its mate. She knew the reason she kept the one; she wondered what their reason was for keeping the other. Had they taken it when they hung him up? Or had they gone back for it later when the news had spread about his untimely death peacefully in his sleep? Had they found it lying on the ground? A dead shoe for a dead man?

Her body shivered. Absently, her hand reached around behind her and pulled the bed quilt haphazardly up around her shoulders. One shoe fell to the floor. A quiet thump.

Cora Lee had cried after Hi was killed, wept as if her body was trying to cull her pain by flooding the earth. Every night, once Rose and Ruby were tucked into bed and stories had been read, cups of water had been refilled and their little feet had pattered across the wooden floors to use the toilet one last time, she would draw herself a bath and sink under the warmth. Sometimes she would let her hands wander, imagining they were Hi's strong farm hands on her skin, the gentleness of his touch.

Sometimes she would stay in the water while it drained around her until her skin wrinkled, her body cold against the porcelain sarcophagus. Sometimes she would see how long she could hold her breath, her eyes open, staring up at the ceiling, under the watered haze. She stopped doing that when the urge to open her mouth wide, to let the water flood her lungs, became too strong of a possibility.

"Cora Lee?" Otis stood in the doorway.

She tilted her head.

He closed the door and walked over to the bed, took the quilt off of her shoulders and set it back in its place, flattening it out with his palm. He held out his hand. "You've been up here this whole time? Let me have that now," he coaxed. Cora Lee sat immobile. He took the shoe from her hand, looked at it a moment, and then glanced down at the other on the floor. "Should I put them back in the same box? Do you want to keep 'em both?" He bent down to pick it up.

Cora Lee bit her top lip and exhaled through her nose.

"Cora Lee?"

"Do you ever think we would have cheated on Hi if he was alive?"

Otis straightened up. "What? Why would you ask a question like that?"

"Look at us. It wasn't more than a year after Hi was gone before we made love in the barn." Cora Lee's voice was flat.

"Yes, but he was gone and not coming back. Circumstances were as they were. No, Cora Lee. If he had been alive, we never would have done that."

"How can you be so sure? If we were attracted to each other then, what would have stopped us from wanting each other even if Hi had been around?"

Otis leaned against the dresser and crossed his arms. "If Hi was alive, you wouldn't have even seen me, that's how I know nothing would have ever happened. You didn't see me. I was Otis, Hi's sidekick, his best friend." He bent his head down then raised it to stare at a spot behind her shoulder on the wall. "And I know you can never love me like you did him."

At this Cora Lee glanced up. "Otis, don't say that."

He shrugged. "Makes no difference. I know you love me in the way that you can, but it won't ever be complete like it was with Hi. Hi is the father of your girls. No tie can ever be the same. I've never had any delusions of it being otherwise. I want you to marry me, and I'll never stop hoping, but even with that I know what I'm getting when I ask. I've never expected more."

She held out her hand to him. "I'm sorry. All these years I thought if I held his death at bay, his real death, I'd somehow be protecting those I loved, making their lives easier. I didn't want them to know the ugliness. The hate." She shook her head. "Maybe Rose has been right all this time. Maybe I'm just scared all around. My excuses were because of my own fear of losing someone else." Cora Lee's voice choked. "Oh God, Otis. Have I been wrong all this time?"

Otis sat down next to her. "Hush. You did right by your girls. Don't listen to Rose. She has no idea what you've been through. And scared? When have you ever been scared? Seems to me you look at the world with one fist pumped to go."

Cora Lee shook her head. "No, I don't. When Hi was here, maybe, when I knew he was behind me with his fists even higher, but I haven't been that Cora Lee for years now." Her eyes filled. "I thought I was doing what was right, for the girls, for everyone, for this town. For me. But all I did was let them win after all. I was so sure that I hadn't given them what they wanted—another notch on their supremacy belt, another death to claim.

"But you know what? I awled that hole, and it was mine and mine alone. I thought by taking him down from that tree that I'd won a victory over their hatred and bigotry, and if the payment was keeping quiet and my head down, in the bigger picture it was worth it because my babies would never know. I let them take away my life, Otis. I let them take my girls' father from them, and I kept quiet. Hi never got justice. My girls never knew the truth. And that's my fault."

"You did what you thought was best."

"Twenty-five years. For what? Change? You've seen the papers. Seen what those kids started in Greensboro all because they wouldn't be served at a counter? They shot my husband and then lynched him, and what have I done about it?"

"Cora Lee." Otis put his hand on her shoulder.

"Someone sent me this shoe. Why now? I've lowered my eyes and 'yes ma'am'd' and 'yes sir'd' until it burned a hole inside of me, made me breathe fire trying to contain it. I've done everything they've wanted, for years, and now they come back with this? What message didn't I get right? What rule didn't I follow? I lost my girls because of it. Oh, yes, their lives are good, and they are doing fine, but I know what they think of me, what they think of this place, their home. And I'm to blame for that, Otis. It was all me."

She stood up and walked across to her dresser, opened the bottom drawer, and pulled out a thick manila envelope from underneath last winter's sweaters. "What more do they want?"

Otis stood up from the edge of the bed. "Cora Lee, we don't know what this shoe means, if anything. It's been years, and this is the first time you've even heard from them. They've kept quiet, too." He looked at his watch. "Now, please. You're tired and anxious is all. Let's go get you a cup of coffee and something to eat. I took Macey May into town for a cheese-burger, and she's out on the porch reading. You've got time to yourself."

Before Otis could get to the bedroom door, Cora Lee had opened the envelope. She shook it until pictures and letters and newspaper clippings floated through the air like dove feathers; they were anything but.

Otis reached over and picked up a few pictures. His eyes softening, a smile formed at the corners of his mouth. "Rose and Ruby are just little in these. I don't understand." His eyes questioned Cora Lee, and she looked away.

"I didn't take them," she said.

He unfurled a letter, then let it fall to the ground after reading the first sentence. He grabbed a newspaper clipping, the headline telling of a young black boy beaten by classmates after he held the door open for a white girl. There were more pictures of the girls, dozens and dozens of them, some taken at a distance, some close, some with their faces crossed out, some with words printed across them that Otis didn't even want to think about. His face went pale and he swallowed, his Adam's apple rising and falling with the gulp. He picked up another picture and then another, his hands consumed with their own voracious appetite. "It's their lives." Otis looked at the pile of paper and photographs around him. "You've been getting these for years? Why didn't you tell me?" Otis put his arms around her.

"Same reason I never told anyone about Hi. Same reason I made you and Denim promise you'd keep my secret. I was trying to protect my family. I understood these warnings. They *took* Hi from me, and they could take the girls, too. But, Otis. I was wrong. We all were."

"Sit down. You need to rest." He tried to guide her to a chair, but she resisted.

"Seems to me I've been resting long enough. Hi's the one dead, not me, and if I had been the one swinging from the tree, the man responsible for it would have been buried twenty-five years ago in the graveyard over yonder. Hi would have made sure of it. You would have made sure of it. Macey May loves this place, and I'm lucky if Rose brings her here three times a year for a visit." Cora Lee stopped and shook her head. "My silence has done nothing more than allow those monsters to win."

She held up one of Hi's shoes in her hand. "Someone wanted to send me a message, but I'm done listening."

"Are you sure about this? How will you tell Rose and Ruby?"

She handed him one more picture.

His eyes widened. "Did this come in the mail?"

Her eyes met his. "Came right through the U.S. Postal System like it was some sort of Thank You card last week."

They looked down again at the photo of Hi swinging from a tree.

Chapter 15

CRAWFORD, GEORGIA
ROSE JOHNSON
1962

ROSE TOOK the last train from Harrison to coincide with Ruby's arrival from the city so Otis wouldn't have to make two trips into the station. She promised Miss Eunice that she would ask Macey May how she was enjoying *Anne of Green Gables* as soon as she got there, but by the time they pulled into the farm, Macey May was in bed, and she didn't want to wake her. Instead she treaded lightly across the hardwood floor in her stocking feet to check on her as she slept, kissing her forehead and tucking the covers up around her.

Rose and Ruby stayed up long enough to hear Cora Lee recite the menu for the Thanksgiving meal and catch up some with Denim about the vet business, but it had been a long day and they were tired. They said good night and were both asleep before either one could even think to ask how life was going for the other.

Now it was morning, and Rose sat the end of her bed viewing herself in the mirror. She and Ruby had stayed in their old room, the light blue wallpaper now faded from the years, hints of flowers scattered across it—ghosts of their former selves. What was she going to tell them about Curtis? He certainly wouldn't be there by tomorrow for Thanksgiving, nor by Christmas. Poor Macey May didn't know yet that they might not be returning to Harrison. Rose cringed at the thought of telling her, of seeing her crumpled face when she realized she wouldn't see Miss Eunice anymore. She had no idea how she'd get their few belongings without a car or where she'd take them once she had them. Oh, she was sure Otis would drive her back to fetch whatever she wanted, but the thought of storing her few possessions in the dirt cellar of her mama's farmhouse felt as devastating to her as if she was burying them alive.

Her only option in Harrison was moving in with Miss Eunice. Rose had survived one slight with dignity when Willie had cast her off. She wasn't sure she wanted to become the town's center of gossip (more than she already was) when Curtis never came home. Staying in Harrison and moving in with Miss Eunice would certainly do that. And her mama couldn't know. Rose wasn't ready to see the "I told you so" in her eyes, the disappointment in her tone.

Rose put on her nylons, making sure the lines were straight up the back of her legs and sat herself up straighter in the chair. If she had to raise Macey May all by herself, she'd do it, but her only job was in Harrison at Adele's. Without it, Harrison didn't have a lot to offer her. She shook her head, trying to excise the words Adele had said to her before she left: the bakery was closing. Rose's head spun. Maybe she'd move them to New York City. Certainly Ruby would let them live with her for a bit. Maybe she could even get her a job at Macy's. In a place so large, it didn't seem like anyone would mind where you came from or who you were. What color your daddy's skin was…or wasn't.

"Rose? You in there?" Ruby tapped her on the side of the head. "Hello."

"Quit it, Ruby! You'll mess up my hair." Rose batted her hand away. "When are you going to grow up anyway?"

"Never if I can help it." She grabbed a tissue off of the dresser and blotted her lips. A bright red pout tattooed the paper. "I don't ever want to be old like Mama."

"I wouldn't say Mama's old."

Ruby shrugged. "Unfashionable, out of style, old—same thing. Here," she handed Rose her lipstick, "you need some color. Macy's says it's proven that women customers will buy more merchandise from other women if they're pretty."

"Then how have you sold anything?" Rose laughed at her own words.

"Shut up." Ruby gave Rose a punch in the shoulder.

"In case you forget, I'm your big sister. I whooped you when we were younger. I can do it again now that I'm—"

Ruby broke in, "—old?"

"Be quiet."

Ruby spritzed some perfume in the air and turned into it. "You'll see. Holiday bonuses are based on performance. Last year, I made an extra thirty dollars in my paycheck. Second highest bonus in my department."

"Thirty dollars, you say?" Rose looked one last time in the mirror and hair sprayed a pin curl along her temple.

"Yes'm."

"Well, I'll remember that when I'm opening my Christmas present from you. Who are you getting so dolled up for, anyway?"

Ruby looked in the vanity mirror over Rose's shoulder and blew herself a kiss. "You never know who might pop in to say hey."

Rose raised an eyebrow at her reflection. "Are you ever gonna stop mooning over Junior? He didn't like you when we were little, he's not gonna like you now."

Ruby plopped down on the bed. "Shows you what you know. He sent me a letter. Found my address in New York City and wrote me. Asked if I was coming back for the holidays."

Rose turned toward her sister. "Asked about you coming home, did he?"

Ruby crossed her arms. "Fine. Asked about you and Macey May too, but he didn't have to write to me. Simply could have asked Mama. He's written me a few times over the years. See what you know."

Rose shook her head. She'd never understand why Ruby pined for Junior the way she did. If Rose thought about it, she couldn't remember a time that Junior wasn't being mean to Ruby—talking above her, talking about her. Long after they were little kids and well out of their teen years, Junior's comments about Ruby still tipped the scale. Rose wondered why she had put up with his baseness back then, why she had sat by him as he ridiculed Ruby's hair, nose, size ten feet. Why she hadn't stood up for her sister. But it had been years since she had done more than be polite in Junior's presence, waved from afar if she was home and passed him in the car. The days of calling to tell him she was back ended the minute Macey May was in her womb.

Rose bent over and fixed the seam on the back of her nylon. "You know, Junior's not—"

"How's Mama?" Ruby interrupted with an abruptness that told Rose that the topic of Junior was closed.

Rose turned on the stool to face her sister and crossed her arms.

"Don't look at me like that. I call the last Saturday of every month. It's just, it's been a long time since I've been home. And you know her. She'd rather spend time talking about the business side of the farm or something that's going on in town than talking about herself."

Rose nodded in agreement. Ruby wasn't saying anything that wasn't truth. "There's mourning air again. Otis told me while we waited for your bus to come in last night."

Ruby rolled her eyes. "How long's it been since the last episode?"

Rose tallied in her mind. "Six, seven months, I think."

Ruby grimaced. "Oh yes, May. Remember. Mrs. Hudson's house burnt down—stove fire, right?"

Rose nodded.

"Mama sure was proud of her mourning air then. Said she knew all along something terrible was going to happen. I wonder how she kept from smiling when she heard the news. What's she think it's about now?"

"Don't know, but Otis says she's been airing out the house for three days straight. Started the morning Macey May came."

Ruby went to the closet and took down a pink cardigan sweater and placed it over her shoulders. "Hand me that pearl stick-pin, would you?" She cleared her throat and turned around to face Rose. "You don't think Mama's going crazy, do you?"

"Wouldn't surprise me. You can't go all your life obeying every 'rule' set before you, bowing your head and your knees at every white man's word, and not find yourself a little off kilter by the day's end."

"Why are you like that?" Ruby's face became stern.

"Like what?"

Ruby shrugged and stretched out her arms in exasperation. "That. That… 'Mama never stood up for herself…' 'Mama kowtows to every white man…' 'Mama has no backbone.' You've never given her a break."

Rose stood and put her hands on her hips. "I give her breaks."

"When? As far back as I remember you've always fought her, tried to show her how easy it is to live like *them*, like everyone could do it except her. You know, Rose, just because you're living with one of them doesn't ever mean you'll be one of them."

Rose stepped back and tears bit at the corners of her eyes.

Ruby exhaled and looked at her sister. "You always had to prove something, Rose. Still do. And the way you prove yourself is by making others feel less than they are. Even though you don't say it, you make them feel stupid."

"I—"

Ruby raised her hand. "I don't need an excuse or an apology, but maybe this visit you could try to take into account all that Mama has done for us and what she's lived through. You seem to forget sometimes that Mama's South growing up wasn't our South. Who knows what she's seen?"

The two stood in front of the mirror and Rose took Ruby's hand in hers. Rose spoke. "Did I ever make you feel…stupid?"

"Of course you did, but you also made me feel loved and protected, so I guess that evens it out."

Rose poked Ruby in the ribs. "We're not really a bad pair, are we?"

"A little taller than I'd like, but no, not too bad."

Hi had given them their height, both 5'8". Cora Lee had given them their slender shoulders and hips that swayed naturally and caused men to take second glances.

"And I still don't think your eyes are fair, at all." Ruby stuck out her tongue.

Ruby had Cora Lee's eyes, dark brown and fawn-like with lashes that didn't need any mascara. Rose's violet eyes came from far back, three generations her mother said, way back to her Great-Great Grandma Hattie, a slave on a Southern plantation. The stories said her eyes saved her, made her a house servant instead of picking cotton under the hot Georgia sun. The mistress of the house believed she was blessed with some power by those eyes, could tell the future, could know if crops would rise or not or whether a storm was blowing in or if a child would be born dead or alive.

"Now, honey," Cora Lee would say when Rose asked for the story again, "Hattie had no such magic, just pretty eyes given to her by God when she had nothing else pretty in her life. Every time she looked in a mirror or saw her reflection in the water, she'd be reminded that she wasn't born to be a slave. God's beauty was never meant to be owned."

Macey May didn't get the violet eyes.

Curtis had blue eyes.

Macey May didn't get those either. Hers were a deep brown, like muddy waters filled with secrets.

Ruby held Rose's glance in the mirror. "So when you going to tell me?"

"Tell you what?"

"The real reason Curtis is gone."

"What do you mean? He's got a good job in California. Called yesterday before I left to check in and wish us a Happy Thanksgiving. Not sure he'll be home by Christmas now. Taking longer than he thought. He—"

"Hmphh. I'm not Mama, and I'm not Macey May. You may have them fooled, but I can see right through you. Always could. So tell me. What happened?"

Rose sat down in the chair in front of the vanity and thought about her next words. Ruby could be fooled. Everyone could. She had managed even, almost, to fool herself for the last few years.

"Did he cheat on you?" Ruby asked.

"Curtis? Never."

"Did he hit you?"

Rose went to shake her head, but Ruby picked up on the slight hesitation.

"Dear Lord, Rose. Curtis beat you?"

"Lower your voice." Ruby always had a tendency to overreact, to be dramatic over the littlest thing. "These walls are thin, and I don't need Mama or Otis knowing my business."

"Did he hit Macey May?"

It was Rose's voice that raised now. "No! Never! I wouldn't have stayed if he ever so much as raised a hand to her. It wasn't like that."

"So you just stayed when he raised a hand at you?" There was no mistaking the sass in Ruby's voice that teetered on disappointment.

Rose turned around to her little sister. Ruby, now living large in New York, independent of life back in Georgia. She had gotten away, managed to leave all the backwardness with which they had grown up. Rose thought she had done the proverbial killing of two birds with one stone when she met Curtis. Helping her own situation and standing up for change by being with a white man. "You wouldn't understand," Rose said.

"You're right there. No man's ever laying a hand on me. And I can't believe you'd let Curtis do you that way. That's not the Rose I know."

"It's not what you think." Rose knew she couldn't explain it in a way that Ruby would understand or accept. Her own mind was still a mess of contradictions. Curtis hit her, yes—but it wasn't her he was hitting.

Ruby turned to walk out of the bedroom, a wave of her hand dismissing Rose's excuse.

"Ruby, wait."

Ruby turned around. Standing in the door frame, arms folded across her chest, she stared into Rose's eyes.

"Sometimes Curtis doesn't seem to remember me."

Ruby leaned into her hip and narrowed her eyes. "What do you mean? Like he looks at you and can't remember you're Rose?"

"No. Like he looks right through me, like I'm not even there."

"You're not talking sense."

"I think something bad happened to him during the war, over in Korea."

Ruby's voice softened. "Didn't something bad happen to everyone over there?"

"Yes, but this is something more." Rose swallowed and closed her eyes. "Sometimes, I think he's still fighting...thinks I'm part of it." She paused, not ready to tell the rest.

Rose stood and went to her suitcase. Tucked underneath her underwear was Curtis's wallet. She fingered the worn leather, the tangibility of it confirmation that he wasn't coming back. "I found this on the kitchen table after he left. No note, nothing. His ID is still in it, his union card. Only thing missing is Macey May's school picture. And there's this."

It had been almost five years since Rose had seen the picture for the first time, five years of contemplating how to bring it up to Curtis. Something she had never managed to do. She had gone into his wallet searching for a quarter to buy a loaf of bread to make it through the rest of the week when the dark sepia corner caught her eye. It was sticking out of the lining behind the bill fold—a picture of a Korean woman holding an infant. She'd like to say that her heart broke when she saw it, that everything she thought to be true between them evaporated into mist. Instead she felt release, an understanding.

He had lost more than just Johnny in the war. Pregnancies between servicemen and Korean women weren't unheard of. Rose knew that many of the girls were looking for a way to the U.S., and many of the men were simply looking for a connection that reminded them they were human. She hadn't faulted him, only wished he had told her. They could have been sending money over, at least making sure that his child's life would be better in some way.

She had studied the baby, trying to tell if it was a boy or a girl, but other than eyes and a patch of black hair, there was nothing that distinguished it as either. She gave it a birthday—October 3—to track its age in her mind, a little more than two years older than Macey May.

Rose stretched out the picture to Ruby. "Here."

Ruby looked at her sister. "His? Did you know?"

Rose shook her head. "Not until I found the picture. He never said a word. Ever."

"And you think this has something to do with why he hits you?"

Rose shook her head again. "No. Once I came up behind him in the living room, went to hug him. Before I knew it, he had me pinned to the ground, his forearm against my neck. I'd never been so scared before—not because he was hurting me but because I could see in his eyes that he wasn't hurting *me*."

"How did you make him stop?"

Rose looked back down at the picture. "*Jebel, Jebel.*"

"Huh?"

"It means 'please' in Korean. I kept saying it over and over."

"How did you know to say that or that it would work?"

Rose cleared her throat. "Curtis has nightmares sometimes. One night I woke up to him crying out those words. In the morning, I asked them what he meant and he told me."

"Did it work?"

Rose's hand instinctively went to her throat as if the pressure were still there. She swallowed. "I passed out. When I woke up he was gone. Two weeks later he came home, all smiles like he had never left. It was the night of Macey May's school annual Bake-Off fundraiser, and we were headed out the door when he walked up the drive whistling. He kissed me on the cheek, picked Macey May up and swung her around, and then proceeded to give away almost all our money at the fundraiser. The way he acted, you would have thought everyone there was his best friend."

Rose bent her head down. "I couldn't make myself ask where he had been, or if he remembered what he had done to me. I couldn't figure out the words. Later that night he told me he'd like a son, someone to carry on his name."

Ruby spoke, her tone quiet. "Maybe this is a boy." She handed the picture back to Rose, who smoothed it out between her hands and put it back in the wallet.

"Maybe."

Chapter 16

CRAWFORD, GEORGIA
CURTIS JOHNSON
1962

THE NIGHT WAS SILENT. So silent I thought for
sure the world was over, like the rapture had taken place and everyone had
been brought up except for me. The stars had disappeared, too. Couldn't
remember exactly what the story said about the heavens needing the stars
when judgment came, but I guess they were part of the package deal.

There was darkness.

There was me.

The ground beneath my feet was wet, the rawness of the night air
seeping into my socks as my toes curled trying to keep it away. I was staying to the trees, concealing myself as I walked, hiding from them. I tried
to remember my commander's orders: flank to the left, stay low, make no
sound, shoot at anything you hear. We were spread out, more than a few
arm's lengths apart when we started our way into the town, each of us
carrying our packs, rifles cocked and loaded. But now I didn't know where
my company was. They were there, and then they weren't.

Johnny had been gone awhile now. I wish he hadn't left. I miss him.
I understood, though, his wanting to draw like he does and all. The Army
doesn't let you do that—what you want, I mean. All these rules about

being here and watching that, standing there and doing this. Sometimes I can't even remember it all. I'm hurt he didn't say goodbye, but I'm happy for him, wherever he got to go to. I imagine he's sitting at home with his mama, drinking sweet tea on the porch and working on being an architect to impress the girls.

Truth be told, I'm jealous. Wish I could figure out how he managed it. One night I'm talking to him at chow about how we need to go to our shift. He says, "The coffee sucks," and they let him go. Gave him a ticket on a plane and woosh…flew him right on home. Maybe that's the unfairness of war they always talk about.

Crap.

I think the coffee sucks here, too, but no one has told me my number's up yet.

Maybe if I had been the first one to say it.

I still eat at our table, the one against the back right, near the door, in the mess. It's tucked in a corner, so when the wind blows, the stench from the trash behind the kitchen doesn't make its way to us like it does to some of the other tables. For a while, I would get Johnny his tray and leave it at the table for him while I ate just in case he changed his mind and came back, but I get the feeling now that that's just wishful thinking on my part. I'll meet up with him again, though; best friends are friends forever, so right now I've decided it's best to make sure I get home alive— or we won't be seeing each other.

There's laughter in the distance, and I stop, one foot raised in a dance with gravity and balance. Where there's noise, there's the enemy. Where there's the enemy, there's a trap you wouldn't even imagine. Thin lines of wire the width of a hair set between trees that will explode your legs off. Bombs buried in the dirt, their triggers underground, sightless, until the toe of your boot makes contact. And then…well, there's no *then*.

The enemy laughs. The men, who I've been told are my foes even though we've never met, laugh. I saw one cry once in fear before his neck was snapped, heard him speak *"jebel, jebel"* from a mouth with missing teeth in it before his voice stopped forever. I can't remember where I saw it, a movie perhaps back in the States, but I did. It made sense to me that he would cry, his life about to be over, but to laugh? I don't think I've ever heard them laugh until now.

I suck in my breath and gingerly put my foot down. In my mind, moving it slower makes it less likely to set off a trap. I know it's stupid thinking that, but this war has made most of us stupid…and paranoid… and scared. My map showed the town was only a few kilometers from camp, and I had been walking near a half an hour with still no signs of the other men. I didn't want to think I was lost. "Lost equals death," our commander told us every morning at briefing. "Whatever you do, don't get lost!"

Did they change the plans and forget to tell me, like Johnny had when he left? Did they want me to get lost?

I know I have a mission, though. That there's a purpose to where I am going, something that I need to do. My gut tells me it's true even if my thoughts can't bring to form the instructions in my mind, even if I can't understand. It's there, at the edge, causing me to walk this way and turn that way, to wait, to move. Biding time. Sometimes I catch a fragment of it. It skirts across my memory and I feel it, deep in my heart, a need for revenge.

So I follow it.

And then it is there in front of me.

He is there in front of me, and I remember.

For a second, I remember.

"Well, well, well. If it isn't Curtis Johnson back from California."

He greets me as if we are friends who haven't seen each other for a long time. I'm close enough to smell his breath, heavy with liquor, and watch his fingers fumble with car keys. He has fixed his tooth. There is no longer a darkened gap in his mouth.

"Doesn't look like you are in any condition to drive," I say, my hand searching my side for my gun, but my holster is gone. What was I doing out on watch without my secondary pistol? I feel my chest for my rifle strap. That too is missing. I shake my head. They're good. They might win this war yet. I don't know how they managed to disarm me without my knowing as I walked, but our commander had warned us about them. Stealing my guns was a dirty trick, but I'd have done the same thing if I had their kind of magic. After all, we are enemies.

"Doesn't look like you should be driving," I say again.

"Oh, it doesn't, does it?" His words slur together.

The keys fall to the ground, and I bend down and take them, securing them in my pocket. "No, it doesn't," I say. If I could stop the use of one of their vehicles, maybe I could save our men on the line.

"Didn't figure you'd come back. Heard what they said, 'He's in Cal-i-forn-i-ay...' " He makes the word breeze across the night air in five syllables, his hands lifted up orchestrating them until the last long "a" morphs into the beginning of a question. "Ay, she know you're here?"

I shake my head, more in confusion than answering the question.

He leans his back against the car door. "Never could figure out what she saw in you. Your skin's just as white as mine. What made you the better choice?"

Head games. We learned about it in basic. The lies the enemy would tell you; the truths they'd twist to get you to break.

I wouldn't play into his hand. "Come on," I say. I take him by his arm and lead him around to the passenger door. "Get in. I'll take you home."

"Always Mr. Polite. That's what you were. More like Mr. Stupid, if you ask me. How's Dr. William Price? Ever ask her about him?" He allows me to help him into the seat, and I slam the door behind him. When I find my unit, I'll hand him over to the commander. There are people better equipped to interrogate him than me.

"Rose, Rose, Rose…smells so sweet." He takes a deep breath in, his words slurring together, and I start the engine.

Names. How do they find out about our lives?

His mouth won't stop. "Curtis. Curtis. Curtis Johnson all the way from California." He is laughing as he says it. Laughing like my name is a joke, like I am a joke, like my life is a joke. The tooth is missing again, and his eyes begin to slant. His hand clasps my shoulder. "It's okay, brother. We all loved her…if you know what I mean." He raises an eyebrow and chuckles to himself.

The truck pulls out onto the road. There is a rendezvous point a few kilometers away, a side lane that abuts brush and overgrowth. I look at my watch. It is a little after 1900 hours. The unit planned to regroup there at 2000.

"Mmm…that Rose. How'd you get so lucky? You know some trick in bed?" His words keep coming, and I wonder if he is even aware that I haven't responded.

Above his voice, I try to concentrate on directions. I've been to the point before, but now everything feels muddled, my mind unable to focus. The road comes in and out of vision, first it's dirt then it's asphalt. When did they put down asphalt? I look out the window as he babbles on inco-herently…*baby…sweet…violet eyes*. I shake my head to clear my thoughts. I knew someone once with violet eyes. They swallowed me whole, those eyes did. Sent me on a course that there was no coming back from. Saved me, at least for a while.

Outside the car window the scenery is changing. Oak and maple are now interspersed with hickory, black gum, and pawpaw trees. My mind is playing tricks on me. Trees from back home wouldn't be here. I think about the last time I slept, the last time my head was on the pillow, but all I can remember is me and Johnny getting ready to go on duty and him saying the coffee sucked.

"Come on now. What's a little sharing between friends?" He reaches over and grabs my upper arm. I shake it off, but the feel of it is still there, the light pressure, the bruising waiting to come up from below the surface.

Macey May.

The name sneaks into my ear, whispering.

"Junior," she had said and then shaken her head unconvincingly.

My foot hits the brake, and the tail of the truck swerves. He falls against me. Johnny had fallen against me.

"Hey man! What are you doing?" He grins stupidly, in his mouth an empty space, dark and menacing. I am out of the car and dragging him from the passenger door. The devil's walking stick is dense and lush. Along with the trumpet creepers, it will provide enough cover for a while, at least. Johnny didn't deserve to die. And what he did to Macey May? Why hadn't I protected her?

Before my mind can even register what I plan to do, my hands grasp my enemy's neck, which, like brittle chicken bones, twists and breaks under my fingers. I feel it but I don't hear it.

There is a short gasp from his mouth, a balloon leaking air, and then his body is limp in my arms.

Chapter 17

CRAWFORD, GEORGIA
MACEY MAY JOHNSON
1962

THE RAIN RAPPED against the windows, its knuckles rat-a-tat-tatting a Morse code I couldn't decipher as lightning streaked the walls with smears of yellow and white. It was crazy weather. "The cousin to mourning air," Grandma had said earlier in the kitchen.

The barometer didn't know what to make of it, and all day, long after the turkey and dressing had been put away and taken out and put away again, Grandma, Otis, Denim, Mama, and Aunt Ruby discussed it like it was some rare phenomenon, as unfamiliar as snow in June. I don't think they took a breath that wasn't tempered with some worry about what more rain would do to the ground that had seen freezing temperatures only a week ago and then bright sunshine for the past few days.

When Mama asked me to go upstairs and get ready for bed an hour earlier than usual, I didn't even argue. I was happy to get away. I didn't think I could stand to listen to one more opinion on the devastation the lack of a proper and full pecan harvest would do to the economy of the area—especially with Christmas around the corner.

Something was wrong with Mama. I could tell. During dinner she kept checking in with me, making sure I had enough cranberry sauce or cornbread or those tiny sweet pickles I loved—like she was making up for something. Usually she focused on my posture and where my napkin had escaped to. This time I knew I could put my elbows on the table if I wanted to, and I doubt she would have said anything.

Otis kept looking at Grandma, a delicate look in his eyes, and I wondered what it was they weren't telling me, what they were trying to keep from me. Even Aunt Ruby, who had been full of questions about my schooling and how I was liking *Anne of Green Gables* when she spoke to me at breakfast, seemed to be preoccupied with Mama once they were dressed and out of their room. There were more "please" and "thank yous" passed around than I had heard in my lifetime. I was old enough to know that politeness covered a multitude of sins and sadness.

"Mama," I said when she put me to bed upstairs. "What aren't you telling me?"

She tucked the quilt down tight around me, and I brought up my knees to loosen the constriction. "Macey May, I'm sure I don't know what you are talking about."

"Are you worried about Daddy?" I thought about him outside somewhere, missing all the fixings of the turkey dinner—his favorite. I wondered what he was eating and if I should have tried to sneak him out a plate. I hoped he had some shelter from the rain.

"No, honey. He said he'd try to be home for Christmas, but, you know, I've been thinking. How'd you like to go to New York and live with Aunt Ruby for a while? Experience something outside of little ol' Harrison?"

My stomach tightened. Was she sending me away again? "Alone?"

She smoothed my hair with her hand. "No, sweetie. The two of us. I thought the city might be fun, new opportunities…an adventure…" Her voice petered off.

My mind thought of Harrison, its quiet streets, school. Miss Eunice. I shook my head. "I don't think I'd like the city. I wouldn't see Miss Eunice every day. I know she has the next book of *Anne of Greene Gables* just waiting for me when I get home. How would I talk to her about it? And what about Daddy? How would he find us? And New York is farther away from Grandma and Otis. What if we weren't able to make it back for the strawberry festival?" My voice was getting louder, and I could feel my heart beating in my ears like it had when I was in the bus station bathroom.

"Shhh…Macey May." She smoothed down my hair. "I was thinking out loud, is all."

"How would Miss Adele get on without you? Wouldn't you miss it?" Mama nodded and stood up. "Yes. I suppose I would. It's just—"

"Just what?" I pushed myself up on my elbows.

"What if we stayed for some extra here? Would you like that? Just until Daddy gets back."

I thought of living with Grandma and Otis. With the cows every day and the tire swing. I thought of dinners where it would be more than Mama and me, and I thought maybe Mama wouldn't look out the window all the time and be able to eat. And maybe Mr. King would deliver here whatever Mama kept hoping our mailman would bring back in Harrison. And since Daddy was already here, he wouldn't need to find us. I couldn't wait to tell him. Maybe once he knew we were staying, he'd feel better letting everyone know his whereabouts. We'd be a family again, and the secrets would be gone. Almost.

"Yes'm. I'd like that. But I think it would make Miss Eunice sad if we never went back. You'd let her know, wouldn't you? I wouldn't want her worrying over us. Maybe she could come on the bus and visit." The earlier idea I had about Grandma making Miss Eunice up a room danced before my eyes. Maybe she could teach me here in Grandma's kitchen.

"What about school?" I asked. There were two more full weeks before we broke for Christmas vacation. I knew Miss Eunice wouldn't be happy about me missing more school after already missing a week. And

Mama normally never let me stay home. Even if I had the sniffles, she marched me out the door every morning telling me I could use a tissue at my desk just as well as I could use one in my bed, and that children rarely ever threw up in school corridors even if they feared they would.

She breathed a sigh. "I bet your teachers could put something together for you. It's something I'm thinking about, that's all. Don't worry, though. I'll tell Miss Eunice if we decide to stay on for a while."

Mama's lips brushed my cheek with a kiss. "Good night, Macey May. I love you." She turned around before she left the room. "Macey May, don't tell anyone about us maybe staying yet, all right? I haven't even brought it up to Grandma."

Another secret. I didn't know where to keep them all. One more and I was afraid they would all spill out of me, a puddle of them around my feet with everyone running around trying to scoop up the ones belonging to them. I nodded. "I won't. Love you too, Mama."

Otis came in a while later to check on me. I expected he would. He knew that storms scared me. He sat at the edge of the bed and counted out the seconds between the lightning and the thunderclaps. "One, two, three, four, five, six, seven— Boom! You know the longer the time between the two lets you know the storm's moving out. Won't be much time now before the sky breaks open, and we see the stars, I reckon. I was counting four between them not long ago, and now it's almost doubled."

Thunder clapped loud outside, and I flinched. "Otis, do you remember when I saw the White Lady last year?"

He nodded. "I remember you telling me."

"Do you think she's still out there in the storm?" I never believed she wanted to hurt anyone, but I didn't want Daddy to meet up with her. What if she told about seeing him?

Otis patted my legs. "No, I reckon she has a place to go, keep herself dry and warm. How about I tell you a story? Maybe get your mind off of the storm and the White Lady?"

I shook my head.

"You sure? Wouldn't believe the trouble that chicken's got himself into since the last time you were here." He smiled, but his eyes looked sad, apologetic.

If only a story would calm me, I thought, but the talking chicken wasn't ever going to be a cat and climb a tree no matter how much it believed it could, and I felt like I had been swimming with my own alligators. And they weren't friendly. "Maybe tomorrow," I said and feigned a yawn. I didn't want to hurt his feelings, but I knew those stories couldn't help me anymore.

"Probably better anyway. Get some sleep, sugar. It's been a long day." Otis kissed my forehead and shut the light off.

I nodded, rolled over, and fell asleep.

A clap of thunder rocked my bed, and I found myself sitting upright, the pillow flung on the floor against the wall. My heart pounded against my chest, and my cheeks were wet with tears. Junior's face, left over from my dream, embedded itself in my eyelids, and I rubbed them trying to make his image go away. We had been in the bathroom, his hand on my leg, his fingers creeping to where they shouldn't be. My throat felt tight and achy like I had been holding back a scream.

Thunder punched the sky. A switch breaking the air before it hit skin. From my bed I could see the rain striking the window, pebbles of water beating it with such force, like nature was mad at being left outside and wanted to get in. A pulsating red light from the yard snuck in through the curtains, creating a ghoulish harmony with the thunder, steady—a beating heart on the bedroom walls. I never remembered lightning being that color. Certainly, Otis had never told me a reason for it. I was surprised that Grandma or Mama hadn't come up to check on me, but then loud voices from downstairs echoed up through the floors overtaking the noise out front. Thunder cracked again. I thought of Daddy.

I jumped out of bed and ran to the window, pulling the curtains aside. A police car sat in the middle of the driveway, its red lights acting as a signal beacon. I cupped my hands against the glass forming a makeshift telescope, and peered through the rain to the outcropping of trees near the water. Out of the corner of my eye, I saw a figure. Daddy? Maybe he was hurt? Or in trouble. I thought of telling Mama. Certainly he wouldn't be mad at me if he needed help. His words formed in my mind. "Macey May," he had said to me, "promise me you'll not tell anyone I'm here. Promise me." I couldn't tell anyone; I had promised. Daddy told me never to break a promise. And he had never broken one to me.

I walked out to the top of the stairs on the second-floor landing. Below, Otis and Denim were talking, and Grandma was telling Mama it was going to be okay. I could see the black boots of the officer standing at the edge of the hallway. There'd be no way to pass them and get out the front door, but I could try to sneak out if they made me go back to bed. I stepped down the stairs, rubbing my eyes as if just awakened.

"Mama? What's going on?"

Mama looked up from her chair at the kitchen table, her eyes rimmed red. When she saw me, she straightened up and blotted her eyes with a handkerchief. "Macey May, honey, why are you up?"

"The thunder woke me, and then I didn't know what the red lights were."

The police officer turned toward Grandma, his hat in his hand. "Sorry, Cora Lee. Didn't even think about it. Let me go and shut them off." He nodded at me when he went by, and soon the red lights were gone, and he was back in the kitchen.

"Is everything all right?" I looked at Otis this time, and he shook his head.

"No, sugar. There seems to have been an accident." He coughed.

"Daddy?"

Grandma put her arm around me. "No, child. Junior."

My skin began to sweat. "Junior?"

Mama cleared her throat and the room quieted.

Denim was the first to speak. "He's dead, Macey May."

A chill ran through me, and I involuntarily shuddered. From the cold or the information, I couldn't tell.

"Officer Paul came to tell us and ask if we had seen him. I guess he told his daddy earlier in the day that he thought he'd come over for a visit and a piece of my chocolate pecan pie. We never saw him, though." Grandma looked again at Mama as if to confirm it. Mama nodded in affirmation. I couldn't tell what the policeman was thinking, if he believed them or not.

"I never saw him either," I said, eager to substantiate their claim.

"Of course you didn't. None of us did. It must have happened on the way here. It's just Junior and I were old friends. I'll miss him." Mama looked tired. "Why don't you go back to bed. We'll move into the living room and close the door so it won't be as loud. There's a little more talking we need to do."

"That's right. I'll bring in some coffee for us." Aunt Ruby stood up and went to the cupboard.

I hadn't even noticed her sitting there at the table, she had been so quiet. When I looked at her now, her skin was pale and she was pushing down her skirt with her hands like Mama did when the nerves got to her.

Otis smiled at me. "Remember to count. It will be fine. Up to about eleven now."

I wasn't sure if I believed him. The claps and flashes seemed as consistent as ever. Louder, angrier even. But I knew the grown-ups wanted me to go so they could talk, and I wasn't eager to stay. "I'll use the bathroom then go up." Mama hugged me one last time, and I walked down the hall.

Through the bathroom door I could hear them making their way into the living room, and finally the big oak pocket door being pulled across but not before the word "murdered" made it to my ears.

I grabbed a towel from the linen closet. If that was Daddy outside, I knew he'd be wet and cold. He couldn't stay out all night in this weather. And with Junior killed, it wouldn't be safe for him to be out there all alone. Now he'd have to tell people he was here. I closed the front door behind me as quietly as I could and ran behind the cruiser, across the yard and into the woods, my bare feet sloshing in the puddled grass. "Daddy? Daddy?" A hand touched my shoulder, and I turned around.

It was her. The White Lady.

She put a finger to her lips, hushing me, and grabbed my wrist. With one hand she pulled me to the edge of the creek, moving faster than I could keep up, the towel lost somewhere behind me. My wet feet slipped, and my knees hit the ground. Mud covered the bottom of my nightgown, the pink gingham turning into putrid gray. My cry momentarily stopped her. The wind was too loud, taking my voice with it as it thrashed against the branches of the trees. She used both her hands to pull me up. "We have to go. Hurry," she said. "There's no time to waste. Hush."

We were out of sight of the front of the house now. I knew no one could see me from the front porch or my bedroom window, and it would be at least an hour before Grandma or Otis even thought of checking on me.

She pulled me down to my knees beside her. We were along the top of the embankment, and I was afraid I'd fall into the water below. "Caroline! Shhh…baby. Mama's here." The White Lady bent low, her knees sinking into the soil next to me. Her voice was high, her words barely audible above the thunderclaps, and I had to strain and focus on her lips to understand what she was saying to me. Lightning illuminated the sky, and for the first time I saw her clearly. I had always imagined her a wisp of a woman, a ghost. A haint that flew on the night air. All the times I had seen her before were from afar. I never believed she was actual flesh and bone.

But here she was. As real and true in front of me as Mama or Grandma or Miss Eunice. Her blond hair was crazed about her face, a patch of it missing from her left temple as if someone had ripped it right out. I instinctively looked at her fingers expecting to see pieces of it tangled around them, a spider web of sorts. A pink barrette, a plastic butterfly like one that came with a baby doll I had seen in the window of the Five and Dime, had attached itself haphazardly upside down to a clump of her hair.

Dark circles surrounded her eyes, and her lips were cracked. The corners of her mouth were etched with blood that at one time had been caked dry but now, because of the rain or saliva, had reconstituted itself and slithered in pink rivulets down her chin and neck. Her skin was white, translucent, and it looked cold, if skin could look that way, and I wondered the last time it had seen the bright Georgia sun.

I opened my mouth to scream, to cry for someone even though I knew it would be fruitless. Nothing came out. Where was Daddy? He had promised I'd be safe now.

She pushed herself up and dragged me with her farther down along the creek. "Come on, we need to get you out. You can't stay there anymore. Mama's here to take you home."

I was crying now, choking, my voice barely audible squeaks, but her grip remained tight. "Please, please let me go. I'm not Caroline. I'm Macey May."

At the mention of my name, she turned toward me, her eyes locking with mine even though it didn't seem like she was seeing me at all. "You are so beautiful. I always knew you'd be beautiful. Just like your daddy.

Your brown skin, your dark eyes." What did she mean? How did she know my daddy?

Above her lightning streaked the sky. She cowered underneath it. "Quick," she said, "before they see us." She was pulling me faster and faster, our feet slick and sliding on the soil. "He never wanted me to have you from the start. He said she was dead. But I heard you cry. I know I did. A mother knows her child's voice." She stopped. "I felt her kick when she left me. Why wouldn't he let me have you? Why did he have to take my baby girl away? I saw him, you know. Saw him take you out of the house out along the water. No one would believe me, though."

We were moving along the edge near the back acres. If someone was in the kitchen looking out the back window, it was possible if the lightning was right that they would be able to see me. "Here. Right here," she said. "Help me." She dropped to her knees, her hands ripping away at the wet ground. Grabbing the bottom hem of my nightgown, she pulled me down next to her, her face close to mine, her breath at once both putrid and warm. "Caroline. I'm here to take you home where you won't be alone anymore. Mama's missed you so." She put her hand on my cheek; her nails were broken and cracked and covered in dirt.

She picked up a flat rock next to her and cut into the ground. I had never seen anyone so determined before. "Hurry. They'll be here soon. He doesn't want me to get her. He wants you to stay down there. That's no place to be. It's dark and wet, and she must be terribly frightened."

I stared into the hole she had dug, remnants of her deranged mission strewn across her face speckling it with bits of earth, her bare arms now dark up to her elbows.

"There!" She grabbed my hand and held it to her chest. "I see it. I knew she was here. I've always known."

Below, the corner of a pink knitted blanket encased in mud emerged from the remains of a plastic bag, an early bulb of some flower I knew instinctively I didn't want to see. The White Lady reached over and fever-ishly excavated the rest of it, her fingers working like hordes of beetles moving the dirt away and up the sides. With both hands she lifted what was in…out.

Animals die on the farm. On highways, they get hit by cars and left on the side of the road. Hunters who shoot but have poor tracking skills leave the animals limping back into the woods for their final breath. Nature does her due diligence as the seasons change. I'd seen skeletons of feral cats attacked by the coyotes and bodies of mice decomposed in the traps. I'd seen whole carcasses of deer picked clean by eagles and vultures until the bone beneath is so sun bleached it's blinding to look at. I'd even seen a dog carrying an entire rib cage down the street, enough bones to last him a month, but I had never seen a dead baby.

I knew that's what I was looking at now.

She held the pink bundle in her arms, the remains of the yarn ripped, frayed, decomposed. A few grubs coiled and recoiled themselves in the weave, upset that their home and dinner had been disturbed. I felt bile rise in my mouth. Wisps of black hair, kinked and coiled atop white bone, stuck out, and as she caressed the strands, they came off on her fingers, stuck there by the glue of the cold rain. A toe, or what I assumed was a toe, protruded out from beneath. "See," she said, holding the bundle out to me, "you are so beautiful. My baby girl, Caroline."

"Macey May?"

I heard my name carried over the rain in the distance.

"Daddy?"

Whether she heard the voice or not, I couldn't tell, but her voice was getting louder, more agitated. "I have to baptize her. The church says she needs to be cleansed. He never washed her. God won't let her in unless she's clean. Mama will clean you, Caroline." She stood up. One hand clutched the bones close to her chest, one clutched me. "I will make you clean."

I didn't know where she got her strength, but her grip on my arm was too tight, and as I tried to pull away, her nails dug into my skin. Sprinkles of red mixed in with the rain, and the blood ran down my arm.

"Macey May, I'm coming!"

I turned my head and saw my daddy running full speed along the tree line. With all my strength, I twisted from her, her nails ripping my skin as I wrenched myself away. "Daddy!"

And then he was there, holding me, kissing my cheeks, my forehead.

The White Lady slid down the embankment and waded out into the creek. The water was high now, the current fast. She slipped once and went under. She came up sputtering, the pink blanket now empty of its contents.

"Caroline!" She screamed in a voice so genuinely pained that, in that instant, I prayed I would never know anything in my life that would cause me to sound that way. I didn't think one could survive it.

"Macey May!" Daddy looked frantic, his hair plastered against his head, his shirt a second skin. "Run to the house and get help."

When I didn't move he grabbed me by the shoulders. "Now, Macey May. Go!"

When I looked back he was running into the water after her.

Chapter 18

CRAWFORD, GEORGIA
CORA LEE JENKINS
1962

THE VOICE WAS SOFT in the distance, and Cora Lee turned her good ear toward the closed living room door, not sure if she was even hearing it. Was Macey May calling for her? Officer Paul was finishing up explaining what had happened to Junior, and try as she may, Cora Lee could not get the horrible vision out of her head. She wondered if it would be there along with Hi's dangling foot whenever she closed her eyes from now on. However, she couldn't protect her girls from this picture. Someone had called in to the station to say that a truck was off Porter's Road still running, driver's side door wide open. When Officer Paul got to the scene, he found Junior's body not far from the road, covered lightly with brush in a small ravine.

His neck had been broken—by someone's hands. Black and blue marks all around the gullet. It had been twisted near backwards. His eyes were wide open, looking at someone or something that wasn't there anymore.

"Whoever did it," Officer Paul continued, "knew how to cover his tracks. Not a stitch of footprints to be seen. Maybe a Green Beret," he suggested. "I knew a few of them when I was in the service…stealthy buggers. Wouldn't know they were even on you until minutes after you were dead." He paused as if thinking back to a particular time, a specific space in his past. "Luckily, they were on our side. There was something else at the scene, though. Strange, really."

Otis rubbed the back of his neck. "What's that?"

"This." Officer Paul reached into his chest pocket and pulled out a photograph. "What do you make of it?"

Otis looked at the picture and passed it to Cora Lee.

"Why'd he have this?" Cora Lee studied the photo.

Cora Lee extended her hand to Rose, the thin black and white monochromatic paper flimsy around the edges, worn.

Rose flinched when the picture touched her fingers. "That's Macey May."

"Is it Junior's?" Officer Paul scratched his head.

Only Cora Lee noticed the hesitation in Rose's response. "Yes. I sent one to him in his Christmas card last year. That's Macey May in fourth grade."

"Must've had it in his pocket and it came loose during the scuffle," Denim said.

Officer Paul nodded.

"Maybe fell out of his wallet?" Otis added.

"Yeah, maybe. Didn't find the wallet anywhere."

"Think this could be a robbery gone bad?" Denim asked.

"If it is, it's the worst I've ever seen. There has to be a lot of anger in a man to almost wretch someone's head off. Seems a bit overkill for a few dollars and some change."

The men kept talking while Cora Lee studied her oldest daughter. She watched as Rose's facial muscles tensed, the jugular vein in her neck becoming more distinct as her jaw clenched tighter and tighter, fighting, it seemed, to keep something down. Her fingers splayed out across the blue material of her dress covering her lap. She sat straight, taut, her gaze set ahead, looking off somewhere in her mind's eye. Yes, Cora Lee thought,

Rose was keeping something from her. A lie, an omission, a secret, she didn't know, but it was evident since she came—evident to Cora Lee, at least, since Macey May's singular arrival on the bus that things were not as they should be back in Harrison. She looked again at Rose, the photo bending under the tautness of her fingers.

Cora Lee knew one thing for certain. There had been no school picture last year. Macey May had been home sick with a cold the day they were taking them. The picture in Rose's hand was from this year. Four wallets. One for her, one for Rose, one sent to Ruby, and one for Curtis. There wouldn't have been any left to send one to Junior.

She replayed Officer Paul's words in her mind. The discovering of Junior's body, the detailed image of how he died. Replayed it all searching for a key. Rose hadn't showed any reaction other than shock and sadness like the rest of them to the news. It wasn't until he mentioned the Green Berets, the service, and showed them the picture that Rose's body had a visceral reaction.

And then Cora Lee remembered. Curtis had been in the service. In Korea.

Ruby sat in the chair near the side table wiping her tears away with a tissue, more tears than Cora Lee imagined were justified for her relationship with Junior. Had Ruby had a crush on him that she didn't know about? She raked her memory. Maybe? Always the younger sister, Junior had treated Ruby as such, pulling her pigtails, asking about boyfriends. That was as far as she could recall it going, from his side at least.

Cora Lee remembered Rose's anger in catching Ruby outside the living room window eavesdropping on her and Junior's conversations through the screen those warm summer nights when he would stop over. Ruby had acted the "bratty little sister" to perfection. But Ruby looked so broken now, and Rose was lost somewhere in her mind, that Cora Lee wondered if she ever knew her girls at all. If in trying to keep Hi's death a fiction to them, she had essentially disavowed herself from being part of their reality.

How many heartbreaks had they suffered while she remained unaware?

The men's conversation leaked back into her consciousness. "At least he had to be in some branch of the service. No one else would know how to do that so well. Heck, they don't even train *us* to do that." Officer Paul laughed a little and then caught himself. He cleared his throat and took his hat off, running his fingers through his hair. "No disrespect meant."

Denim had been pacing the floor listening to the story. "Did you check at the bar? Had he been drinking there? Playing cards? You know Junior can get downright impudent when he combines the two. You would think with it being Thanksgiving he would have held off, stayed home. Tom doesn't need this. It's bad enough poor Abby...I mean Abigail...with Mrs. Walsh the way she is...damn it."

Officer Paul looked down at his feet. "She didn't take the news well either. Started hitting Tom so I stepped in to restrain her, but he waved me off. Told me her nurse was scheduled to come any minute, and he said he'd make sure they sedated her. She's supposed to go back to the sanitorium later tonight—only home for the day, I guess. You should have heard her, though. Talking crazy. Blaming him for taking her children from her. They only have the one. Had one, I mean. Junior. Man. Not sure I can talk about him in the past tense just yet. I told Tom I'd stay until she got calmed down, but he told me no, that he wanted me out there finding his son's killer."

He rubbed his chin. "And then she started wailing. Never heard a woman cry like that before. Made me think I was trespassing in a conversation I had no place hearing. Don't know how Tom has dealt with it all these years."

Otis got up from the chair and stood next to him, his hands on his hips. "If someone from out of town was at the bar…well, you never know what they might do…might have done. Especially if they caught him cheating or got tired of hearing him talk the way he does like he owns this town. Any strange cars around today? Although I suspect with the holiday there's probably more than usual."

It was well-known throughout town that not only was Junior a mean drunk, especially when he was playing cards, but he was also a cheat. More than once he had spent a night in jail after getting in a fight with some-one who found him cutting the deck. His daddy always came in the next day and posted bail, asked with the lowering of his head and voice if they could "see fit" to keep this little indiscretion under their hats. It wouldn't have made any difference, the news was out long before anything could be covered up, and besides, a leopard didn't change its spots. Most people never understood who Mr. Walsh was trying to fool.

"The bar is my next stop. Wanted to come here first and see if I could establish a timeline. He left not too long after dinner, and they ate early. Thought he might have stopped over here to say 'hey.' He'd been gone almost four hours since he was home."

Cora Lee stood up and spoke. "I did invite him to come on over for pie, but he never showed. No time specifically, just mentioned it to him when I bumped into him at the bus station a few days ago. I was picking up Macey May. He likes my chocolate pecan."

Officer Paul looked at his watch. "I need to get going. Thank you again and Denim, Otis, if you hear anything…"

Otis and Denim both nodded.

"I'll show myself out." Officer Paul tipped his hat.

No one moved as they listened to his footsteps down the hall-way and heard the door open and close. In the distance, the cruiser engine turned over. Outside the rain continued. It was coming in sideways now. It lashed against the windows creating a vision of a blurred world.

Rose stood up, the photograph of Macey May fluttering to the floor. "I need a glass of water." She was on her way to the kitchen when they heard the scream.

"Help! Otis, Grandma. Help!"

This time the voice wasn't soft, and Cora Lee wasn't the only one who heard it. Denim ran to the window and looked out. "My God. It's Macey May."

Rose shook her head, a look of confusion across her face. "Macey May? Outside?"

Cora Lee was out the door and onto the porch before anyone could stop her. There was Macey May standing on the lawn. Her nightgown was dirty and wrapped around her wet skin and water dripped off of the ends of her hair and down her face. Even from the distance, Cora Lee could see the cuts on the tops of her bare feet. "Child, what are you doing out here? What's wrong?" she shouted.

Otis raced past her into the rain, picked up Macey May, and brought her into the house. "Quick, Rose, get a towel. Poor thing's soaked to the bone. And so cold. Ruby, put some hot water on. We've got to get her warm." He reached to the back of the couch and pulled down the afghan that was there, covering her in it. He looked again at Ruby who seemed paralyzed. "Ruby, now. Go!"

Cora Lee sat down at her feet, rubbing them together with her hands. Why had she gone out in the storm in only her nightgown and bare feet? Macey May was shaking, her teeth chattering, her toes blue and purple under the dirt. She tried to push herself up off the couch. "No." The words gritted themselves between her teeth. "Help."

"Shhh, baby. Help is here. Grandma's gonna take care of you."

Ruby's scream came from the kitchen. "Curtis!" She was in the living room now, her eyes wide. "Out the kitchen window. I swear I saw Curtis down in the water and there was someone—"

Cora Lee looked at Otis in confusion. Curtis was in California now, far away from this. Wasn't he?

Rose ran in with the towel. "Curtis?"

"The White Lady," Macey May finished. "She's out there and going to drown if we don't help Daddy."

Otis looked at Denim and spoke quickly. "Grab some rope from the shed and a flashlight. We're going to need 'em."

Macey May pushed the afghan off and put her feet on the floor. "No, baby," Cora Lee said. "You're staying here."

Cora Lee looked at Rose, at her daughter. "Rose. Stay with Macey May." When Rose didn't acknowledge her, Cora Lee walked over and put her hand on her cheek. "I know, baby. I know. We're gonna get rid of all these secrets, the two of us, but not right now. Right now you've got to be strong for your baby." She took her by the hand and guided her to the couch. "Now, you both sit right here. Ruby, get on the phone and call the sheriff. Tell him to get Officer Paul back over here. Call Dr. Walters too. Looks like we'll be needing him."

Cora Lee met up with the men outside. The rain hadn't slowed, and the clip in which it came down made it even more difficult to see. "Stay away from the edge," she reminded them as they worked their way toward the creek. "Ground doesn't hold up well in this rain, and it's likely to cave in. There's a place a bit up where the rocks are more stable. We can access the water there."

The White Lady. For years Macey May had spoken about her on her trips to the farm. Otis humored her, listened to her stories, but Cora Lee didn't. Wouldn't hear any of it. Even with her belief in mourning air, she never believed Macey May's ghost was real. A figment of her overactive imagination. Now, she wished she had listened.

The thunder sounded like a train barreling full speed down the track, the power of it moving into the soft ground, reverberating up their legs. Flashes of lightning along with the bluish hue of the full moon illuminated their steps. It was a night for ghosts—past and present.

When they came to the water, Cora Lee stopped in her tracks.

The White Lady. And there was no mistaking Curtis, a few feet away from her, his hand outstretched to her. He was a long way from the West Coast.

The spectral image splashed around in the water, an inhuman howl emanating from it. Spinning and turning in a frantic motion, her arms were entwined in what looked to Cora Lee to be remnants of a pink blanket. Curtis stepped closer, touched her shoulder. She reeled away as if his touch was fire, her screams getting louder. "Where is she?" she cried.

Cora Lee heard the words. Was there someone else in the water with them?

"Please, my baby! She's alive. I know she is."

The White Lady lost her balance in the current and went under the water.

"Abby!" Denim screamed.

Cora Lee watched as Denim quickly tied the rope around his waist and then around a tree. In seconds he was running toward the water.

Curtis reached down to grab the White Lady. She was beyond understanding what he was trying to do, and her frantic motion caused him to lose his footing. Her arms were wild, fingers clawing at him, pushing on his head while she flailed in an attempt to keep from being dragged down by the current again. Her screams didn't stop. Cora Lee remembered hearing once that the biggest issue with saving someone from drowning was not being drowned by them in their panic. Watching Curtis in the water, she believed it.

Otis slid down the side of the creek and jumped into the water as both Abigail and Curtis went under. "Keep the flashlight on me, Cora," he said.

"Abigail!" Tom Walsh's voice boomed across the creek, a roar of thunder in its own right.

Abigail bobbed up a few feet from Denim's reach.

"Curtis?! Do you see him, Cora Lee? Where did he go?" Otis screamed.

Time stopped. Cora Lee watched the goings-on in slow motion. Otis desperately searching the water for Curtis, Mr. Walsh running toward them, Denim stretching out his hands toward Abigail, calling her Abby with the same level of fear in his voice as in her lament for her missing baby. Cora Lee caught her breath. Mrs. Walsh was the White Lady. How had she not realized it before? Abigail was the ghost that Macey May had been seeing all these years.

Curtis's head emerged from the water and went back under. "Otis, there!" Cora Lee screamed and moved the light. "Behind you. Curtis!"

With both arms Denim grabbed Abigail and held her to him, his arms encircling her chest, his voice speaking something into her ear that seemed to calm her down. Cora Lee watched her collapse into him. He smoothed her hair down with his hand and kissed her cheek, her forehead, her lips. Cora Lee blinked, not sure what she was seeing.

Life moved fast forward, sped up to match the noise and chaos around it.

Denim had just kissed a white woman.

The remains of the pink blanket washed onto the shore. In the corner of her memory, a scene worked its way in. She was sitting at home surrounded by reams of pink and blue yarn. Hi had asked her why she was making both. "A dead bunny still doesn't tell the sex, now does it?" she replied. "Since I don't know what Mrs. Walsh is having, I'm making two blankets—one of each color." She had given the pair to Mr. Walsh, but they never got to use either one. Mrs. Walsh's second child—a daughter—was born still.

After that, Mrs. Walsh hadn't been right. Cora Lee couldn't blame her, couldn't imagine what the loss of a child that late in a pregnancy would do to a woman. From what she had heard, Mr. Walsh was the only one home when it happened, and Mrs. Walsh delivered the sad thing on the bathroom floor with him helping her. When he realized the baby was dead, he took her away without even showing her. Poor woman never even got to hold her baby girl or feel her skin against her cheek, smell her scent.

Cora Lee couldn't understand what made Mr. Walsh do that—not allow her to see her own child. It seemed to her it would make the grieving that much more complicated. It hadn't helped none either that he wouldn't allow for a proper burial. The child wasn't buried anywhere, not even a grave to mourn at. He said he had the coroner dispose of the body, and then he made it seem like she had never existed. Most people nodded their heads in a knowing way the first time the ambulance had to come and take Mrs. Walsh off to the sanatorium for a "rest"; most people eventually stopped nodding as the years went by.

"Get your black hands off my wife!" Tom Walsh's voice barreled across the storm matched with the short barrel of his pistol pointed at Denim. Mr. Walsh turned toward Cora Lee, his eyes filled with a hate that she had never seen before. "Did you know? Did Hi tell you about them? Him and my Abby? I couldn't let them get away with it. Did you think I was going to allow one of those in my house, under my roof, eating my food? Walking through this town making me a laughingstock?"

He cocked the gun and nodded at Denim. "And I'll take care of you, too."

She looked over at Otis who was diving under once again searching for Curtis, unaware through the rain and thunder what was happening on shore. Mr. Walsh's words fused together. *Hi and Abby?* Her head screamed *no* back at the thought. Her heart screamed it back even louder. Cora Lee looked at the strings of the blanket. A pink baby blanket knitted by her hands for Abigail's new baby girl. What had she been screaming? *The baby wasn't dead...she had felt it move.* Cora Lee closed her eyes. Hi's foot swinging from the tree. A bullet hole through the chest. Mr. Walsh's gun pointed at Denim's chest, his words still clinging to the rain. *He couldn't let them get away with it.*

"Denim! I need our baby. I need Caroline." Abigail's words wrenched themselves through the air, finding the crevices of space between the thunder, exposing themselves through the illumination of the lightning. "Where is our baby? She was alive. I know she was. Denim, I heard her cry."

Mr. Walsh staggered on a root and the gun went off into the ground. Abigail screamed. He looked at Denim. "Your baby? No. It was Hi's, I tell you. I know it was. I—"

"Tom! Tom! Put the gun down." Officer Paul was ten yards away, his revolver pointed at Tom.

Tom whipped around, the gun's aim now erratic. He lifted one hand to his face and wiped the rain from his eyes.

"Come on, Tom. Before someone gets hurt." Officer Paul's aim remained steady.

"It's too late for that."

Cora Lee became aware of the passage of time, of the other present that was unfolding before her. She watched as Otis's movements slowed in the water, saw his arms empty. And she wondered how she would ever tell Rose and Macey May.

Curtis.

He had been under too long.

Officer Paul walked slowly toward Tom. "What are you talking about, Tom? It's never too late. We can figure this all out. No one blames you. You're hurting over losing Junior. You're not thinking straight. And the stress is making Abigail talk nonsense. Now, hand me the gun." He reached his hand out.

As if by magic or God himself wanting everyone to witness what was about to happen so there would be no question, no misunderstanding regarding the events about to transpire, the rain stopped and a clap of thunder loud enough to break open the earth quaked the ground around them. Lightning lit the sky. Abigail screamed, her mouth an "O", her eyes terrified. Cora Lee followed her gaze and saw Tom lift the gun into his mouth and pull the trigger.

Chapter 19

CRAWFORD, GEORGIA
ROSE JOHNSON
1962

ROSE WAS SITTING on the couch with Macey May when she heard the first gunshot. Her body felt it as if the bullet had ripped through her skin, and her leg kicked up in reflex. To verify it wasn't thunder, she looked at her sister. The fear reflected on Ruby's face confirmed it.

"Watch Macey May, Ruby."

She was out of the house on her way to the creek before Ruby had a chance to argue. From the distance she could see Otis down a ways in the water searching for something, his hands splayed out in half circles reaching under and coming up empty. Denim stood chest high in the murkiness ten yards away from him, his arms wrapped around Mrs. Walsh, her cries blending with the storm itself. She saw Mr. Walsh staring down at them from the edge. Even from her distance she understood that he was crazed, a gun in his hand, pointing first at Cora Lee and then at Denim.

Mr. Walsh was speaking, his words garbled through the rain. She watched his mouth form the sentence. "I couldn't let them get away with it."

She had never seen Mr. Walsh without a tie and jacket, his hair meticulously combed to cover the spot at the top of his head when it wasn't covered by a hat. This man was no one she had seen before. His shirt, once tucked in and proper, had expelled itself from his belt, a few busted buttons exposing a white T-shirt underneath. There were mud stains on the knees of his pants from where, Rose assumed, he had stumbled on his way to get there. His wet comb-over, plastered now by the rain, escaped into his collar and left the top of his head bald.

I couldn't let them get away with it. What did he mean?

Officer Paul was trying to get him to put the gun down. He motioned with his hand that he wasn't going to harm him. And then Mr. Walsh did it—killed himself—right there in front of all of them.

Cora Lee stood unflinching as if she had made her peace with whichever way Mr. Walsh had chosen to point the gun.

"Mama!" Rose ran over to Cora Lee.

Denim emerged from the creek, a watery leviathan with two heads and four legs. Abigail's arms were wrapped tightly around his neck, her body in his arms. Her shoulders continued to shake, but her wails had lessened to a whimpering that trailed them both. He set her gently down on the ground and sat himself down right next to her, never letting her go.

Otis had skittered up the embankment to Cora Lee and embraced her. Rose reached out to touch her mother's hair. "Mama? Mama? Say something." Cora Lee didn't move, her gaze fastened on Mr. Walsh's body a few yards away.

"Otis, is she okay?" Rose's eyes narrowed, her lips set.

Cora Lee batted her hand away from her hair. She pushed her way out of Otis's arms and walked over to Tom's dead body.

Rose looked down along the tree line and scanned the water. *Curtis?* She thought back to Ruby. Maybe she had been mistaken. The distance from the kitchen window was far, the weather awful. Perhaps she only thought she had seen Curtis; maybe it had been Mr. Walsh all along. But Macey May had said it herself, that Daddy was there in the water trying to save a woman.

"Otis, where's Curtis?" Rose knew the answer before he said it, felt it rip through her like the sound of the bullet had moments earlier.

"Honey, I'm so sorry. I couldn't…"

The speed of the water was slowing with the passing of the storm. *He came back,* she thought. It was true. She hadn't believed it would happen, was sure that this time was it. But Curtis had come back to them. "If anyone can survive this, he'll do it," she said.

Officer Paul interrupted them. "I'll call in and get some men to start looking downstream. They'll find him, Rose." He paused and looked over at Cora Lee standing over Mr. Walsh's body. "I know I saw it with my own eyes, but I still can't believe it."

Cora Lee moved closer to the body.

Officer Paul held his hand up and raised his voice above the last droplets of rain as he made his way over. "Cora Lee, you need to step back. This is a crime scene. I can't have anything disturbed until we've checked everything over."

"He's dead, Paul. You saw what he did. What's to check?"

He shook his head. "I know, but there's protocol, laws."

Cora Lee scoffed. "Laws? You're going to talk to me about laws? Seems to me there've been laws about killing, about lynching, but no one seems to enforce those."

"Honey?" Otis stood behind her, his hand on her back. "Come on now. This can be done later."

"Mama." Rose reached out and squeezed Cora Lee's hand; it was cold and wet. "Otis, we need to take her inside. The doctor should be there by now."

"No." Cora Lee's voice was soft but strong, strengthening in its reserve when she spoke again. "No. I don't need the doctor. I'm fine. I'm more than fine."

Rose looked at her mother and was sure that if Cora Lee could, she would spit on Tom Walsh's body.

The storm had left with the end of their own tempest, and now the air stilled. Before Dr. Walters had left, he had assured Rose that Macey May would be fine, physically. She only suffered a few cuts and scrapes that would heal within the week. He wasn't sure how long it would take for the other healing to take place.

"Rose," he said. "This I do know. Children are resilient. They come through situations that would leave a grown man paralyzed. Give her time and she'll come around." He had given Rose some sleeping pills to take for a couple of nights, for both her and Macey May, to make sure they got the rest they needed. "Remember, that girl's going to require everything you can give her right now. You've got to take care of yourself." She had given one to Macey May as soon as he left but hadn't taken one herself. She needed her wits about her if any of it was going to make sense. She still couldn't understand everything that had happened that night; she had been trying to put the pieces of the puzzle together and kept coming up a corner short.

Rose sat motionless in the rocking chair on the porch, her feet placed square on the floor in front of her, her eyes staring off across the yard seeing nothing. Macey May slept on the cot under blankets a few feet away. Rose was glad that the medicine had worked. The voices of Ruby and Otis whispered through the window behind her. Denim had followed the ambulance that had taken Abigail to the hospital. Another ambulance had taken the body of Mr. Walsh. There had been no news about the search for Curtis.

"Honey?" The screen door opened with a yawn and closed quietly behind Cora Lee. "Thought you might like some sweet tea? Brought you a sandwich, too. Bacon and tomato." She placed them down on the table next to her. "You've got to eat. These next few days going to be tough ones for a lot of reasons."

"I don't understand it. What was Mr. Walsh talking about, Mama? And what you said to Officer Paul about murder and lynching? What's going on?"

Cora Lee looked out into the night. "I'll explain it later. I don't have it in me right now, but I promise."

"And then Denim, in the water with Mrs. Walsh…calling her Abigail. I saw him kiss her. Mama, were they lovers?"

"I think so."

Rose shook her head. "Did you know?"

"Nope. Seemed to be happening right under my nose for years, and I never saw it."

Rose absently took a bite of the sandwich and a sip of tea.

"I believe there's a lot that happens in front of us that we never see for what it really is until we are far enough away from it to look at it differently." Cora Lee sat down in the chair and began to rock.

"Mama, I think Curtis did it."

"Did what?"

"Killed Junior."

"Rose, what makes you say something like that? Curtis is a hero. He was trying to save Abigail…he did save Abigail. She would have drowned if it hadn't been for him."

Rose shook her head. "No, I know that, but…"

"What is it?"

"That picture."

"The one of Macey May?"

Rose nodded. "It belongs to Curtis. He carries it in his wallet." For a moment Rose looked down at her hands. "Mama, he wasn't always right. I mean…I don't know how to explain it. Sometimes back home, he wasn't there with me. It was like he was still back…in the war." Rose studied Cora Lee's face. She saw lines around her mouth, a strain behind her eyes, gray hairs speckling her temples, signs of aging she'd never paid attention to. "Mama, if they find him, if he made it and is running, what will they do to him?"

Cora Lee stopped rocking. "I don't know about that, but, Rose, the water was fast. Otis saw him go under. He tried to grab him before he was swept away. I just don't want you—"

Rose cut her off. "I'm not ready yet, Mama. Not ready to look Macey May in the eyes and tell her that her daddy's dead. I can't do it, can't think it. It's too much." She stood and walked to the edge of the porch and leaned into the post. "Mama, how'd you do it so easy?"

Cora Lee stopped rocking. "How'd I do what?"

"Making living after Daddy died seem easy, like it was no problem?"

"No problem? Honey, it was a problem, a big one, but I had you and Ruby to look after, same as you have Macey May. Not saying I didn't grieve. Oh, I let myself have that time for sorrow, but that was private time. Didn't need to burden you girls with that."

Rose turned to face Cora Lee. "You know, I never saw you cry."

"Sure you did. You just don't remember."

Rose shook her head. "No, not about Daddy. I used to watch you, waiting for it, anything that showed me how much he meant to you. That it was okay for me to cry. Then you stopped talking about him, wouldn't answer our questions. Made me think you didn't love him, Mama. When the time comes, Macey May's going to see me cry. She'll know I loved Curtis."

This time Rose didn't hide the accusation in her voice.

Chapter 20

HARRISON, GEORGIA
CURTIS JOHNSON
1953

I'M NOT SURE I ever intended to make a life with Rose at first; after all, I understood the world. Harrison had afforded me a long leash, though, and for that I was grateful. No doubt, the job building the railway with some of the locals was a benefit, but I think Rose being who she was helped me the most. She had that power about her, the ability to hold her head high and stare down men who I've seen others cross the street to avoid. She made no apologies.

It was early, a good half-hour before opening when I walked to the bakery to say goodbye, to tell her I was going, leaving for a while to figure things out. I had been forgetting, minutes really, periods of seconds, but enough that I was starting to get scared. I would come back, though—I needed her. And when I came back, healed and whole, I'd bring a ring with me. I knew legally it would stand for nothing, but to me, and I hoped to her, it would mean everything.

The sun streamed through the front window and even behind the counter, standing slightly in the shadow, I could see the green hue to her skin, a paleness to her cheek.

"Honey, you all right? You don't look so good," I said a little bit above a whisper.

"Oh, she's not all right." Adele's voice was loud even from the back of the store. Rose rolled her eyes and sat down on a stool. Adele's feet stomped to the front. Her eyes looked me up and down, her bottom lip sticking out in a know-it-all pout. "No, sugar, she's not fine at all." She wiped her hands on her apron and walked over to me, close, her arms crossed like a bodyguard ready to throw me out the second the boss nodded his way. She craned her neck toward Rose. "You going to tell him, or you want me to? Not sure this one could figure it out on his own. He's gonna need you to spell it out for him. They usually do."

Rose's voice was firm. "Adele, stop it. This is between me and Curtis."

Adele glanced back. "Is it now? Seems to me my only employee can't stomach looking at cakes or smelling pies baking. No, I'd say this is beyond the two of you."

Rose stood up and grabbed her jacket off of the coat rack. "Come on, Curtis. Let's take a walk. The fresh air will do me good."

"It's almost—" Adele sputtered before Rose cut her off.

"Adele, I'll be back in ten minutes. Plenty of time before the first customers get here. Now, please, give me a minute."

Pregnant. Baby. I knew what the words meant, but they didn't make sense. Rose and I had been seeing each other for six weeks, almost every night since I had followed her into the store, but we had only had sex once in her place when she knew the landlord wouldn't be around. I wasn't expecting it. If truth be told, she made the first move. I hadn't even been with a woman since I had come back from Korea—just couldn't seem to think about it the way I used to.

I used protection even though she didn't want me to, said she knew her cycle and it wouldn't matter. I had an old one in my wallet, put there the night of prom three years ago, but in my mind it was better than nothing. I didn't think I was carrying anything around inside me, always made sure I used something in country (the army actually supplied them), and I tried not to kiss the women on the lips either, but sometimes…well, sometimes I needed to feel close. Those times I'd call them Susan or Mary, whatever name reminded me of home. It didn't seem to matter none as long as I paid them. Funny how a kiss felt closer than sex. And I wanted to kiss Rose. Boy, did I want to kiss her.

I felt foolish listening to her, embarrassed that she was needing to air her private life to me, to make excuses, to apologize. I should have known from the start that we wouldn't amount to anything. Rose was out of my league—especially those lavender eyes. Not sure what guy could find himself in that league. I put my hand up to stop her. She didn't owe me this, and I didn't want to hear any more. My mind searched for some way to save my dignity. She was telling me that she was choosing to be with her baby's daddy. That's it. Over.

I knew about her history with Willie Price, heard about that from the guys even before I met her. She had never spoken of it, but we stayed clear from talking about our pasts, like we both were trying to forget—an unspoken agreement. I know why I hadn't thought about her other guys, the ones she no doubt saw when she was looking at me. Same reason I tried not to think about the war.

I could see her lips moving, but the words tumbling from her mouth evaded me. She was leaving me, just like my grandma had, just like Johnny. I'd be all alone in the world again. Sweat broke out on my forehead, and I wiped it off with my handkerchief. I looked down at my shoes, trying to slow down my brain. Time with her made me forget everything—a drug of its own that kept me grounded; how could I give that up? Without her, well, without her the war had won.

There were hints that it already had.

"So?" Rose was looking at me stern-like, her eyebrows creased.

"What?"

"I know this is sudden, but aren't you going to answer me? Have you been listening to anything I've been saying?"

I swallowed, trying to understand what she was saying and why she was asking me anything. It seemed like all she needed to do was to say one last goodbye. I looked at her, and she looked so scared. I cleared my throat. "It's not a lot, but I've got some cash. It's yours if you need it."

"Excuse me?" There was a sharpness in her voice as if I had insulted her, like what I had said was an affront to her decency or just an example of my own stupidity like Adele had said.

I lifted my arms up in surrender. "Rose, I don't know what you expect from me..." *Shouldn't you be talking to him? Whoever him is*, I thought.

Rose sat down next to me and took my hand. "Curtis, look at me." She spoke slowly then. "I'm pregnant with *your* child."

Whether she paused or not to let her words sink in, I don't remember. Perhaps she went on talking, explaining herself, inventing a time frame that even she could make herself believe. I smelled the crispness of apples in the air and new pine waiting for its place on the calendar before it came in full force. I saw the colors change in the sky as the sun heightened, purples and pinks opening up to blues. I felt her hand in my mine, grasping on to it as tightly as her lie.

Your baby, she said.

My baby. I let the lie sit in my brain.

Maybe she hoped Adele was right, that I wouldn't be able to figure it out on my own.

"What are we going to do?" Her voice trembled a little. "Curtis?"

It amazed me how my name could be said in such a way that it took on a hundred meanings, a hundred suggestions and pleas all incorporated into six letters with a lilting of it at the end.

When I thought about it later as we walked through the streets that night planning out our future in Harrison, I know why she did it, why she lied to me, protecting herself the only way she knew how. What other choice did she have? It was 1953.

I knew the simple math didn't work out. Contrary to what Adele thought, I wasn't stupid. Got As in both physics and calculus in high school as well as biology. But it's funny how sometimes one question is all you need to hear to get all the answers you were ever looking for.

"You love me, don't you?" She asked it in earnest, a trip in her throat.

I looked into her eyes. They were so lovely.

"Yes, I do."

That deep unnatural violet.

Those eyes made me believe in God.

For a while at least.

Seven and a half months later when Macey May arrived and her deep brown eyes opened to look into mine, I knew then that it would never matter to me—a calendar, a timeline, none of it. The war, Johnny, Rose's lie to me...all of that was washed away by her little face. What did it matter who her father really was? I'd be her daddy and always protect her.

And I thought, hoped, that those eyes would be enough to keep me.

Chapter 21

CRAWFORD, GEORGIA
MACEY MAY JOHNSON
1962

I THOUGHT I KNEW what chaos was. Chaos was Mama on Sunday mornings when we were running late for church, and she couldn't find her hat to match her purse. Chaos was Thanksgiving afternoon when the oven temperature was erratic and the sweet potato casserole was almost done, but the turkey had at least another hour. Chaos was when Daddy was gone "on a job," and we didn't know when he was coming back, yet I knew the rent was due because it was circled in red on the calendar, and the jar of extra change on the windowsill had been emptied days before, and Mama's eyes were circled dark.

Once they came back to the house, Mama, Grandma, and Otis all rushed to my side, touching my forehead, kissing my cheeks, hugging on me like they wanted to make sure I wasn't some sort of ghost who had come back from the dead only about to disappear into the darkness again. Aunt Ruby looked on me with sad eyes, shaking her head and holding my hands when I asked about Daddy, and they told me they couldn't find him. "I'm sure he'll be okay, though, Macey May," Mama had said. "Your daddy always is." She bit her bottom lip, her eyes swimming in tears close to breaking.

Grandma gave her a look then, crossed between sadness and disapproval, kind of like one Mama had given me when she found out I had been in a fight with Suzy Turner on the school yard during recess. Suzy had referred to Mama as something I couldn't repeat. When I told her and Daddy about it later that night in the kitchen, I had seen that look before she turned around to check on the potatoes she had boiling on the stove.

Sadness and disapproval.

Back then I could understand the disapproval, but I wasn't sure about the sadness. Now I understood the sadness but not the disapproval.

Mama thought that Daddy had been washed downstream with the current or had trod up the bank on the other side when he saw Officer Paul arrive and was hiding away somewhere in the woods, waiting for a time to show himself. I didn't know why seeing a police officer would make Daddy hide no more than I understood why Mama was trying so hard to ignore the truth. I knew he was dead. I could feel it in my heart, in the empty space that had never been there before. I didn't want to hear those words come out of my mouth, like not saying them left a possibility that they weren't truth.

I was sitting in the corner of the living room in the wingback chair, my legs tucked up underneath me, when Aunt Ruby brought me a cup of tea with honey, the steam rising up in miniature clouds, warming my face as it passed. "Now, be careful. That's hot. Don't go burning your throat by drinking it too quick. Little sips, remember?" I nodded but she was already gone, walking to the front door to help Uncle Denim who was trying to get in, but his hands were full.

"Get blankets," he said, his voice loud and urgent.

When I saw bare legs hanging from his arms, I realized he was carrying the White Lady.

Grandma whisked over to the cedar chest and took out two quilts and just as quick had them around her. "Here you go, Abigail. Let's warm you up with these and then we'll go get you some dry clothes." Her calm voice contradicted Uncle Denim's, and her look spoke nothing but sadness. "It's going to be all right. Everything's just fine," she said.

I couldn't tell if she was talking to Uncle Denim, the White Lady, or all of us.

Otis led Denim to the couch and propped pillows up behind her as Denim set her down. Back in Harrison when Daddy was home and feeling good and Mama was happy, they'd sit on the couch together, close like, and Mama would look at him, and her eyes would say words that I understood but couldn't explain. Uncle Denim's eyes were doing that.

"Our baby," the White Lady murmured. "Our baby."

He put his hand against her cheek. "Shhh…Abigail. I know. I know."

I looked away, afraid I was seeing something meant to be private.

Officer Paul came in not far after them, wiping his brow and looking whiter than any white man I'd ever seen. He kept saying, "I can't believe he done it. Dear God, have mercy. Did you see him? Why'd he do that?" Like Grandma, I wasn't sure who he was talking to. It seemed everyone was just talking…to the wind, to the wall, to themselves, to everyone, to no one. He kept taking his hat off and running his fingers through his wet hair. He was pulling at his collar like it was tight and choking. I got up from my seat, and Otis had him take it. "Otis, I just can't believe he done it," he said again even though by then Otis had gone into the kitchen with Grandma.

I stood in the corner, my mug of tea now lukewarm in my hands. I had heard of people saying they'd like to be a fly on the wall in certain situations. I felt like I had become that fly. Uncle Denim and Mrs. Walsh were on the couch, Denim's head bent over hers, their fingers entwined; Officer Paul sat on the chair, his elbows on his knees, resting his head in his hands; Mama stood at the big window, her arms crossing her waist, looking out into the darkness; Aunt Ruby stood behind her, a hand gently placed on her shoulder. Grandma and Otis returned from the kitchen, her carrying a coffee pot and him with a tray filled with mugs and sugar and cream.

"Now, get yourselves warmed from the inside, all of you," she said. This time it was evident she was speaking to everyone. I watched as heads pivoted toward her voice. "It's going to be a long night. I'm making some sandwiches, and I expect you all to eat them."

An ambulance came along with the sheriff, both sets of lights igniting the sky like the fireworks that Old Peeper used to set off in the grocery parking lot on the Fourth of July. I faded even more into the background of the noise and adult talk. I think Aunt Ruby was supposed to be watching me, but she got to pouring coffee and comforting Mama. The food came out—leftover turkey on white bread and potato chips—and I reckon she forgot.

I slipped out of the living room, sandwich in hand, my feet bare and quiet down the hallway. I held the handle of the front door between my fingers, pushing it open slowly so as not to let it crick as I made my way out to the sleeping porch. The rain had stopped, and the air was still. Almost seemed like the earth was settling again, breathing deep, erasing what had happened. Mist floated on the grass, a layer of mystery and fine white.

If I had known for sure then that he wasn't ever coming home, I might have run back into the living room right into Mama's arms and let us cry together and get all the grief out that had started to fill up my throat. But I had let Mama's hope become mine, and I found myself straining to see forms and shapes in the shadows. I half expected Daddy to come walking through them asking me for a bite of a sandwich and making me promise not tell anyone he was there again.

I would have promised anything.

"Macey May, honey?" Mama was sitting next to my bed, her hand caressing my hair like she did when I was running a fever. I swallowed and my throat felt sore. "You about ready to get up? Grandma's got some biscuits with butter and sausage gravy. She'll fry you an egg too, if you'd like."

"What time is it?" I rubbed my eyes and sat up. The sun was shining behind the curtain, a pale yellow sheen peeking through the sides.

"Almost ten. Found you asleep out on the porch cot last night and brought you up here." She patted my head. "Expect you needed the extra rest." She smiled weakly and looked at the door. "Probably better that you slept. It's been a busy morning round here with…" Her voice drifted away, and she stood up to go.

"Mama, wait." I threw the covers off and ran beside her. "The White Lady?"

She nodded. "Abigail Walsh…Junior's mama. They took her to back to the hospital last night to get checked out. She'll have to stay there now with no one to look after her. Probably better that way."

That wasn't the question I had intended when I asked about her, and it seemed to me that Uncle Denim would want to be looking after her.

"I'm sorry I never believed about your ghost all these years." She smiled at me, but her eyes stayed looking inward like she wasn't really seeing me.

I shrugged and looked down at my bare feet. How did I ask what I was needing to know? "She must have been wandering around here at night when she was home visiting from the sanatorium," Mama said.

"Sanatorium?"

"It's a special hospital, baby, for people who…" Mama paused as if she were searching for the right words that would make sense of it all. "For people who have experienced too much pain in their life. Sometimes people need extra care, more than even those who love them can give."

I waited for her to mention the baby, Caroline, the one the White Lady was missing on. The one she had pulled up from the dirt wrapped in plastic and a pink blanket. The one she thought I was. In the chaos, no one had asked me anything last night—about how I knew Daddy and the White Lady were down in the water or what I was doing out of the house. Now it seemed like they, or Mama at least, had forgotten my part in it all.

Mama hadn't stopped talking even though it didn't seem as if she was speaking directly to me. It was more like she was piecing information together for herself, connecting some dots in her mind's eye. "Maybe she missed the creek. I know I missed it when I first moved to Harrison. Your daddy never could understand that about me—missing the light brush of that low running water when I complained about the farm all the time, the coolness on my toes on a hot summer's night. You can't trust that water, though. It's fierce in a storm. Your grandma's right to tell you to keep away."

It seemed Mama wasn't waiting for a response from me, which was good since I wasn't sure what she was saying really. I stayed quiet.

Downstairs I heard the porch door open and the squeal of the springs as it shut back in place. Muffled voices on the porch swarmed around and then Grandma called Mama's name. She patted me on the cheek. "Got to go see who that is. There'll be lots of people coming 'round here today, Macey May, and there's plenty we need to talk about, but we'll do that as a family once they all clear out. Why don't you stay up here for now and read one of your books, okay?"

I nodded. She headed toward the door, and my mouth opened before I could stop it. Words came out that I didn't realize I was going to say. "Daddy's dead." I hadn't meant it to be a statement, but when I heard it out there, my ears knew the truth.

Her voice was low and sad across the room, and she didn't turn to face me, just kept her hand on the doorknob. "Macey May, don't say that. We don't know yet. There's still hope."

I ran to the window once she left and pushed the curtain aside. The sheriff's car was out front. I closed my eyes and waited for what I knew would be coming. What he was here to say.

By the time Mama's foot hit the last step downstairs and her cry battled the walls, I knew.

They told me Daddy had drowned while trying to save Mrs. Walsh from drowning herself. The water had carried his body a ways down until it got tangled on a copse of broken tree branches that had dammed themselves up in the middle of the creek. I held onto Mama for the rest of the day, afraid that if I let her go, she might be washed away too. My head ached from crying, and my stomach kept rolling in on itself. Grandma hugged me tight and brought me chicken soup and crackers, but I could only take a few sips. The crackers were dry and caught in my throat.

I was used to Daddy being gone; I wasn't used to knowing Daddy wasn't ever coming back. Mama made me take a pill around seven and took me up to bed. When I woke up the next morning, she was still sleeping right beside me in her clothes from the day before.

I spent the next few days with the cows, mostly letting the adults have their space. Sometimes grown-ups needed to carry the heavy burden and didn't need me around to remind them of the smaller ones.

Daddy's funeral was planned for Monday as there wasn't no need for an autopsy, it being pretty obvious to everyone how he died. There was no one from out of town to invite or notify, although Mama did call up Miss Eunice to tell her. She didn't have Johnny's mother's number or address, although I imagine Johnny knew before any of us. Mama decided to have him cremated and tucked into a silver urn. I thought we'd scatter the ashes out in the creek, seeing that that was where Daddy had been heroic, but Mama wanted them near her. Maybe it was her way of making sure he didn't go away again.

I had never been to a funeral before and even though Daddy's was going to be in Grandma's parlor and not in a funeral home, I still felt uncomfortable. They hadn't let me say goodbye to him. Otis had gone with the sheriff to make the identification and said he had made my goodbyes for me then like he knew I would want. He told me that I didn't need to see Daddy the way he was when they found him, that it was better to keep him in my mind's eye the way he had always been. I chose to picture Daddy winking at me, his mouth spread wide in a smile, my name on his lips.

Grandma had run into town and found me a navy-blue dress with a white bow at the waist, and she had laid it out across the chair in my room. My white knee-highs and penny loafers were next to it waiting for me.

"Macey May?" Mama knocked on the door before she opened it. "You about ready?"

"No," I said. I knew I needed to be dressed, but my legs and arms didn't seem to want to work. I had managed to put on my slip, but that was it.

Mama walked into the room and picked up my dress. Without saying anything else, she unzipped the back of it and looked at me. My arms went up in the air automatically, and she came and put the dress on over my head. Next came my socks and shoes. Mama bent over in front of me putting them on my feet. "Up," she said. "Turn." I turned and she zipped me up. Before I could stop myself, my arms were around her waist. She hugged me back so hard I thought my insides would break. "We can do this, Macey May. Your daddy wouldn't want any sadness."

She wiped my eyes with her thumb and swept her hands along my shoulders. Her dress was black, and she looked beautiful. Daddy always said there was no one prettier than Mama, and he was right. I slipped my hand into hers, and this time she held it and squeezed it.

I only knew the family at the funeral. Some of Grandma's church ladies had brought cornbread, greens, and ham along with an apple pie and something called 'chocolate delight.' They stayed for the service, choosing folding chairs against the back wall so they could be quick to serve when it was over. Reverend Wheeldin hadn't known Daddy, seeing that we didn't visit that often, but his words were nice. Daddy was in heaven, he said, up on a cloud with Jesus. I liked that picture of Daddy sitting high up above me on cotton candy in the sky. It made me want to go outside and look for him.

Aunt Ruby came over to me while people were sitting around the parlor, plates balanced on their knees, cups of sweet tea standing on the floor beside them. I was at the table. Mama hadn't wanted me to spill.

"I'm headed back to the city Wednesday morning. I told your mama you're both welcome to come visit whenever you need, and stay if you want. My place is small, but we'll make do. Macey May," she took the seat next to me, "your daddy was a good man. Don't you forget that."

How could I ever forget?

Chapter 22

CRAWFORD, GEORGIA
CORA LEE JOHNSON
1962

CORA LEE STOOD at the kitchen window the next morning, mindlessly fingering the curtains over the sink, trying to construct words in her head that could claim sense.

It wasn't the conversation she imagined having so early in the morning, but when Ruby suggested that she would be heading back to New York the next day, she didn't need to look at Otis's reproving glare over bacon and toast to know she had to speak up. What was she holding back for, anyway?

"Girls," she said. "I've been keeping something from you all these years…and it's about time I stopped that…stopped hiding things thinking that I could control outcomes if I controlled what you knew."

Rose put down her coffee cup and sat straighter in her chair. Ruby wiped her mouth with the napkin. "Okay, tell," they said.

Otis cleared the table as Cora Lee spoke, allowing the girls to learn their history, for Cora Lee to speak her past.

And as she spoke, she watched them without watching, her focus somewhere beyond into a time that was no longer a secret. For better or worse, the farm would never be what it was to them anymore. She would never be what she was to them. In that one moment, as the secrets rolled off of her tongue, she had changed their lives forever, just as she had changed them when she had closed her mouth to the truth over two decades ago.

When she was done, she nodded—an official ending to the telling. "There you go."

The table was quiet—the strawberry jam waited to be spread, the drip of coffee down the side of the mug suspended as if it had the power to prevent itself from falling. Cora Lee's words impacted it all.

Rose spoke first. Cora Lee wasn't surprised since Rose was never one to hold back. All the years the girls were little, Rose would erupt while Ruby would wither under her sister's words, trying to claim some for her own and always failing. It would be later, long after both girls had been tucked into bed, that Ruby's tiny bare feet would wander into Cora Lee's room to be heard.

In a strange way, she found comfort in the fact that her news hadn't changed the status quo among them, and she braced herself for Rose's impending tirade.

"Mama?"

Cora Lee lifted her chin and looked her in the eyes, her hands clasped together as they hung in front of her. She was ready for whatever words Rose felt she needed to say, knowing she deserved every last one of them. She had lied to her girls almost their whole lives, and Cora Lee was certain Rose had no intention of sitting quietly with that information.

"Mama." Rose's voice gripped itself, and the rest of the words pinched and squeaked their way out. "I'm so sorry. I was awful...oh, God, I was so awful to you for years, Mama."

Cora Lee's face crumpled. She hadn't wanted to cry. She had hoped that she would make it through her telling as matter-of-factly as she had made it through the past twenty-five years without Hi. It was how she had survived.

In an instant, as the words found their place in the present, Cora Lee saw the past—Hi hanging from the tree, the bullet hole through his chest. But new images pressed themselves in, taking over the others: Hi playing with the girls outside in the summer on their front lawn while the lightning bugs started their nightly parade; Hi lifting Rose above his head, spinning her around like an airplane, her laughter roaring through the clouds. She saw Ruby's hands stretched up to him. *Me, me, Daddy.* Cora Lee saw Hi's strong hand in her own as they watched the girls sleep tucked securely in their beds, and she felt his skin against hers. She felt him.

Rose ran to her mother, the woman she had purposely distanced over the years, the woman whom she now understood had sacrificed everything for her to keep her safe.

"Oh, Mama, why didn't you tell us? Why did you hold onto this for so long?" Ruby's words mixed with tears as she wrapped her arms around Rose and Cora Lee.

Cora Lee's shoulders heaved. Her babies, they understood.

Cora Lee braced herself for their questions, knowing now that honesty was all she had to give. The conversation would be long. "Did you know Mr. Walsh was responsible? Did you have any idea through the years? Any at all?" Ruby refilled their coffee cups.

"No, baby. Didn't know who had done it. Didn't care. What difference would it have made? Otis, Denim, and I assumed it was the Klan."

"Why didn't you report it?" Rose reached out and took Cora Lee's hand.

"Why didn't I ever tell anyone? Why didn't I ever go to the police? Otis wanted me to, said so right away. It was a different time then. I had you and Ruby to protect. Your daddy was gone. It wouldn't have done any good to find myself swinging from the same tree. No, Otis was with me when we found him, and then we told Denim. Let everyone else believe he had died in his sleep. Told you that and your sister…even myself through the years."

Cora Lee's mind was still putting together the pieces, the ones that Rose and Ruby didn't need to worry about: the extent of Mr. Walsh's deception, his manipulation of her trust. When she thought about it her faced burned, how he must have been laughing at her every night. And to think, he had come by the house to offer his respects after Hi's funeral service. The thought made her sick.

What had he been thinking when he dropped Junior off with her, saw him running hand in hand with little black Rose? Was he biding his time, waiting, hoping to see her fail, the farm sold?

He had thought Hi was the father of the baby. Bashed the poor little thing's brains in because she was part black. Buried her on Hi's acres in a trash bag. Always wanting to buy the land to hide his crime. The baby hadn't been Hi's, though. It was Denim's. A love child, one that Cora Lee had come to find out over the past few days had been the product of years of love. The times hadn't allowed it, though, and Abigail wasn't strong enough to go against society, so she had married Tom. But her heart belonged to Denim and his to her. He kept to the corners of her life, living on stolen moments when he and Abigail could find them.

Ruby stirred some sugar into her coffee and took a sip. "Did you know about Denim?"

Cora Lee shook her head. "Should have, but can't say I did. Knew he wasn't interested in any woman I wanted to set him with. Couldn't even name but one or two who he did take into town on occasion. A movie, pie…nothing of any importance. Always seemed more of an obligation on his part to keep me off his back. To make people not talk.

"He seemed content, never needed any companionship other than us and his animals. But oh, how he loved playing with you two. Other than your daddy, I don't think I've ever seen a man more taken by you two little girls. But truth be told, my eyes were on the both of you and running this farm. Didn't give much thought about other people's lives, never mind their hearts."

The sun was out, the day poking its head through kitchen curtains. It seemed impossible that the days before had even happened. The death that they held. Cora Lee looked at her girls and began to clear off the table of the breakfast plates, needing to get moving. To get life moving.

As if on cue, Denim poked his head around the doorway. "You ladies doing okay?"

Ruby and Rose smiled.

"Come in here, Denim, and have a cup. It's fresh." Cora Lee walked over to the stove and lifted the percolator.

Denim waved his hand. "Nah, don't want to intrude. I know there's not much time left before Ruby needs to be going. You spend that together. Rose, when will you and Macey May head back to Harrison? I told her she could come by the clinic and see the batch of new kittens. Wouldn't want to go back on my word."

Cora Lee took down the flour from the cupboard and some butter out of the fridge. She'd make a pound cake that night for dessert. One last nice meal together before her girls left. They hadn't had time yet to talk about Rose's choices now that Curtis was gone. What would be best for her, for Macey May. There was something Rose wasn't telling her still, but she wasn't about to push. They had all been through too much, grown closer together over the revealing of secrets. She didn't want to lose that.

"I'm not sure, Denim. Adele's closing the bakery for good after Christmas, which leaves me without a job. Other than Miss Eunice, I'm not sure what Harrison holds for us anymore. Maybe I'll leave Macey May here and go on back to see the closing through and then return for Christmas. There's only two more weeks of school until break starts up again.

She doesn't need to be traveling back and forth. I mentioned to Macey May about staying on here at the farm for a while until I sort things out. Silly thing. So worried about Miss Eunice back in Harrison by herself."

Cora Lee smiled as her hands broke apart the butter into the bowl, her girls talking at the table behind her. Rose mentioning perhaps they'd stay. Rose and Macey May there with her on Christmas morning. Everything she had longed for, hoped for, seemed to be closing in around her. As it always should have been.

Ruby walked to the sink and rinsed out her mug. "I work through the twenty-second, and the Christmas party is the next night, but I don't need to go. I can take the overnight bus from the city and get here by morning." She picked up a dishcloth and wiped some flour off of the counter. "I don't know the last time we all spent Christmas under the same roof."

Cora Lee knew. Rose had been nineteen, Ruby sixteen. It was the year she had given them matching pearl necklaces. Rose had been upset. She didn't think Ruby was responsible enough for such a grown-up gift. By the next Christmas, Rose was in Harrison with Willie and didn't make it home until after the new year. Once Ruby graduated high school, she was off to New York, and Cora Lee was lucky to have her babies together for the strawberry festival. And even that wasn't a yearly guarantee.

A knock from the kitchen door made Cora Lee jump. There had been too many knocks of late, too many people needing to come in, and none with good news. She wasn't expecting anyone.

"Hello? Cora Lee? Anyone home?"

Through the closed kitchen door, the faded voice battered her brain. It had been years, but she recognized it. Her eyes caught Rose's. Rose recognized it, too.

Dr. William Price.

There he was on her back porch, his jacket slung over his shoulder, his hand in his pocket, standing like he had over a decade ago when he had entered her kitchen carrying a blueberry cobbler for the picnic and then left with her daughter.

Chapter 23

HARRISON, GEORGIA
ROSE JOHNSON
1953

ROSE HELD HER BREATH for a moment, trying to clear her head. She had been sitting on the bench across from the bakery for long enough to feel the slates' indents on the back of her thighs through her dress. Seven minutes—that's what she had left before she was due at work. Forty minutes had gone by with nothing, not one resolution coming to light, only more confusion in her mind, which seemed more muddled by the hour. If only she could come up with an answer, a way out, it might be all right. Anything to save herself from the humiliation.

She was closing the bakery that night, working the register for the last hour then staying after Adele left to make the pies for the next morning's rush. Most Saturday mornings there'd be a line outside the door waiting for pies, *her pies*. There was a difference. Adele's were good, but Rose's pies were better and she knew it, everyone did. And everyone knew that Rose made them on Saturdays.

A line wasn't an answer, though. Neither were sold out pies. There weren't enough pies in the world to raise a baby on her own.

If she turned her head to the left and stretched her neck, she could just make out the corner building where Willie's apartment used to be.

Instinctively her hand went to her stomach. Still flat, really. And why wouldn't it be? Barely a month past at most if her cycle was accurate. It was hard to imagine there was anything in there that would eventually be a person. Rose closed her eyes. She couldn't track Willie down at Howard. He had left her. He had made his decision. Bringing a baby into it wouldn't make a difference. He hadn't wanted her. That's all Rose needed to know.

Harrison's Main Street wasn't ever busy; today was no exception. Across the street, two women entered Old Peeper's grocery: one pushing a baby carriage, the other followed by a little girl in pigtails playing imaginary hopscotch. A dinner fixing run, no doubt, for that one missing ingredient, or not enough milk for tomorrow morning's breakfast.

The town, its slowness. Rose wondered why she hadn't left, why she hadn't hightailed it out of there and hopped a train for Ruby and New York City the minute Willie decided he had no backbone and left her alone there. She could have gone back to Junior in Crawford and wrapped him around her finger. Oh, how that would have riled her mama. Instead, she had stayed, looking for any other choice or any new chance to come her way. She was still looking.

A pickup drove by and honked at the man who had come out of the garage at the filling station on the corner. He waved a hello, scratched his shoulder, and lit a cigarette before turning around and walking back to the bay, his blue overalls and embroidered red company patch visible from where she sat across the street. She could make out a green car raised onto the lifts. He flipped the sign in the window to *closed* and unwound the rope that he used to pull the garage door down.

The tower clock struck five, and Rose's pulse began to race. It was a race against time to get everything set before it ran out—before talking would commence, and adding of dates and calendars and shaking of heads; before any choice she hoped to make was made for her. There was only so much that people would accept in the end, what they were able to turn their eyes from, what lies they would allow themselves to believe. An unwed mother would not be one of them.

Rose stood and smoothed down her maroon chiffon skirt and adjusted the flower in her hair. The pickup had circled around the town green and then stopped for her while she crossed the street. Their low whistles emanated from the front windows, lowered for the breeze and the exact purpose of letting her and the other ladies know that they were seen. Rose knew these boys. Elwin. Lucas. She knew their mamas. She knew their mamas' mamas, and that was why there were no options for her in Harrison.

The muffler rumbled as the truck continued past.

"Pardon, miss." The apology carried across the air from the open tailgate of the pickup and whispered into her ear like fate had decided to step in and direct. A hand to the tip of the hat, a reverential tilt of the rim. Out of the corner of her eye, Rose caught the buttoned shirt with a tie, the cuff on the pants, the white skin, darkened in the sun to a warm brown, under the rolled-up sleeves.

An option?

She wasn't telling Willie, and she'd do whatever was needed to not go back to the farm, to her mama's disappointment. She had two lives to think about now—hers and her baby's. She brought her shoulders back and lifted her chin and sunk her hips into a sashay that her mama always said would get her into trouble one of those days.

Now it might just get her out.

When she heard the hand beat against the side of the truck for it to stop and shoes hit the pavement, she knew there was a possibility. When she tied the apron behind her back, turned to ask Curtis what he would like to try, and saw the puppy dog look already in his eyes, she knew she had found her answer.

And Willie would never know.

Chapter 24

CRAWFORD, GEORGIA
CURTIS JOHNSON
1962

DEAR ROSE,

I never knew when it would end for us, only that it would, but I wanted to be able to say what I wanted to say and what I needed to say before my memories swallowed me up whole to the point where I couldn't find my way back. I'm gone, or you wouldn't be reading this. I made Dr. Price promise that he'd only give you this letter once I was dead. I hope that I haven't destroyed what little love you had left for me before I went.

I wanted to thank you for doing what you did all those years ago when we first met, telling me Macey May was mine even though she wasn't. For the longest time, I believed you chose me because I was there, a ready-made answer to a problem that you thought was bigger than you could handle on your own. In a selfish way I'm glad you never understood that you didn't need me; you were large enough all by yourself. But after a few years, I began to think that maybe it had nothing to do with you at all, that maybe it was fate intervening on both our behalfs, giving you what you thought you needed and giving me what I did—a family.

Macey May Johnson.

Macey May Price.

Ten fingers and ten toes for me to count and hold. Ten fingers and ten toes for me to feed and clothe. Ten fingers and ten toes that loved me without reservation. A purpose for my mind.

I don't think you ever felt that way about me, Rose, and that's okay. I never expected you to. Maybe you did a little once you saw me becoming a daddy. I'm the most proudest of that, being a daddy to Macey May. I think I did all right.

Don't worry about her. She'll be okay.

She has you, Cora Lee, Otis, Denim, Ruby…and Willie.

You have to give him back to her, Rose.

But don't wait to explain things. Don't make him your friend "Dr. Price" or "Uncle Willie." He's her father. Tell her now; tell her everything. Keeping secrets never did anyone any good.

I should have told you my secrets. I should have told you that my mind goes missing for days sometimes, and I hear the gunfire from the war. There are times that I see the enemy in front of me as clear as deer under the bright moon. I don't know what you could have done, but it pains me to think that you might have believed you were the cause of my leaving.

I pray I never hurt you.

Rose, you were always strong. I wish I had a teaspoon of the courage that runs through your veins. Maybe then I would have been able to pull myself back from the edge, fight more when I felt the darkness reaching for me. I never seemed to be any good at doing that after Johnny died. The war follows you, stays with you like the smell of fire in your clothes that doesn't wash out. They don't tell you that when you sign your name, tell you what you are really signing away.

I love you, Rose, truly, always. You are the most beautiful woman I have ever seen. I was yours the minute those lavender eyes looked at me, and the gift of Macey May, well, it allowed me to know happiness. Not many men get to have that.

I'd like to think that as you read this letter you are sad at my death but proud also. I'd hate to think that I brought you any more pain in the way I left this earth or caused you any more embarrassment. Perhaps in my last moments, I did some good, helped someone, made amends somehow. I'd like to think that the war didn't win after all, didn't fully destroy who I was or wanted to be. I wanted to be someone you could love and someone Macey May could look up to. I hope you remember me like that so Macey May remembers me like that. Perhaps I made a difference at the end. I'd like to think I did.

—Curtis

"Rose?" Willie looked at her intently. "Don't hate me for keeping it from you. He asked me as a doctor. I couldn't break my oath." The kitchen was empty except for the two of them now—Willie and Rose, Curtis's words between them. It had taken Rose a while to comprehend why Willie was there in her mother's kitchen. It had been a surprise to see him, to hear his voice on that back porch, yet it hadn't. It seemed like even in his death, Curtis was trying to take care of her and Macey May.

"Do you know what it says?" She flattened the paper on the table and placed the envelope next to it like it was an exhibit under glass, some sort of imaginings that people would want to read hundreds of years later. "Did he tell you what he was going through?"

Willie shook his head. "I didn't read it, Rose. That letter was for you."

"But did you know?"

He hesitated. "Yes. He came in a few months back before he left. After hours—never when Odella was there. He told me about blacking out, spaces of not remembering, but it wasn't until last week that he told me about the hallucinations."

273

"Last week?"

"You had already sent Macey May on, and you were heading back here the next morning when he came in. It was almost six, and I was putting the trash out in the alley. When I opened the door, there he was. I tried to get him to stay, to let me call you. Told him I'd get him help, that you'd come in looking for him, any word of him, but he was worried that he'd hurt you or Macey May if he didn't go…afraid he already had."

Rose looked down at her clasped hands. "He never hurt Macey May—ever."

Willie put his hand on her shoulder. "You?"

"I always knew it wasn't me he was hurting, if that makes any sense." She stepped back from him, his fingers slipping off of her shoulder. She walked out the kitchen door into the back yard before he could respond.

The afternoon had stayed warm like the weather itself was lost in a state of confusion, wondering what it was supposed to be doing right then in the wake of everything that had happened over the past few days, in light of the letter. Curtis had said no secrets anymore. She thought for a moment about where her life would be if he hadn't walked into Adele's so many years ago, if he hadn't been so willing to accept the lie she offered up. An unwed mother—another reason for shaking of heads on porch rockers, another 'mmmm…hmm, anyone could have seen that coming' gossip tag during a covered dish at church. She knew those conversations, spewed them out of her own mouth more often than she cared to remember with no regard for the life on the other end marred by her words. It made her ashamed. She hoped she hadn't raised Macey May to be that cruel. She knew Curtis hadn't.

And she had come to love him. Not in a breathless way that most young women long for, like she had experienced with Willie. In a comfortable way, like choosing a bed and deciding you'll take the one *that will do* rather than the one that costs more than your paycheck but makes you feel like you're floating on air.

No, with Curtis, her feet had remained on the ground. It was a blessing to her that it had happened, her loving him. She'd known other women who hadn't been so lucky, even those who had known their men years before marrying them. Curtis had made it easy. Every Friday night he'd come home with a spray of flowers, sometimes store-bought carnations, others wild daisies from a field. He'd thank her after every meal she ever cooked and kiss her on the cheek. Sometimes on Saturday nights after Macey May had gone to bed, he'd set up the transistor on the porch and sway with her to sounds of big bands.

She could never be sorry about her choice. They had created a family together, the three of them. A home. Her hand went to her belly. A home that would be adding another person.

Rose walked until she reached the edge of the creek. Willie hadn't followed her. She knew he'd stay back, giving her space. She also knew he'd be down eventually, and she'd need to tell him. Lies had only brought her family unnecessary pain. All these years she could have understood her mother rather than pushing her away, could have helped Curtis find some peace, and could have let Macey May know her father.

The water was calm, the torrential current from the days before only left in memory. The paradox of nature, like humans—the power to heal, the power to destroy. Rose looked across to where Otis had been searching for Curtis when he went under, where Mr. Walsh had stood, crazed, eyes frantic with a gun pointing at Cora Lee, where Abigail had clung to remnants of pink yarn that had once held her baby girl. This was why her mama protected her from the truth of her father's murder, why she hid this hatred from her and Ruby. She hadn't wanted her girls to know it, to live in it. All those years.

She heard Willie's footsteps behind her and found comfort in the fact that she had been right that he'd eventually follow. She still knew him.

"Rose, can we sit?"

Rose turned and looked at him. "There's more, isn't there?"

Willie nodded and led her over to the bench. He reached into his pocket and handed her two more envelopes.

"Do you know what these are?" Rose's fingers touched her name typed formally on the top of the envelopes. What else had Curtis done, she thought.

Willie nodded again. "He told me. Wanted you to read his letter first before I gave you these. He was a good man, Rose. A good father."

Both letters were from Hankle and Mitchum law offices. Rose had never heard of them before. The address underneath their names read Dobson. Dobson, so that was why Curtis had gone there. To see lawyers.

"Why did he give these to *you*? Why did he give *you* that letter?" She let the weight of the two envelopes fill her hands. Light. Is that what Curtis's life came down to? A wisp of paper in an envelope?

"He understood more than he let on, Rose. Knew more than you thought. I guess he figured he could trust me, that if something happened to him that I'd come to you." He leaned over and put his elbows on his knees, his hands clasped together. "He was right."

Rose put one of the envelopes down beside her and opened the other. Her shoulders raised and lowered with a deep breath, fortifying herself for whatever the words would tell her. Her eyes ran back and forth across the black print, and she brought her finger to it as a guide, stopping and starting again at points. "Willie, does this say that I own a house?"

Willie turned his head toward her. "Not outright, but come January once it's finished being built, you and Macey May have a house to move into in Harrison. Three bedrooms, one bath and a one-car attached garage. Down payments already been made and your name is on the deed."

Rose placed her hand on the papers in her lap as if they were sacred relics that needed to be touched in a reverential fashion. Her eyes filled. The last down payment made was for $537.00. All the money in his sock drawer. "He always said he was going to buy me a house someday. Guess I should have believed him." For a moment, she allowed herself to stay in that space—a space where the horrors of the past few days and the uncertainty of the past two months didn't exist.

Willie picked up the second envelope and handed it to her. "He loved you and Macey May…don't ever doubt that."

The tears started soon after she read through the second paragraph. A life insurance policy naming her sole beneficiary of $30,000.00. She could pay for the house and put money away for Macey May's college. Maybe even buy the bakery from Adele. They could stay in Harrison near Miss Eunice. Macey May would be so happy. Rose looked across at Willie. She could stay in Harrison near him. Maybe that had been Curtis's plan all along.

Rose wiped the tears off of her cheeks and folded the policy back into the envelope. "It's getting to be that I'm not sure you ever know anyone. Mama. Curtis."

She thought about what she had kept from Curtis, but what he had known all along. She thought about what she had kept from Willie and in turn Macey May, never giving him the opportunity to truly know his own daughter, never giving her the opportunity to have one more adult to love on her.

And she remembered Curtis's words in his letter, *Give him back to her, Rose.* She stood up and walked to edge of the embankment. Water was water, but this water that had taken Curtis's life while he saved another. It had changed her life forever.

"I'm done with secrets, Willie. I can't hold them in anymore and don't want to. It seems like they've surrounded me all my life, and then I insulated myself and Macey May with them as if they were some magical talismans that would keep harm at a distance. I loved Curtis, I did. In our way we were good, and you have to know I was happy because I was. When he was okay, in his right mind, we were good. At the time, he was my only choice, the only one I could see, and I'll be forever grateful that he jumped off the back of that pickup and walked into the bakery that night. You had broken my heart, Willie. Broke it in so many pieces that I expected cuts on the soles of my feet whenever I walked, and I wondered why the whole world wasn't bleeding along with me. Did you know how much I loved you?"

Willie bowed his head.

Rose cleared her throat. "Still do if we're truth telling. Don't believe I ever stopped. Oh, in my head I did. Fought it every day with everything I had. Told my heart that I was stupid to have followed you to Harrison, even more stupid to think you'd have me as your wife. Said so many things in my mind to make me hate you, that just your name made me see red."

"Rose, let me—" Willie stood up and walked to her.

She shook her head, her back to him, her eyes looking out over the running water. "No. I need to say this. I made you into something you weren't, someone I needed you to be to justify my own actions. It gave me reason to not be truthful with myself, Curtis, Macey May…hell, everyone. But mostly it allowed me to not be truthful with you. Willie," she paused and turned to him, "lies creep up on you, don't they? Slip into your mouth so easily they become like truths until you believe them and all the reasons you had for creating them in the first place. Curtis wasn't Macey May's father. You are."

If he had walked to his car, started it up, and driven away without ever looking back, she wouldn't have judged him. Would have nodded her head in agreement and returned to the house to say goodbye to Ruby and help Cora Lee start thinking about dinner. If he had yelled at her, cursed even, she wouldn't have thought him vile. Would have lifted her chin high to allow his words to hit their marks. If he had broken down and cried, wept like loss was eating him up, she would have begged on her knees for him to forgive her.

But when he stepped close to her, held her face in his hands and looked into her eyes, she felt her strength begin to fade. "Those eyes. Curtis was right. They are fairy eyes…a man could get lost in them, want to stay lost, and do whatever he thought needed to be done to keep himself there. To have those eyes look away from me again might just kill me."

"You knew?"

Willie let his hands fall to his side, but he kept his eyes locked on hers. "I'm a doctor, Rose. Calendars don't lie. Also knew you were making a new path for yourself, and I didn't want to be the cause of more hurting. I wasn't strong then. I'm ashamed by it now. Was ashamed then, but not enough to speak against my parents' wishes. And then you were with Curtis. And you seemed happy. I figured I hadn't given you anything I had promised you. The least I could do was give you the future you had chosen with him."

"All this time you let Curtis raise her, love her…let her call him Daddy?"

"That was your choice." Willie took a few steps back and sat back down on the bench. "I'm not sure what you are hoping to hear, Rose. Yes, I did. I accepted your lie. I watched him hold her hand as they walked down the street, swinging their arms back and forth. I watched her riding on his shoulders when he came to pick you up from Adele's some nights. Her smile when she was up there, so high, almost touching the clouds… and her voice when she called for him…she adored him. Never knew a voice could sound like love until I heard her say his name."

Rose stood still. Not wanting to move, to speak in case she said the wrong words. She thought back to the day she knew she was pregnant with Macey May, the decision she made then to not speak. To not tell

Willie. It had worked out, mostly, but was life supposed to be that—just something that worked out? Couldn't it, shouldn't it, be more? This time it couldn't be her decision alone.

"What do you want to do?" she said.

"Curtis raised my child for me. And for that I'll be forever grateful to him." Willie walked up behind her, and when she turned around he was there, inches away. Gently he placed his hands on her stomach. "I think I need to repay the favor. If you'll let me."

By habit Rose's mouth opened to speak, to deny it, to continue the lies that had been flowing freely for years. As words began to tumble out, she covered her mouth with her hand to stop them. It was over, for her mother, for her, for all of them. Not again. Not ever.

Willie moved her hand away.

"I never told him." Rose choked the words out. In the back of her mind she wondered if that would have made a difference. If Curtis had known, would it have been enough to keep him there with them, or would it have made him leave even faster knowing he had three to protect from his nightmares.

"He knew, Rose, or suspected. He said so when he came to see me." Willie laughed a little. "Said he noticed extra jars of dill pickles in the fridge, just like when you were having Macey May. I'm sure that's why he did this all, why he sent me to you. This baby will know about Curtis. You'll make sure it. We'll make sure of it." Both of his hands were on her cheeks, her tears running between his fingers. "We'll tell Macey May everything and answer any questions she has. I've lost enough time with both of you. I don't want to lose any more."

Chapter 25

CRAWFORD, GEORGIA
MACEY MAY JOHNSON
1962

"MACEY MAY, are your presents packed?" Mama grabbed the empty lunch plate off of the kitchen counter and wiped the crumbs into the sink. When she stood sidewise, I could see the bump in her belly holding my baby brother or sister. The past week leading up to Christmas seemed to announce the impending arrival. There was no mistaking she was pregnant.

"Yes, Mama. Now can I go help Otis in the barn?" I grabbed my sweater off the back of my chair. I hoped she wasn't going to make me wear my winter coat and hat or worse, mittens. Christmas had brought little change in the Georgia weather, but Mama had always demanded clothes be dictated by the expectations of the calendar rather than what was going on outside the front door. "He's got the heater on," I said for good measure.

Mama shook her head at me but didn't say anything. I can tell I've been wearing her down these last few weeks we've stayed on with Grandma and Otis. Just the other day I forgot to take my shoes off after playing outside. Walked right into the living room and plopped down on the couch before I realized they were still on. She shook her head at me then too.

281

"Fine, go. But remember, we leave for Harrison tomorrow, so you've got to be all packed up. Your daddy—"

I coughed, my way of reminding her. We had made a sort of bargain, the two of us, after she told me about Dr. Price being who he was. I didn't want Daddy looking down from heaven and watching me share his name with Dr. Price. To me they weren't interchangeable, and I didn't think they ever would be.

She started again. "Willie will be here by dinner and then we are leaving early tomorrow morning. I've got a bakery to reopen." She said the last part smiling, and I was happy for her. It had been a long time since I had seen Mama with a genuine smile on her face.

Mama had returned to Harrison a week after Daddy's funeral to meet with the lawyers and used some of Daddy's insurance money to buy Adele's. Our house would be ready for us shortly after the new year. Mama needed to go shopping to fill it up, and I needed to start school again now that vacation was coming to a close. We'd be staying with Miss Eunice until it was all settled. I was beyond excited to see her.

I had read four of the *Anne* books since coming to Grandma's. Miss Eunice had sent Mama back with *Anne of Avonlea* and *Anne of the Island*. *Anne of Windy Poplars* came through the mail to Grandma's just in time for me to open on Christmas Eve. I think Mama knew what it was, so she let me unwrap it early. I read it through most of the night waiting for the morning to come. I hoped beyond hope that Miss Eunice had *Anne's House of Dreams* waiting for me. Her Christmas card hinted that she did.

Anne and Gilbert were to be married in this one, and I couldn't wait to read it. I thought it would probably be wise of me to learn all I could about weddings. There was something in Mama's eyes when she talked about Dr. Price that made me think it wouldn't be too long before they sat me down again to have another talk.

I circled Mama in a hug before I left. She was getting better at receiving them and giving them, and I grabbed an apple for Mabel out of the basket on the table. She was healing up fine, and Otis had promised that I could feed her a treat.

The barn smelled good, like sweet hay.

Otis came out of his office. "There you are. Weren't sure you were coming." He held up two cups of steaming cocoa. "I hoped you were, though, or I was going to have to drink both of these myself." He sat down on the side of a square bale pushed up against the wall and motioned for me next to him.

The cup was warm in my hands, and I held it up to my nose allowing the chocolate steam to cover my face. I didn't want to think it, but Mama was right. I should have worn my winter coat.

"Otis," I said, taking a sip of the hot chocolate. "Mama asked me to call Dr. Price 'Daddy,' but I don't think I can do it."

Otis got up and went over to his desk, fished around in one of the drawers, and pulled out four cookies. I smiled. Grandma would kill him if she knew he was hiding cookies in the barn. "She did, did she?"

"Yes, sir."

Otis always carefully weighed his words before he spoke them. Once I counted a full six minutes waiting for an answer. I knew this time would be no different. I watched as he dunked a cookie into his cocoa, tapped the excess off into the mug, and then popped the moist sweetness whole into his mouth. "You understand why she wants you to?"

I nodded.

He handed me a cookie.

" 'Daddy' is a pretty special word, isn't it?" he said.

I nodded again. My throat was beginning to feel tight like it did before tears came.

Otis waited. I watched him repeat the process of dunking the cookie. I knew he was waiting for me to gather myself.

"I know Willie is my father, but he's not my daddy. Only Daddy can be my daddy."

He nodded this time. "There's importance to names, to the ones we're given and the ones we choose. You know, though, there are other forms of 'Daddy' like 'Papa,' 'Pop,' 'Father,' 'Dad.' Maybe one of those would fit." He took a big sip of the hot chocolate and let out an "ah" for effect. Otis was always being silly.

I hadn't thought of using another name. I leaned back against the wall beside him. I needed to do some thinking on this. " 'Father' is much too stuffy. I'm not even sure I could say it without laughing. 'Father, can you pass the peas, please?'" I burst out with a chuckle then and Otis smiled. " 'Pop' sounds like something I could use if I was a boy, and 'Papa' makes it seem like I'm in Avonlea with Anne." I tapped my fingers against the mug. " 'Dad' might work. I'm getting older, you know, and 'Dad' does sound more mature. It doesn't feel the same as saying 'Daddy,' not all soft and warm, but not cold either. Different."

Otis took the cups and walked them over to his desk. He took out his pocketknife and cut the apple I had brought into pieces, then he picked up a brush and held both out to me. I spent the next hour with the cows brushing their soft coats and feeding apple chunks to Mabel. A small part of me wished that Daddy hadn't bought us the house, so we could stay with Grandma and Otis on the farm. But Mama had already promised that our visits would be more frequent, and I could come stay over school vacations. It seemed like everything was going to be different now.

"Macey May," Otis's voice sing-songed over the herd, and his head popped up a few cows over. "Why don't you go on back to the house and finish packing up your things. I know your mama and dad want to head out early. I'll be in for dinner." He disappeared out of vision before I could reply.

Otis was like that. Sneaky. Using 'dad' as if it was natural, allowing me to hear it, get used to how it sounded in the air before I said it myself.

Dr. Price sat across from me at Grandma's dinner table. I studied him when he wasn't looking, trying to see traces of myself in him. We had the same eyes. He ate every last morsel Grandma put on his plate and then accepted her seconds. He made a point of telling her that her buttermilk-pecan pralines were even better than the ones his mother boasted about. He took two when the dish was passed around and another when it was passed back. I watched Otis take only one and wink at me, our secret of the cookies safe.

Dr. Price was almost a foot taller than Daddy, and his voice was louder but in a good way. I watched him look at Mama. It was the same way Daddy used to. Dr. Price would never be Daddy, but I thought he eventually could become Dad.

I helped Grandma clear the table. Mama said she wanted to go out for one more walk along the creek, and Dr. Price went with her.

"I'm proud of you, Macey May," Grandma said as she passed me a plate to dry.

I dried it and set it on the counter. Grandma kept the plates high up in the cabinet, and I wasn't tall enough yet to reach it.

"Why?"

Her hands stopped in the sink, the soap suds' tiny mouths opening and closing around them.

"You've been through a lot these past weeks. And I'm sorry for all of it. I'm afraid we weren't there for you, me and your mama, the way we should have been. Had issues of our own needed looking at, healing." She turned the water back on for a second. "Things will be different now, I promise. You'll be coming here, and we'll be visiting you in Harrison so much that you'll get tired of me and old Otis and beg us to leave you alone."

For some reason her words made me happy and sad at the same time. She must have sensed it because she wiped her hands off on the dish towel and enveloped me in a hug. "Macey May, you are more loved than you will ever know."

Later that night as Mama tucked me into bed, she told me to close my eyes and put out my hand.

When I looked there were two gold rings.

"Those were Daddy's and mine. I know you can't understand everything right now, Macey May, and when you're older we'll talk about it again. But no matter what the world says, your daddy and I were married, husband and wife in our eyes, and I believe, God's. We were a family. I want you to have these. When we get back to Harrison we'll go into town and find you a nice gold chain to put them on so you can wear them. Would you like that?"

I let the rings double up on my thumb; they were too big even for that. I nodded.

"Good. Now go to sleep. Morning will be early."

The door clicked shut, and I listened as her slippered feet shuffled along the hallway and down the stairs. I strained and could hear her talking to Grandma in the kitchen, although I couldn't make out the words.

I pulled my legs from out of my covers and walked across the cold wooden floor to my pile of belongings packed for our trip back home. Mr. Jumpers sat atop the suitcase, and I grabbed him up. The bruises on my arms had faded, forgotten, it seemed, by most. The reason for Junior's death remained unsolved but dismissed in people's minds, replaced with Daddy's and the story of Abigail's baby and Mr. Walsh's suicide.

I stood at the end of the bed, counted to three, and jumped onto the mattress. I was almost ten, but sometimes monsters underneath in the dark still felt real.

I snuggled under the covers and closed my eyes with Mr. Jumpers nestled under my neck if I needed him. Most nights I didn't. Some nights I did. Mama's conversation from the kitchen muted even more, my lids fluttered closed, and I could hear Junior's words in my ears, his breath whispering across my neck.

I knew the truth of Uncle Denim and Abigail, the White Lady. I knew about their baby, Caroline, and what Mr. Walsh had done to it. I knew what Mr. Walsh had done to Pap because of what he thought Pap had done. I knew every secret that Mama, Grandma, and Otis had chosen to tell me. But I also knew that there were things they kept to themselves. All secrets are not meant to be told.

There was a soft click as the outside bathroom door locked, and then appeared the tips of men's black shoes, freshly shined, across from mine. I pulled my feet up onto the toilet seat and tucked my head into my knees.

A girl who swam with alligators. A chicken who thought it was a cat. 2x2 is 4. 3x3 is 9. 5x5 is 25.

I closed my eyes.

I knew I didn't need to worry anymore.

Daddy had seen to that.

AUTHOR'S NOTE

ALMOST A DECADE AGO, a character came into my mind—a little nine-year-old African American girl from Georgia— Macey May Johnson. She refused to leave, so I sat down at my computer and wrote the first chapter of *Threshing of Straw*, and then unsure as to where the story was headed, I put it away and left it there for years.

Macey May was never far from my thoughts, though. She played in the recesses, asserting herself, and asking me when I was going to finish her story. It was a few years later that the rest of the novel came to me with the characters, the lives I felt I needed to write, and the relationships I wanted to explore.

I am aware of the position in which this novel places me. I am not African-American, nor am I from the South. I am a New Englander transplanted as of late to the Midwest. Some will argue that I have no right to pen a story from the point of view of a person whose skin does not match mine or from a place from which I have no roots. Some will argue that the job of a writer is to step into spaces outside our own and see through other lenses.

This story is about a family, the secrets they keep from each other, and the way they reconcile their past in order to live in the present and have a future. If readers come away connecting with the characters' brokenness and hope, then I have done what I set out to do. If readers find themselves propelled into the larger discussion regarding cultural appropriation in literature, then I have done much more than I thought possible.

ACKNOWLEDGMENTS

I ALWAYS HOPED a book that I wrote would find its way to publication, and it finally has happened. Even now, as I think about the people I want to thank, it seems surreal that I get to do it. As any writer will tell you, writing is a magical, exhausting, and personal experience. A private endeavor that takes place, for me anyway, mostly in my head, long before the words find their place onto paper.

I will be forever grateful for all of the mentors who helped guide me through my MFA program with their encouragement and belief that this day would come to pass and to the Ohio Writers' Association Great Novel Contest for giving new unpublished authors the ability to get their stories out there. Thank you for choosing mine.

It's a bit frightening to ask someone to read a book that you've spent years of your life cultivating. It's even more scary when you ask them for honesty. Thank you to friends and family whose insight made this book even better. To those who heard I had written a book and asked to read *Threshing of Straw* before it was published and then asked to be able to pass it on to their friends, thank you. You made me feel like a writer.

To my husband, Darren, who didn't laugh twenty years ago when I set out to the library with a notebook and pen to write a novel, thank you for your unwavering support. To my children, Peyton and Beckett, who tell their friends that their Mom is a writer as well as a teacher, the recognition means so much. Now you have to read my novel!

To my parents who had books in the house as I grew up, and to my father who is the first writer in the family. Thank you for making words a part of my life.

To Kristyn and Julie for decades of friendship, and to Charlene for even more years and answering some rather strange medical questions via text. I am honored to call you friends.

And to Krista, Lynda, Susan, and Vici—my Ladies. I hope you know; I hope you just REALLY know.

ABOUT THE AUTHOR

KIM CATRON has an MFA in Creative Writing, a Masters in Education, and has taught English for almost thirty years. Most of her life was spent in Massachusetts, but she now resides in rural Wisconsin with her husband, two children, her dog Jane Austen, and Dudley the cat.

Blog and book reviews: kimcatronauthor

Email: kimcatronauthor@gmail.com

Facebook: Kim Catron Author

Twitter/Instagram: kimcatronauthor

CPSIA information can be obtained
at www.ICGtesting.com
Printed in the USA
LVHW041813150523
747037LV00004B/798